the
BLOODY BLACK FLAG

the
BLOODY
BLACK
FLAG

A Spider John Mystery

STEVE GOBLE

SEVENTH STREET BOOKS®
AN IMPRINT OF PROMETHEUS BOOKS
59 JOHN GLENN DRIVE • AMHERST, NY 14228
www.seventhstreetbooks.com

Published 2017 by Seventh Street Books®, an imprint of Prometheus Books

This is a work of fiction. Characters, organizations, products, locales, and events portrayed in this novel are either products of the author's imagination or used fictitiously.

Cover illustrations © Shutterstock
Cover design by Nicole Sommer-Lecht
Cover design © Prometheus Books

Inquiries should be addressed to
Seventh Street Books
59 John Glenn Drive
Amherst, New York 14228
VOICE: 716–691–0133 • FAX: 716–691–0137
WWW.SEVENTHSTREETBOOKS.COM

21 20 19 18 17 • 5 4 3 2 1

Library of Congress Cataloging-in-Publication Data

Names: Goble, Steve, 1961- author.
Title: The bloody black flag : a Spider John mystery / Steve Goble.
Description: Amherst, NY : Seventh Street Books, an imprint of Prometheus Books,
    2017. | Series: Spider John mysteries ; 1
Identifiers: LCCN 2017014064 (print) | LCCN 2017029567 (ebook) |
    ISBN 9781633883604 (ebook) | ISBN 9781633883598 (softcover)
Subjects: LCSH: Pirates—Fiction. | Murder—Investigation—Fiction. | Revenge—
    Fiction. | BISAC: FICTION / Mystery & Detective / Historical. | GSAFD:
    Historical fiction. | Mystery fiction.
Classification: LCC PS3607.O27 (ebook) | LCC PS3607.O27 B58 2017 (print) |
    DDC 813/.6—dc23
LC record available at https://lccn.loc.gov/2017014064

Printed in the United States of America

For Gere, the star I steer by.

I

OCTOBER 1722

Spider John Rush resigned himself to the hard truth—he was returning to a world of cut and thrust, hide and pounce, blood and smoke, pitch and tar.

He had been foolish to think of leaving that world; Spider John belonged in no other. Ezra had said as much, but Spider seldom wished to concede that Ezra was right.

Spider tugged gently at the oar and watched the dark shoreline recede. The oar had a few rough spots, and a splinter poked the scabby knob on his left hand where his small finger used to be. That scab had bothered him already; it always did in cold weather, and this was October off the New England coast. Spider winced, tugged the tiny spear out with his teeth, then spat it into the chilly night air to vanish in the deep. He'd smooth out the oar later. For now, he focused on being quiet and doing the work.

Spider hoped the converted whaler they rowed toward would be in a better state than this damned leaky boat. It smelled of rot. He suspected the partially rotted bench he sat on might give way any moment. He wondered how the thing endured Ezra's weight. Ezra, who stood well over six feet, shared the bench with Spider, rowing on the port side. Ezra sat with his ridiculously long legs tucked up near his chin.

The sea, dark as velvet and painted with a ribbon of moonlight, reminded Spider he was thirsty. Aft, Addison peered into the darkness, sipping now and then from a leather flask and glaring at any oarsman who made a splash that broke the silence. That would happen with eight men rowing, and some of them a bit drunk. Other than that, they were as silent as ghosts, just as Addison had commanded.

A whiskey scent wafted from Addison's flask. Spider caught Addison's eye and nodded toward the flask in hopes of coaxing a swig, but he got a sneer in return. "Just row, and be quiet about it," Addison hissed in a whisper.

Spider was new to the crew, and had never seen the ship they rowed toward, but he did not doubt that Addison had reason for caution. The man likely had smuggled some things ashore, given that the English and French did battle over the Acadia border far north of Boston, and there probably was not a man aboard the boat who did not have crimes on his ledger, including himself and Ezra.

So they all were running from something, Spider supposed, even the chubby surgeon with rum on his breath who also was joining the *Plymouth Dream* crew, and whatever hazards they left ashore, they were headed toward new ones. That was the nature of the piratical life Spider and Ezra had led, and the life they were resuming. They were blood brothers against a hostile universe, and they were given very little choice in the matter.

As they rowed, in a rhythm they'd reached without the aid of a cadence or chantey, Spider threw many a nervous glance shoreward. He sought signs of a lantern or torch, and listened for shouts or musket fire. They were well away from the Massachusetts Bay Colony coast now, and the full moon showed nothing but its own shining trail on the expanse of ocean. In the distant north, lights from Boston looked like a small swarm of orange-and-yellow fireflies on the horizon; it would not be long now before those lights were extinguished and Boston settled down to sleep. Most of the city was in bed by now, he presumed, but brothels and taverns still plied their trades. He saw and heard nothing, however, near the secluded cove from which they'd launched, a good deal south of Boston proper. Spider spat overboard now and then as a charm to make his luck hold.

He had not been so lucky on other accounts. He had no jacket, for one thing, and wore two shirts against the October breeze. He hoped to buy a pea coat from storage or from a shipmate once aboard *Plymouth Dream*, and for once he had a bit of coin in the leather pouch fixed to his shabby belt.

He did not look forward to the deadly trade ahead, but part of him was relieved to be at sea again. On land, he could always feel the looming noose. The crowds, the doorways, the alleys all could hide crouching dangers—an agent of the law, an eyewitness to past misdeeds, or just a man with a knife and a need for bread. On the sea, Spider could see most hazards from a distance and could meet them with sword and gun in hand if he could not outrun them.

That was not true on shore, where Spider was out of his element.

He wished Addison would pick up the pace.

Addison, though, was not concerned about speed. The man consulted a battered watch occasionally, tilting it to catch some moonlight to read by, but seemed satisfied with their progress. Nor did Addison peer rearward at the shore, ever. Spider began to wonder if the first mate's demand for silence and the occasional touch of the flintlock pistol tucked into his belt were merely a show to demonstrate he was in command.

Addison was perhaps twice Spider's age, somewhere in his forties, and spoke with a voice as deep and rich as molasses. He was balding, and heavy, but his hard blue eyes still gave the impression he could kick a younger man's ass if it became necessary.

Spider's personal concerns faded with each stroke of the oars. Once he was certain they hadn't been followed, he began to relax. He stared greedily at Addison's flask.

Ezra wagged a finger and shook his shaggy red head, flashing a broad grin. He knew what Spider was thinking, no doubt, and had a good joke—or lecture—in mind. But Ezra had the sense to keep his mouth shut, what with Addison showing no signs of tolerance. Ezra already had a fresh, shallow gash on his nose, a souvenir from the scrape that had prompted them to chase after Addison and accept his proposal to sail with *Plymouth Dream*. Ezra would just as soon avoid trouble now, if he could. Spider sighed. Finding passage to Nantucket and seeking a life ashore had been his foolish dream, and Ezra had gone along despite misgivings.

Fate, as always, had other ideas.

Spider nodded slowly at Ezra, and then they both focused on their work.

Spider had no idea how long they would have to row in silence. Addison had kept those details to himself, as was proper, given the circumstances. But at the end of the rowing would be a ship, hard work, and distance between himself and his pursuers. There would be bloody work, too. There always was. But he could handle that, as he had done most of the last eight years, and as distasteful as it was he preferred it to being burned or hanged. He had seen hangings, and watched the way the pious bastard officers of law and order always delayed the deed with preaching and speeches. He had seen the doomed men shake in dread until the very gallows shook with them, and he had heard the dreadful crack of the lever, the deathly squeal of the trapdoor hinge—and the horrid snap of the neck, the very sound of finality.

And burning? He could not even bring himself to think of it. The dread of it haunted him in nightmares.

He would take any quick death by knife or musket or pistol over that. Anything but that.

Those dark thoughts made him touch his neck, and his fingers found the leather strap and followed it to the pendant. It had been so long since he'd seen Em. And what of his son? Little Johnny had to be about eight years old by now, perhaps dreaming of the sea himself. Spider hoped not, for the boy's sake. Such dreams had led Spider onto a whaler, and eventually onto a pirate sloop. His carpentry skills had saved him, or else he'd have been cast away with the rest of the whaling crew after the pirates had subdued their vessel. His dreams often showed him the visages of the poor souls who had been deemed useless, and thus had been cast overboard to swim until their muscles failed or sharks devoured them.

He brought the pendant up quickly, kissed it, then tucked it back beneath his shirts. He wondered if he would ever see her again. Ezra had warned him it would be foolish to try, and events had proven Ezra correct. But he would send money, if he could. No long letters, no admissions, no promises, no revelations—nothing that might hurt him one day in a court of law, nothing that might tie him to bloodshed and crimes of piracy—but such help as he could send. And the heart pendant. He'd carved it from ivory, for her. He planned to send her that, too, along with a lock of his hair and a note, if he could find someone to write it for him.

It was little—so little—but it was the best he could do, and so he would do it.

They rowed until the shore was beyond sight, and Spider had no sense of time left. There was nothing but the roll of the boat, the splash of oars, the salt-tinged air, and the stream of moonlight. Ezra and Spider were the new men, along with a surgeon who pretended to row while others did the actual labor. Spider and Ezra exchanged several glances while the surgeon barely dipped his oar into the sea.

Boredom set in, until Addison corked the flask and tucked it away, then reached into a sack at his feet.

"I have our goal in sight, gents," Addison said. "Twenty degrees to starboard, if you can manage that. It ought to be a simple maneuver, aye, but . . ."

The oarsmen, despite the doctor's miscues, managed the maneuver with little difficulty.

"Forward all," Addison said.

They found their rhythm again and proceeded in that fashion for a few minutes, until Addison spoke again.

"Ship oars," he said quietly. The command was followed, though one or two fellows were slow to heed and a couple of men groaned as if they'd been hauling bricks. The surgeon let out a huge sigh, as though he were Sisyphus watching his stone roll downhill.

Spider imagined old Lieutenant Bentley lashing a forehead or two with his knotted rope and opening bloody gashes. Even after leaving the navy for the whaling trade after losing an arm, Bentley had insisted on being addressed as lieutenant, and on wielding that damned rope. Spider did not miss Lieutenant Bentley one damned bit.

Addison grumbled, scratched his gray beard, then removed a cowbell from the sack at his feet. It made no sound even though Addison dangled it about somewhat carelessly, and Spider figured the clapper was gone from it. Addison pulled a dirk from his belt, grasped it by the blade, then tapped the cowbell with the wooden hilt—twice, thrice, then once. He hit it hard, and the notes rang out against the otherwise silent night. The first mate peered ahead the whole time, moonlight shining off his bald pate.

Spider turned to look over his shoulder and saw the vessel in the distance, standing dark with sails furled. She had three masts and good lines as far as he could judge in the darkness. With her long bowsprit cutting the night, she looked like some surfacing narwhal aiming for the sky. *Plymouth Dream* had been built for the whale trade and long voyaging, and would serve well if maintained with care. Spider hoped that was the case, but Addison had said she'd been without a decent carpenter for a good while. Addison had overheard Ezra and Spider talking in Boston and deduced Spider was a carpenter. That had led to the invitation to join *Dream*'s crew.

They had declined, at first. Circumstances eventually had forced their hands.

Ezra's quiet laugh brought Spider back to the present.

"Well, we're not rowing all the way to Jamaica, then," Ezra joshed softly, flexing his fingers and flashing a grin toward the vessel.

Mention of Jamaica lifted Spider's mood. Walking ashore was less dangerous there for a man on the account than striding through Boston, although not without its hazards, and there was a good prospect of finding a northbound merchant vessel that needed able hands. His hoped-for rendezvous with Em might happen, eventually. For the moment, Spider contented himself with the memory of the way her nose crinkled when she flashed her bright smile. He would simply have to wait, and endure. He was good at both.

"Not rowing to Jamaica in this thing, for certain," Spider said, placing a hand gingerly on the bench. "Surprised this leaky bucket floats at all. I believe there are more worms than wood in this god-damned thing."

"It got us here," Addison said tersely. "Ye can see to making it better tomorrow, right, carpenter? Earn your keep?"

Spider nodded, though he doubted the boat would serve even as firewood. He would salvage what he could and give the rest to the cook's fire kettle.

"Well, then," Addison said. "If ye can all be quiet as ghosts for a bit, perhaps I can do m'own damn job. Else, you get to swim. Understand?"

Spider bowed his head in acknowledgement. Ezra covered his gap-toothed smile with one hand and raised the other in supplication, bowing his head until his ruddy beard brushed his grimy pea coat.

Addison repeated the series of notes on the cowbell, the tones spreading like waves in the darkness. Spider chuckled as Ezra winced at Addison's lack of rhythm. Ezra couldn't play a note on any instrument, but figured he could be a great musician if life had only given him a fiddle and time to practice.

Addison repeated his unmusical taps once again, and a reply came moments later, the same sequence on a bigger, deeper bell. Addison grinned and reached back into the sack, trading the bell for a wide-brimmed hat that had seen too much salt and sun. "Amazin' what ye can hear when the hands is all proper silent and respectful. A'right, then," he said, placing the hat over his bald head. "We can head in and not get shot. Back at the oars now, and ye'll earn a drink or two."

That sounded good to Spider. The aroma wafting from Addison's flask enticed him like a beautiful woman.

"Didn't they know we were coming?" Ezra tilted his head as he asked the question; it was too dark for Spider to make out his raised eyebrows and puckered lips, but he was well acquainted with his lanky friend's confused expression.

"We could be us, or we could be someone not so welcome, far as Cap'n Barlow knows," Addison said. "Pays to be cautious on an outlaw sea, boy. Don't want to be mistaken for spies, or worse. Old George's ships are all over the water, ever since they got Roberts. They got him, so they think they can get us all. Navy smells blood, like a shark smells blood. But Barlow is uncommon smart, and uncommon cautious. And so, for that matter, am I. You shall see."

Spider winced. Bartholomew Roberts, the notorious pirate captain, had eluded his predators for four years, capturing prize upon prize almost under the Royal Navy's very nose. And yet they'd caught up to him at last in February, capturing his *Royal Fortune* at Cape Lopez on the African coast. Roberts died quickly with grapeshot in his throat, a better fate than most of his men received. More than fifty had been throttled at the gallows.

Roberts's death represented the end of a pirate era to some, but Addison and Barlow saw it as an opportunity.

Spider uttered a silent prayer, in hopes of never being hauled to a gallows himself.

He and Ezra traded glances as the crew went back to work. Ezra swallowed hard, then shrugged. Spider did likewise. Neither of them wanted to return to life on the account, but there were no other roads open to them, not here, not now. Grim humor and fatalism won the day.

"We won't get shot tonight, maybe," Spider whispered. "But what of tomorrow, eh? Or the day after?"

Ezra grinned. "I would stand behind you," he whispered, "but you're not so big as to make much of a shield." Indeed, Spider was of less than medium height and was accustomed to staring up into other men's faces.

"I don't have to be big, just quick," Spider said. "You tall fellows, you make for good targets."

"Is that so?"

"Oh, yes," Spider said, grinning. "You're a dead man, certain."

Spider, with his pitiful cutlass dangling over his back in a wooden scabbard hung on a thin rope, clambered over the rail just behind Ezra.

A pair of lanterns, far apart and swinging from the lines, provided the only light, too dim to allow Spider to make out much of *Plymouth Dream*'s condition. But Spider smelled plenty of good cedar and oak along with pitch and tar and damp sails, and the gunwale had felt sturdy and smooth as he climbed aboard.

Spider, Ezra, and the elderly gent who claimed to be a doctor headed toward the foremast on Addison's order. The newcomers stood near one of the lanterns, and Spider squinted against the light. Men, most of their faces hidden in shadow, crowded the gunwale and hoisted aboard crates and sacks of supplies from the boat below.

The rest of the boat's crew headed one way or another, receiving nods of greeting and slaps on the back from the dozen or so men already standing on *Plymouth Dream*'s deck. Spider, his eyes slowly adjusting to the lanterns, tried to pick out Captain Barlow in the crowd, but he saw no one who seemed to be in command.

A chicken clucked somewhere, and a yellow-white cat stepped across Spider's foot before vanishing into the darkness.

"Well, then, Addy. You were able to fetch what we needed?" The voice, pitched low and rich as good whiskey, came from somewhere forward. Spider turned toward it and beheld his new commander, Captain William Barlow, climbing down from atop the forecastle.

Spider had never heard of him before meeting Addison, but the first mate had given Barlow high marks for boldness and ingenuity.

"Aye," Addison answered, bowing his head slightly and doffing his hat. "And a bit more."

Men milling about the deck made way. Barlow approached, slowly, in measured steps. As the captain came into the light, details emerged. Tricorn hat, white or pale gray. Six feet of height, or more, certainly taller than Spider. About twice Spider's age, too, somewhere in his forties. A long cane, held in the right hand and resting over his right shoulder. A salt-and-pepper beard in a face with deep-set, dark eyes. A long English naval coat, which Spider immediately envied. A sardonic smile that seemed to lend something sinister to the October chill.

"Introduce us, if you please," Barlow said to Addison, while pointing his cane toward the newcomers. Spider thought the cane to be ash and guessed it could give a damn good whacking. He tried to discern whether it concealed a dagger or a short sword, but the dim light thwarted him. In any case, Barlow did not seem to need it to get around. He moved with an athletic grace.

Spider also noted a pistol handle peeking from beneath Barlow's coat. The gun was tucked into the man's belt, within easy reach and placed so that it would be most efficient to draw left-handed. Noticing such details had kept Spider alive to this point, and he practiced the skill diligently.

Addison pointed at Spider. "John Rush, Cap'n, called Spider. Don't know why. He's a carpenter."

Barlow's grin widened, but it did not grow any warmer. "Well. You'll find *Dream* in fair condition, I do not doubt, but we've got some hatches and spars in need of attention, and our boats are a wretched lot. Had some rough seas of late. A lot of things got knocked about."

"Wicked wind, that was," Spider said, "if you mean about a month ago."

"Aye," Barlow said. "Rigging and masts came out of it well enough, though. We were locked in a harbor for too damned long setting things aright, though, and there is yet more to do."

"Same gale put me and Ezra here ashore." Spider nodded toward his friend. "We were on *Lamia*, and she did not fare so well as you."

Indeed, *Lamia*—dangerously overladen with goods badly stowed, in Spider's view, after she'd seen much successful hunting—had gone down once the rudder had ripped apart, and she'd turned herself broadside to the heavy rushing sea. He and Ezra and a few others had been able to get boats launched, and he'd seen men tossing about in the stormy dark, but he had no idea how many had lived and how many had died. He and Ezra had escaped in an overloaded boat that got swamped; the two of them had arrived ashore clinging to a random spar and thanking Jesus whenever they could spare a breath. They had no idea what had become of the other men in their boat, and had spent much of their week of hiking toward civilization discussing the nature of God and why some were spared while others were not. They had finally decided it would take wiser men than themselves to figure that out.

Spider and Ezra had eventually learned that others had made it ashore, too, though they might have preferred drowning—they'd been caught and dragged in chains to Boston, and were hanged for the entertainment of a mob. Spider and Ezra had decided not to watch.

At least one man from *Lamia* had been free when they chased Addison down and accepted his offer. Spider wondered about Scrimshaw's fate. They had left him in a lurch, out of necessity.

Barlow cocked his head. "*Lamia*. Bent Thomas, captain?"

"Aye."

"Knew him, in Jamaica, a while back. Decent cuss. Good ship, if I recall. Bermuda rig, aye?"

"Aye on all accounts. Don't know if Cap'n Thomas lives, sir," Spider said. "The ship certainly does not. It was a mad rush to get away once she took on water so. She was heeled over good, and last I saw of Bent Thomas he was diving from the rail. Our boats all got blowed and tossed separate ways. There were many men in the water, and no gettin' to them."

Murmurs swept amidships, and a short man with a wooden leg walked away cursing, his peg sounding a dirge drumbeat on the deck.

He passed a scarecrow of a man, with lanky gray hair draped around a gaunt face and a scar where his right eye should have been, who leaned forward and peered at Spider. The man was at least sixty if he was a day, but seemed to be fit as a fiddle. He leered oddly and laughed a harsh, dry laugh.

"Stow that, Odin," Addison said tersely.

The one-eyed man, still laughing, wandered off.

Barlow whispered Bent Thomas's name, paused a moment, but showed no sign of sadness. Violent deaths were expected among men who sailed under a black flag, and a stormy demise was a better death than hanging. "We've a few other vessels in need of work," Barlow said at last. "You know a thing or two about cutting down a vessel to accommodate guns?"

"Aye," Spider said. "Done it a few times."

"Good," Barlow answered. "Very good. We've tools, if you have none."

"Good, sir." Spider nodded. "My tools went down with *Lamia*."

"You still have a couple of tools, at least," the captain said, his dark eyes widening. The cane came forth slowly. First it tapped the bone-handled dirk tucked into Spider's belt; then it rose in a slow half circle to touch the rope that held the scabbard and sword. "Do you know how to use these?"

"Aye," Spider said. "When I must."

"The knife you may keep, of course," Barlow said, turning his back to Spider and slowly pacing away. "A sailor is useless without his knife. The cutlass, though, that we must put away until such time as you need it. We've a crew with high spirits. I prefer to avoid trouble. When the time comes, you'll have trouble plenty enough."

Spider noted again the pistols Barlow and Addison carried, and felt ill at ease surrendering his weapon, but he slowly removed the scabbard from his shoulder and handed it to Addison. "Of course," Spider said.

Barlow spun quickly and stared at him. Spider could not tell whether the man was pleased with his quick acceptance of the rule, or disappointed. The captain then quickly turned his attention to Ezra.

"Ezra Coombs," Addison said, hooking a thumb toward Spider's friend. "Able-bodied seaman, merchant and navy, and some time spent on the account. Looks big enough to hurt someone, aye?"

"Well met," Barlow said, and although he was a tall man himself, he had to glance upward to look at Ezra's face. "Quite the large bastard."

Ezra said nothing. Spider glanced toward his friend and noticed Ezra's attention was focused beyond the captain, on a figure just within the circle of lantern light. That figure seemed equally engrossed with Ezra. The mystery man wore a long cloak, of the sort some monks wore, and Spider could not make out whether there were any weapons beneath it. The man's face, however, promised danger. He was shaved bald, and his head and face were covered with strange tattoos—dots and whorls and intersecting lines. His eyes were fired with menace and fixed on Ezra.

Spider nudged Ezra slightly. "Aye, Cap'n, well met," Ezra said. "Thank you for having me aboard. I shall not disappoint." He said it in his gentlest voice, the one he used to put people at ease. Ezra's sunken eyes, prominent cheekbones, red beard, and old scars that showed white against the tanned forehead gave him a sinister appearance. Combined with his towering height, it meant people tended to fear him at first appraisal. He had learned to compensate with polite manners and a soft voice.

"We shall see," Barlow said.

Spider watched the tattooed man stare at Ezra. The captain moved on to the next new arrival.

"And this?" Spider thought Barlow's voice held just a bit of contempt.

"Doctor Eustace Boddings," Addison said, "late of His Majesty's Navy."

"His Majesty," Barlow said. "May he bugger a goat!"

Cheers went up at that, and Spider and Ezra joined in, but the doctor nodded sharply. "Pleased, Captain, and ready to serve."

"You have been served yourself, it seems to me," Barlow said. "I believe I detect a huge stench of liquor on your breath."

"A nip, sir, no more," Boddings answered. "A toast with a lady friend before my departure, is all it was."

"You've seen long service, I judge," Barlow said. "Is your mind sharp, still?"

"As a scalpel," Boddings replied. "The Lord has blessed me."

"Voyaging won't wear on you?"

"No more so than any other hand," the doctor said. "You may rely upon it."

Addison cleared his throat. "He heard me mention Jamaica, sir, and inquired about our accommodations. Doctor Boddings seeks to work his passage to the island, sir. He has ample medicines with him, and I've talked with a few in Boston who have sailed with him. He's an experienced hand."

"A quality to be sought in a surgeon, I assure you," Boddings said.

"We may be a long time coming to Jamaica," Barlow replied. "We've some prowling to do, and hunters to avoid." The captain and his first mate exchanged knowing glances.

"I understand," Boddings said. "As a Christian man I shall take no part in bloodshed, of course, but I shall do my duty afterward, to be sure. And as for any conduct that might transpire, well, judge not, the Good Book says."

The doctor, a dour and gray man of too much weight, spoke well, if slowly, but his eyes did not seem to focus on anything. Spider wondered what compelled a man of his age to throw in with a crew like Barlow's.

The captain snorted. "You may well take part in the bloodshed when you find a cutlass at your windpipe, I dare say. Many a Christian man will cast his teachings aside when it comes to a choice between someone else's life or his own."

Barlow scratched his chin and paced back and forth.

"I've never had a physician aboard. We've an extra berth in the officers' bay, a small one used for stores right now, but it seems fitting a man of education ought to have it," Barlow said. "It is yours, provided you do some cooking and other chores when you have no patients to tend."

Boddings stiffened. "See here, Captain Barlow, I spent more years at sawing arms and stitching wounds than you have been alive. I am no common ruffian for you to assign to a galley...."

Barlow moved swiftly, and his nose was in Boddings's face in a heartbeat. "You are part of this crew," the captain said, "and you will not sit idly by waiting for someone to cut himself doing real work or get sick in the weather. You will serve me as more than ballast or you will serve me as chum, do you understand?"

Boddings nodded slowly. "Aye."

Barlow pressed closer and sneered.

"Aye, Captain," Doctor Boddings added hastily.

Barlow paced a dozen steps away from the newcomers, then turned and placed his cane back on his shoulder. "You all know what we do here? Our line of work, if you will?" They nodded, and Barlow continued. "We take what we need, where we can find it. Some chose this life. Some did not. Makes no matter. We are outlaws, marked men, and now so are you, if you weren't already." Barlow's eyes blazed at Spider and Ezra, even as his voice grew quieter and his cadence slowed. "If we are caught, we will swing. Simple as that. And I tell you this . . . I'll not hang. No, sir. I will run, or I will fight, but I will not hang. And you will run with me, or fight with me. Do not become a liability to me, gentlemen, and we'll all make some fine money as a reward for our risk, and one day we shall live like kings. We've a good deal of profit aboard already and just may see a good bit more before we reach Kingston. Just work hard, obey orders, and see to it that I am never forced to choose between your life and mine. You will lose that toss of the dice, lads, every time."

Spider listened to the cold words and wished he had his cutlass.

"You answer to no one but me, as our articles make clear," Barlow said, after a lengthy pause. "And I answer to no one, not man nor God nor devil. I do not know who you've sailed under before, but I do not go in for votes and lengthy deliberations and holding councils as some do. You may tell me what you think, and I'll ponder it. But I rule in the end, and we've all done well by it. Have we not?"

He raised his cane high, and men cheered loudly. Then Barlow continued. "You'll be paid according to our articles, which you'll hear and mark yourselves. We'll do so come dawn. Do you have questions?"

Spider noted that Ezra and the tattooed man remained locked in some sort of silent communication, while Doctor Boddings seemed tense. "None, Cap'n, save wanting a look at the tools," Spider answered.

"Come daylight, for that," Barlow said. "You and Coombs will be on Addy's watch, go to work at daybreak. Doctor, Addy will show you your berth and the galley. For now, welcome to *Plymouth Dream*. Addy, some ale all around, and weigh anchor. Dowd, get someone on the halyards and let us put on some sail. I think we have been anchored long enough. Helm, south by southeast, if you please."

"Aye," said a broad-shouldered black man, as tall as Barlow and wearing only pants, boots, and a shirt, open despite the chill. Dowd pointed at the short peg-legged man and called out a few names. "You heard the cap'n. Move." The man spat tobacco on the deck and watched to see that his orders were obeyed; apparently, Dowd commanded the night watch.

Barlow spun and headed aft, vanishing into the night once he moved beyond the lanterns' reach. Men climbed into the dark night and went to work, and the mainsail filled with wind, white as a ghost in the moonlight. Other sails followed, and soon Spider could feel the vessel move against the ocean. He could not venture a guess as to the ship's company, but he could tell *Dream* was crowded.

Addison called for a keg to be tapped, and Doctor Boddings seemed much more interested in the proceedings than he had been a moment before.

Ezra's mystery acquaintance, the tattooed man, was nowhere to be seen.

"Well," Spider said quietly. "You've a friend aboard already, I see."

"Not a friend," Ezra said, whispering. "His name is Tellam, and he hails from Salem. I know him from way back, and he knows."

"He knows?"

"Yes. He knows of my witch blood."

2

*S*pider sat on a four-pounder next to Ezra, in a spot as far from the lantern light as was feasible. Shadows danced upon the sails, and oily smoke tickled Spider's nose. *Plymouth Dream* forged southeastward with a gentle lift and drop, lift and drop, that made Spider feel at home again after their brief stay in Boston.

He'd selected a leather jack from a barrel full of drinking vessels, and Ezra had a mug of pewter. Both were filled with lifeless, lukewarm beer.

"To Bent Thomas and *Lamia*," the peg-legged man, standing nearby, said somberly.

"Aye, Peg, to Bent Thomas." That reply came from Odin, the ugly one-eyed bastard. Both Peg and Odin nodded at their new shipmates, and Spider nodded back. All manner of drinking vessels were lifted high, and there was a second or two during which only the wind and the snapping of sail and creaking of timber were heard—until Odin laughed and swallowed his beer.

"To Bent Thomas," Spider said quietly; then he drained his ale in a couple of swallows and turned to Ezra. "So, this fellow Tellam knows."

"Aye," Ezra said. He took a whiff of his drink, then winced and poured the contents into Spider's jack. Spider nodded appreciatively and took a sip. "Peter Tellam is his name."

"That's likely to be trouble, I suppose, judging by the look on your ugly face," Spider said after wiping beer from his chin.

"Aye," Ezra answered. Ezra's grandmother had been hung during the witch madness in Salem, and his mother had been hung sometime later. Spider's family tree held similar secrets; his own gram had been accused and set afire by a drunken, fearful crowd before he was born, but his mother had escaped to Boston. Such dark pasts were a big part of the bond between Spider and Ezra. It was something they could each share and understand—or not understand—together.

It also was something neither man shared with others, if they could help it. Their current situation showed plainly why that was necessary.

Their haunted past had led to the latest troubles ashore, the pursuit that had compelled them to seek the sea again. After learning the horrid fate of other *Lamia* survivors, Spider and Ezra knew they needed a real plan. So as they ate decent crab and cod near a warm tavern hearth, they tried to devise new names and identities for themselves, with a hope of arranging passage to Nantucket, and to Em.

But others huddled in the tavern began to speak of witches.

"You can tell them by the smell," one said. "Like an old grave."

"They can only turn to the left, never the right, my ma says. That is as sure a sign as any, I say."

"Wolves sire their children," another said. "Witches marry wolves."

That had been too much for Ezra, who stood up despite hissed warnings from Spider. A moment later, fists and chairs started flying, and Spider and Ezra found themselves outnumbered. Spider had drawn his battered and partially rusted blade and cursed beneath his breath.

As others joined the fracas, Spider had felt a queasy, fearful knot in his stomach. He and Ezra both had dipped their hands in bloody water many times, and the *Lamia* survivors may well have talked before their executions. Spider and Ezra stood little chance of avoiding the gallows if taken, and this incident was exactly the kind of attention they did not need.

Then things got worse.

Ezra grabbed Spider by the collar and turned him toward the door. He pointed to a man who had just slammed the door shut before moving to a window and peering anxiously outside.

Ezra spat and whispered. "Is that Scrimshaw?"

"Damn," Spider said. "Sure as I'm a cursed man, that's Scrimshaw."

Scrimshaw had been a topsail man aboard *Lamia*, and he had lost a fair amount of coin and chores to both Ezra and Spider in dicing and other contests during idle moments. He had vowed more than once to slit their throats if given a chance.

The fighting had quieted around them, as the tavern's company eyed this newcomer and noted the drawn blade in his hand. An increasing wave of noises from outside drew their attention, too, and men peered out of windows to see what was commencing.

"Damn me, now I hear horses, riding hard," Ezra said.

Spider listened. "And orders. Drums. Troops! Looking for Scrim, no doubt."

"And the blackguard will sell our souls in a heartbeat," Ezra said. "Won't even ask the Admiralty for mercy in exchange for our hides. He'll do it for spite."

"We must run," Spider said nervously as the sounds grew louder.

They bolted for the door, Ezra taking a moment to drive the hilt of his blade into the back of Scrimshaw's head, once to start him falling, and a second time to be certain he stayed down.

After that, they had rushed out of the tavern, commandeered a wagon, and driven the horses away from the martial sound of drums until the beasts lathered and stank. Then they had abandoned the wagon and made their way in the dark toward the small inlet Addison had described, both thanking and cursing a bright moon and clear sky. They were able to see their way, but the light made hiding difficult.

Heading deeper into Boston had not been an option. Aside from the troops between them and the rest of the city, Ezra's height was a liability—he was nearly seven feet tall. They could not simply find a crowd and disappear into it.

Nor would Spider feel comfortable in a crowd under the best of circumstances, and these were hardly good. The fracas in the tavern and the attack on Scrimshaw would prompt a diligent, wide-ranging search. Staying in the area almost certainly would have meant a noose.

But at least they had known of a place to go.

The day before, the stranger Addison had made quiet inquiries, seeking a ship's carpenter for a vessel he described as "hopin' to avoid His Majesty's valiant fellows, that we might do some enterprises."

They'd rejected his offer then, but the skirmish and hard words in the tavern had made them desperate.

Fortunately, Addison had given them a rendezvous point and a deadline to reconsider.

So they'd tracked Addison down in a mad rush, with Spider imagining the rope at his neck and lead balls in his back the entire time. They'd accepted the offer to sail with *Plymouth Dream*, and warned Addison that trouble likely was not far behind them. Now here they were—back on the account and surrounded by suspicious people again.

Spider glanced around the ship and saw no friendly faces.

"Yes, trouble," Ezra said. "Tellam will be trouble. But I will handle it."

"We will handle it," Spider corrected him. "I suppose swimming ashore is a fool idea."

"A bit far," Ezra said. "And damned cold."

Spider rubbed the itchy scab on his left hand where his small finger once had been. "All them markings on that gent's face. He been to the South Seas?"

"Worked a whaler, the *Persephone*, had some island folk aboard," Ezra said. "So people told me, anyway. He let them mark 'im like that. It's all over 'im, I hear. Even his pecker."

"Looks a bit crazed, if you ask me." Spider drained his beer. It was bland, but he could feel the effects.

"Tellam can be intense, I'd say," Ezra said. "Full of Jesus and fervor."

The cat, carrying a dead rat, jumped up beside Ezra and stared at him. Ezra took the rodent, patted the cat's head, and tossed the rat carcass overboard. The cat streaked away as suddenly as it had appeared.

"That's a good cat," Ezra said.

"If you say so," Spider replied. "The damned things spook me."

Spider tried to get the attention of the man wandering about with a wooden pitcher, filling cups, but soon decided he and Ezra were being ignored. "Ho there," Spider called. "Thirsty men here. Promised drink, we were."

The tall man approached. His face was hidden beneath the brim of his hat, and he said nothing, but he filled Spider's jack.

"Well met, and thank you," Spider said. "I'm Spider, he's Ezra." Ezra, lost in thought, grunted a hello and stared out over the rolling sea.

"Weatherall," the man said without looking up. "John Weatherall."

"Been with Barlow long?"

"No."

The man moved to fill Ezra's mug and glanced up just long enough for Spider to make out a tight-lipped sort-of grin framed by a black beard just beginning to thicken, and eyes squinting in the dim light. Then the man finished his task, and his face vanished again beneath the brim. He scurried off quickly, as though to escape a sudden rain.

"Well, then," Ezra said. "Not in a mood to visit with us, I suppose."

"Perhaps Tellam has been spreading gossip," Spider said. "We may be in for a long, unpleasant voyage."

"Or a very brief, unpleasant voyage," Ezra answered, handing his mug to Spider. "Drink up."

Plymouth Dream's new recruits did not wait until morning to sign the articles, after all.

"My work in Boston was tiring," Addison said, "with many arrangements to be made and much vital business to conduct. Very profitable business, I might say." He winked. "Thus, lads, I shall not wish to be up with the goddamn roosters."

Spider, Ezra, and Doctor Boddings gathered with Addison beneath a swinging lamp hung above a barrel near the mainmast. A rather handsome black man, who wore his dirty long coat and rakish, yet battered, hat with the air of a toff, brought the first mate a salt-ruined leather tube, a pot of ink, and a quill. Spider wrapped his arms around himself in an attempt to fight off the chill.

"Thankee, Elijah," Addison said, and the man bowed and left. A sweet aroma floated in his wake.

Addison reached into the tube and pulled free a worn, rolled parchment. He dropped the tube onto the barrel head, unfurled the document, and began to read: "Articles of Mutual Agreement Pertaining to All Crew of *Plymouth Dream*, Cap'n William Barlow Being in Command."

Addison sighed, spat, and wiped his brow. "Weary as a bonny lass after the fleet comes in," he muttered, handing the parchment to Doctor Boddings. "You read it."

Doctor Boddings took the document and began reading in a sonorous, Sunday sermon tone.

The articles were mostly familiar to Spider John; every outlaw vessel he'd ever called home sailed under some sort of written agreement. *Plymouth Dream*'s articles dealt with matters such as disposition of plundered goods, accounting for all plunder, duties to defend vessel and crew and the rights of men aboard, punishments for cowardice in action and the like, but they gave considerably more power to the captain than articles Spider had signed in the past.

On most pirate ships, crews voted on matters such as destinations and general courses of action, and the captain wielded unquestioned authority only when the ship went into action, when there was no time to take a vote. *Plymouth Dream*'s articles left all such matters in the hands of her captain. And only Barlow and Addison could go about armed with anything more lethal than a work knife or two, or other tools necessary to do the daily work of keeping a ship afloat and in trim. *Plymouth Dream*'s crewmen went about mostly unarmed, unless the vessel was preparing for battle.

It made little difference to Spider what the articles said. He could sign them, or he could be tossed overboard. Turning back now was not an option at all. So he signed them. He wrote in a crabby hand, "John Rush," and was proud he was able to do that much.

"I can't read nor write," Ezra said. Addison took the quill pen, dipped it, and wrote out "Ezra Coombs, ABS, his mark." Ezra added a large "X" beside it.

Boddings signed with flair. All three men had marked the back of the parchment, which, like the front, contained many names—a large portion of which had been crossed out. Many crossed-out names had small skulls drawn next to them.

"Well then, lads," Addison said, initialing each name and adding the date, then clamping the lid on the ink pot, "the three of you all belong to *Plymouth Dream* now and shall share in any spoils we take from this day forward. You will not share in the profit from our business in Boston—Spanish guns sold to a French trapper on behalf of Indians fighting the English over a lonely stretch of northern border, ha!—but there is always such business to be had, and there always shall be, bless the powers of this world. May they never come to agreeable terms!"

Ezra coughed. The man always seemed to have one malady or another, from coughs to diarrhea. Spider had often offered advice to improve Ezra's health, but it went ignored. Spider shook his head.

"Let us hope we all never share a spot on the gallows," Addison said. "I am off to sleep. You may do the same. Forward for you two. Doctor, follow me."

Spider and Ezra ambled toward the crew hold. "Our captain does not run the most democratic of ships, Spider."

"Indeed. Still, I've known others to ignore what we've all signed when they could do so without consequence."

"True. Not many we can trust."

They reached the hatch, and Ezra headed down first. "Good Lord above, this place smells like a dead French whore!"

"You should try living harlots, Ez." Spider climbed down swiftly, then coughed. "You spoke the truth, though. Damn!"

They watched wide-eyed as Elijah, the fellow who had delivered the articles for their signatures, aimed a small bellows into the crowded chamber of huddled men, dirty hammocks, frolicking shadows, lantern smoke, wooden chests and burlap sacks, shirts and coats hanging about, off-tune fiddle music, rolling dice, and a cat's mewing. From the bellows wafted a perfumed scent that did nothing to mask the odors of sweat and urine; it only added to the revolting mix to render it even more wretched.

"A gift from a friend, who frowned upon the idea of me among so many unwashed and uncouth sea hands," Elijah said in answer to their puzzled stares.

"It is no improvement, as near as I can tell," Ezra said.

Others growled, and several men tried to wave the offending perfume away. One fat fellow bent at the waist and farted loudly, eliciting loud laughter. Spider could not detect the man's gas because of the overwhelming perfume.

A toothless scruff approached Spider, who still shivered in his two shirts. "Got an extra pea coat, for a price. I am Robert Dobbin." It took Spider some effort to make out the fellow's words. Aside from not having a tooth in his head, Dobbin talked at twice the rate of most folks, as though he was merely rushing through a formality because no one would understand his words anyway. He accompanied his speech with numerous gestures, including a finger pointed toward a scratched and battered sea chest.

"I ain't got much money, but I got some," Spider said. "Let me see the coat."

The gray coat was of good wool, had only a few holes in it, and, incredibly, didn't smell as though it had been wrapped around a feverish horse for a week. They haggled a bit, and Spider thought he'd made a good deal.

Ezra found an empty hammock and hunkered down for sleep. Ezra could sleep anywhere, regardless of odor or snoring or dirty berths. Spider found a spot, looked about to see if anyone had staked it out as his own, and then doffed his outer shirt. This he tossed onto the hammock before donning the coat he'd purchased.

He expected inquiries. New men aboard any vessel ordinarily were pelted with questions, as the crew sought news of the world. That was true aboard any ship, but especially so when sailing beneath a pirate flag. These men were outlaws and courted death if they stepped ashore, but they were men, too, and usually had loved ones somewhere. They normally would wonder about their welfare. Had the crops been good? Were the Indians on the move? And they always wanted to know about any amorous adventures ashore. Sailing was lonely business.

But Spider entertained no such queries. Instead, he got piercing gazes that were quickly averted once noticed. Men talked quietly, but among themselves—not to him.

It was unsettling.

Spider went back on deck for a while to stare into the darkness off the starboard bow. Out there in the distance was Nantucket. Sometime the next day they would pass it by, but probably not close enough to see it as Barlow was tacking well southeast, away from the colonial coast. Spider kissed Em's pendant and blew two kisses toward where he supposed Nantucket to be. Then he went below and tried to sleep amid the snores, coughs, odors, and Odin's ominous laugh.

Spider decided to sleep with a knife in his hand.

3

*A*fter far too little shut-eye, Spider rolled out of his hammock, which was too close to a bulkhead for real comfort. Ezra was already above, apparently, but other men stirred slowly and grumbled. Barlow called down the hatch. "Move, lads. *Dream* won't sail herself."

Men responded slowly to the captain's call. This was a far cry from naval discipline. Old Lieutenant Bentley, the former navy man, would have clouted a couple of these sluggards by now, Spider reckoned.

Spider emerged into sunshine and a sharp chill in the wind. His exhalations formed clouds that rushed away on the breeze. Gulls perched on the bow, calling to comrades who hung in blue sky, seemingly as motionless as the white clouds farther above. *Plymouth Dream*'s bow rose and fell in a gentle cadence.

Addison had said the ship's company included more than seventy men, more than was strictly necessary to sail her, but providing ample manpower in a battle. The sun had lured most, it seemed, out onto the deck or up into the trees. She was a crowded vessel.

Despite missing a chance to go to Em—he cursed the panic that had consumed him ashore at the approach of English soldiers—Spider had to admit to himself he enjoyed being on the ocean. Yes, it was cold now, and he had to bundle up against the icy spray thrown up each time *Dream*'s bow hit a trough, but soon enough they would be in warm, southern air, and after that they'd be working in sweltering, equatorial heat.

And chill notwithstanding, he had a vast expanse of sea between himself and anyone who might decide to hang him. Spider wandered aft, where sails might shield him from the icy splashes. He took a deep breath, tasted the salt, and closed his eyes for just a moment.

A tug at his sleeve turned him around. "You are Spider John, sir?" It was a boy, maybe thirteen or fourteen, blond and freckled and earnest, wearing at least half a dozen shirts in a desperate bid to block out the October wind. Spider pondered, for a moment, whether to set the poor boy in a boat and tell him to row for shore as hard as he could, before this hard life on the account swallowed up his soul. But he knew the boy wouldn't listen, and the land likely was out of reach anyway.

Spider sighed. "Yes, Spider John Rush."

"Why do they call you Spider?"

"I climb good, is all." It was a lie, although he was, in fact, a fine climber; he was called Spider because, as a boy, he used to eat the eight-legged pests just to hear his sister scream.

Spider tucked his wild blondish mop of hair into a blue scarf and deftly knotted it behind his head. "Who are you, boy?"

"Hob. Really Hobart, but Hob."

"Got a surname, Hob?"

The boy lowered his head. "Not anymore," he answered quietly. "Da wouldn't like me using it, not on this ship."

Spider nodded. He didn't want to bring shame on Em or anyone back home, either.

"Well, then, Hob it is," Spider said, tapping him on the shoulder.

"I'm to show you the tools." Hob pointed. "This way."

They trod the deck, as sails snapped and men hummed. Spider judged *Dream* to be about a hundred feet long, and perhaps a shade over a quarter of that abeam. Her masts looked solid and straight, but the deck was worn and in need of a good scrubbing. She was not particularly speedy, and not as maneuverable as the numerous pirate sloops he'd served aboard, but *Dream* had a cavernous central hold, where men once did the messy work of whaling. The odor of whale oil seemed infused into the very wood; it lingered, ghostlike.

Spider knew Barlow commanded a small fleet of vessels and figured the man sent his swift sloops and frigates out in search of prey, then stored most of the booty here. Spider hoped that was the situation, in any case, for it meant he and Ezra might miss out on most of the killing. That would be fine with Spider.

Spider followed the boy forward, where a large chest was lashed against a hatch by the foremast, with a boat to either side. One of the boats was the wretched thing they'd rowed from shore. It looked worse by daylight. The other boat was not much better. Spider would apply pitch, brace what he could, and try to make them respectable. He rather hoped *Dream* would take another vessel prize and simply replace these leaky vessels.

The cat sat on the better boat, licking itself. "Shoo, Thomas," Hob said. The yellow-and-white critter stared at Hob as though the boy had no right at all to issue orders.

Spider picked up the cat, tossed it to the deck, and said, "Go on, then, Admiral Thomas, you creepy bastard." The cat scurried off.

Spider opened the unlocked chest to reveal a horrid jumble of rope, broken wood, and rusty, dull tools—mallets, chisels, pliers, files, nails, pegs, saws, drills, clamps, knives with no handles, spare metal from guns. Adding to the clutter were candle scraps, leather straps, and whetstones—items that would serve, it appeared, although it would take him a good while to sort it out and put things where he could find them as needed.

Spider sighed, figuring he'd spend a good deal of time finding tools and repairing them before he could use them to repair anything else. "Is this the whole lot?"

"Aye, except some hammers and such strewn about among the lumber stores. I can go looking."

"Who was carpenter before me?"

"John Benker was his name," Hob said. "He got shot dead."

"Good," Spider said, looking at the mess. Things were tossed about haphazardly, and precious space was being wasted.

Spider asked Hob to fetch him a bucket. The boy did so quickly, and Spider put the best-looking mallet he could readily find into the empty container. He fished about for a decent file, then cursed and decided a smoke was needed. "I am going aft, boy, and will grapple with this mess later. I might use a good hand, if you are free."

"I am supposed to help the doctor with the meal," Hob said. "After that, maybe, if Cap'n says."

"Well enough." Spider grinned. "Let us find the cook. I'll need his fire."

Wandering aft on the gently rolling deck, Spider pulled free the pipe tucked into his belt and filled it from his slack pouch. It would be his last smoke for a while, unless he could filch or purchase some tobacco. Amidships, *Dream* had a fire box, a brick oven where crews had boiled the blubber from their long voyages. Spider could see where two more such ovens had flanked this one, but those had been removed. The remaining oven, belching smoke as the doctor struggled to close the iron door without burning his hand, served as the galley.

"Good morning, Doctor," Spider said, whipping the kerchief from his head and wrapping his hand. He opened the door swiftly, shoved some tinder from a bucket into the box, and lit it. Then he put it to his pipe to bring it to life.

"Good morning it is not, I dare say," Boddings growled. "The Lord meant me for finer things than to be ship's cook." He tossed a ladle into the deep pot swinging from his right hand, splashing hot water that sizzled on the deck.

"I will not bother you further," Spider answered, patting Hob on the shoulder before taking his leave.

Bright sun washed the deck, and the sails swelled with good wind. *Plymouth Dream* was meandering her way southward, at about eleven knots, and Spider was glad of it, for there would not be many more bright days such as this at this latitude. He missed the Caribbean. Spider replaced the scarf on his head and gazed into the starboard distance, but he could not make out the coast. He had no idea how far off the land was; in any event, it was unreachable. It might as well have been a million leagues.

He craned his neck to look about as men shuffled to and fro in confusion, some working, some dangling nets in hopes of capturing fresh fish, others trying to amuse themselves with dice or arguing about politics or theology. Amid the chaos he was able to determine *Dream* mounted six four-pounders on her main deck. One cannon had a carriage with a nasty crack that would not survive many more firings. A couple of small swivel guns were placed above the forecastle, where they could harry any ship *Dream* pursued. The four-pounders were mismatched but all carriage-mounted; they were locked down tight now, but could be moved in a hurry. The rail had been cut to accommodate the weapons.

A glance over the gunwale showed him a dull white hull trimmed in bright, bloody red, with paint mostly in good condition but in need of care here and there.

He looked about for Ezra and spotted the tall fellow aft at the tiller. He headed that way, a cloud of smoke from his clay pipe streaming in the wind, a pair of chickens crossing his path.

Spider climbed onto the poop deck and waved at Ezra. "Well, then, they found honest work for you, did they?"

Ezra grinned. "I suppose you've been busy pretending to fit one piece of wood to another in some useful fashion, Spider John."

"I've been pondering the proper fate for a messy carpenter. It involves brimstone," Spider said. He pointed at the wheel. "How does she feel?"

"It's like dancing with a pig," Ezra said.

"Ah, then, you know a thing or two about that, I'd say."

Ezra nodded and winced. "She goes where you tell her, but not as easily as she ought."

"I'm going to go and put together a decent kit of tools, then give the ship a look. Storm probably knocked things about, I'd guess, and her previous carpenter wasn't one to work too much."

"Feels that way," Ezra said. "I noted a hatch cover missing in the crew hold. Some night a drunk will step in it and bust his head further below."

"I saw that," Spider sighed. "Got other stuff to see to, first, so watch your step."

"Aye." Ezra nodded. Wind blew his red mane all around, and he looked genuinely happy to be at sea once again.

"I shall give the rudder a look, when I can, see if I can make her dance more like a lady," Spider promised, turning. He found himself face-to-face with a wild-eyed Peter Tellam.

The tattooed man roughly shoved him aside and glowered at Ezra. Behind Tellam stood a broad-shouldered but short man. Spider thought he'd heard him called Jenkins. That man had a knife in his hand and glared at Ezra, but Tellam did all the talking.

"Jesus consigns your soul to hell, Ezra Coombs." Tellam no longer wore the long cloak, nor did he wear a shirt. Spider wondered what sort of zeal prompted the man to doff his shirt and coat in this brisk October wind. The whorled tattoos covered his sun-browned upper body, and they wriggled like snakes as he moved. So did the muscles in his arms.

Ezra laughed softly. "Aye, but the Lord is happy to watch you go about the sea robbing and killing, then?"

Tellam sneered. "I am not without sin, but I can make amends and try to free myself of this life. You, though, will always be Satan's spawn.

"I prayed on it, Coombs, and decided I cannot remain silent. You should not have brought your Satan taint aboard this vessel."

"No taint," Ezra said calmly. "I rebuke the devil, praise the Lord." He brought his hands together quickly in a prayerful gesture, then returned them to the wheel. "I've no wish to trouble you, Peter Tellam."

"You do not fool me," Tellam said.

Odin, sitting low on the mizzenmast ratlines, chuckled quietly, shaking his head and squeezing his lone eye shut.

Spider, behind the interlopers now, slowly pulled his own knife free. He concealed it beneath crossed arms and measured the distance between himself and the necks of the two men confronting Ezra.

"Not tryin' to fool anyone," Ezra said. "Just need to live, and sailin' is my trade. This is the only job I could find."

Tellam turned to address a slowly growing crowd on the deck below. "That is all you are, eh? Just an honest sailin' man? Did you tell them your ma was a witch, Coombs?"

Jenkins snorted, and his fingers fiddled with the knife in his hand.

"She was not," Ezra said, controlling his anger admirably, but Spider could detect the signs in his posture and in his voice, and was glad to note Ezra glanced at Jenkins's blade. "They hung her, but she was no witch."

"They hung your ma's ma, too, didn't they? I suppose she, too, was no witch?"

"That is true, she was no witch." Spider and Ezra made eye contact, and Spider showed him a brief glimpse of the knife he concealed at the ready. Ezra kept at the tiller. "Men do foolish things sometimes, and people die," Ezra said. "Sometimes innocent people."

Tellam faced him again. "Oh, yes, innocent people die. I know that. They die around you, don't they? Have you told these good gentlemen of the *Trusty*? How she went down? Showed them your mark, have you?"

Spider heard a few gasps and muttered curses. Most men of the sea knew the tale of the ill-fated *Trusty*, a Royal Navy brig lost on her maiden voyage from Plymouth. Powder in the hold had exploded, and most of the hull forward had shattered in a heartbeat. The rest of her sank quickly enough. Very few survived. Ezra Coombs was one of the lucky ones.

Ezra raised his right arm and pulled at his coat and shirt sleeves, revealing a tattoo: the words "Trusty, 1716" engraved on an anchor.

"Yes. I was aboard *Trusty*, part of her one and only crew. Damn tragedy. Good men lost."

"You weren't lost, though," Tellam said, sneering.

"Calm this storm, lads." That came from a voice in the crowd on the deck below, and Spider spotted Weatherall. The man had been unfriendly when pouring their ale, but he was acting as peacemaker now. "The Lord will sort it all out, no need for us to fret." Weatherall then turned to whisper something to Peg and toothless Dobbin.

"I was lucky," Ezra said. "I could have been killed as easily as anyone else."

"Lucky, you say," Tellam spat. "Can't say the same for your shipmates, now, can we?"

Jenkins snorted again and tightened his grip on the knife hilt.

"I had nothin' to do with the blast, damn you," Ezra said. "If you've a point to prove, let's have a go." He nodded at a fellow who had been smoking aft. That man took over the tiller; then Ezra stepped back and plucked his dirk from his belt.

Tellam smiled. "Let us do just that." He drew his own knife. Tellam showed no fear of Ezra's size.

"Thou shalt not suffer a witch to live!" That came from someone in the crowd. Toothless Dobbin bellowed something incomprehensible in reply.

"Whoa, lads, whoa!" Elijah waved his arms, spinning in a circle, addressing all aboard from a spot near the poop deck ladder. Spider could smell the man's perfume. "The Lord has a plan. It is not for us to judge. Perhaps Ezra was spared because it was the Lord's will."

Some crewmen nodded. Others seemed dubious. Odin, his one eye shining brightly, laughed at a joke only he could hear. Spider saw no change in attitude from the pair confronting Ezra, however.

"Cursed witch!" Jenkins was in motion even as he said it, the knife aimed at Ezra's throat. Tellam stepped back, and Ezra moved to defend himself.

Jenkins lunged with a shout, but Ezra stepped aside and clubbed him hard on the shoulder with the bone hilt of his own knife. Jenkins stumbled but regained his footing quickly and spun about. Ezra was taller, and certainly stronger, Spider judged, but Jenkins was quick.

Spider figured Ezra would handle Jenkins, so he tried to keep a weather eye on Tellam. That man stood back, grinning and muttering. Spider thought he made out the word "Jesus" once or twice.

Jenkins feinted left, then moved in again, bringing his knife upward in a big sweeping curve that started low and drove toward Ezra's belly. Jenkins's left hand slipped behind his back and brought forth a second knife while Ezra grabbed the attacking arm with his left hand. Spider shouted a warning, but Ezra didn't need it. When Jenkins stabbed with the second knife, Ezra's blade was there to parry, and Ezra's knee drove upward into his assailant's crotch.

Jenkins howled, doubled over, and got a knee in the face. Bloodied, he fell backward. Spider silently willed Ezra to go ahead and kill the son of a bitch, but Ezra stood grinning.

"If you'd like to dance some more, I will oblige," Ezra told Jenkins, who was coughing and snorting blood.

"Belay that!" Barlow shoved his way through the surrounding men and climbed the ladder to the poop deck.

"Son of the devil," Jenkins hissed, rising more quickly than Spider expected and lunging with his knife at the ready. Ezra squared for battle again just as a thundercrack made Spider jump. A large hole erupted in Jenkins's forehead. The man's legs went limp, and he fell nose-first onto the deck.

"Damn and blazes!" Barlow roared, a smoking blunderbuss in one hand and his cane in the other. The first mate Addison followed, pistol in hand and sword drawn. No one else made a move, nor uttered a word. "When I say belay, goddamn it, belay! What in hell goes on here?"

Tellam spat. "Coombs is a witch's son!"

Barlow raised his eyebrows. "Well, now. True, is it?" He stared at the dead man and shook his head slowly.

"Aye," Tellam said. "*Trusty* sank under his curse! Jenk was goin' to throw his cursed ass overboard!" Tellam turned toward Ezra, as if to avenge his friend, but dropped his knife as Addison raised his pistol and said quietly, "Think, man."

Barlow glanced at the dropped blade and smiled. "Well, damned silly thing to lose an able-bodied man about." He tapped Jenkins with the cane. "Dead. For nothing. Goddamn ye, Tellam. I don't believe in curses."

"Ask Bent Thomas about curses, then." Tellam's eyes were wide and gleaming. "*Trusty* weren't the only ship this bastard cursed. Coombs was aboard *Lamia* when she went under, too. His friend said so, aye? Two ships lost with this bastard aboard. Shall we be the third?"

Barlow spun slowly, pointing his cane at Ezra and glancing quickly at Spider. "That is true enough, now ain't it? Bent Thomas took you on, and his ship is gone. Maybe he's gone, too. Good man, Bent Thomas."

Ezra nodded. "Aye, a good man," he said, breathing hard but keeping his voice calm and even. "Hope he lives yet. I've seen more than my share of troubles, it is true. A lot of us have, I reckon. Dangerous work, aye? Being a sailor, a pirate? But I've sailed aboard a number of ships, and most of them didn't sink."

"He doesn't belong on this vessel, I say," Tellam said. "He deserves to burn."

"Should he, now? Should he?" Barlow seemed lost in thought for a moment. "Well, I will be damned," Barlow said at last, spinning slowly as he talked so that all could hear. "And so will all of you, and it ain't nothing to do with anyone's ma or witch blood. I'd say most of us have earned our own hellish fates twice over. If there is a hell, it was made for us, gents. You, too, Tellam. You, too."

As the captain spoke, he randomly pointed his flintlock here and there, so each man could imagine a ball flying through his brain. All hands quieted. Spider returned his knife to his belt; Ezra did likewise.

"We prevail through strength in numbers, gentlemen," Barlow continued. "We can scarce afford to be ripping up our own strength." He stared at Tellam. "We all know you can fight, Tell. Jenkins could fight, too. He could handle gun and blade, but we have lost that, have we not? Over nothing? And now," he said, turning toward Ezra. "We know Coombs here can fight as well. So we've lost one, and we've gained one. Very good. Scales balance, gents, and that is about as fair as any of us has a right to expect. Maybe more so. Let us not wager more," he added, glaring at Tellam.

"We're stronger together, gents, stronger together," the captain said. "We make our own luck, and fucking fight together, and need every fucking able hand we can muster. Roberts is done, his crew hung, so many wolves have fled these waters. We've got the prey all to ourselves, if we be smart. Have we made money, men?"

A few cheers went up.

"Have we made money, I ask?"

A louder, more enthusiastic chorus rose.

"And we will make more. Much, much more." Barlow lifted his cane to the sky. "I do not believe in witches, or curses, or bogeymen, or mermaids, or little fucking fairies, but if this man proves to be unlucky"—he aimed the pistol at Ezra's head—"I will shoot him myself, without hesitation, without remorse, just as I shot Jenkins for disobeying my order. Until such time as I deem it fit to shoot this man, though, we will all keep our pretty little knives tucked away where we don't get hurt, and we will use our strength and our daring to make us all rich men. Agreed?"

Men nodded and cheered.

"Now, then, Tellam. You see to your friend. Distribute his goods, per the articles. Spider John, have you work to do?"

"About to get to it, sir."

"Do that," Barlow growled. He gave Ezra a long look. "You can fight, for certain. Save it for when we need it. Don't go lookin' for more trouble."

"Aye," Ezra said.

The captain climbed down the ladder and stalked off. "Out of my way, Peg, damn ye!" The man with the wooden leg jumped aside, quite nimbly, and his peg thunked hard on the deck.

Addison picked up Tellam's knife and gave it back to him. Tellam glared at Ezra, then knelt by Jenkins's corpse. Ezra went back to work at the tiller.

Spider stood by Ezra's shoulder. "This is not good...."

"No," Ezra said. "Not at all good."

They sat together later, Spider athwart a four-pounder and quaffing bad beer, Ezra whittling on a walrus bone as he sat on the gunwale. The workday had been long, but Spider had been right about the rudder needing some care. *Dream* had been idle most of the day while he opened her up below and replaced a cracked brace, but she was under sail again now and behaving herself admirably. Barlow, who had grumbled ceaselessly while Spider worked, was all smiles and nods once *Dream* was catching wind again. She was not a bad little lady, Spider had decided of this craft. He deemed it a shame her decks went almost entirely without washing. Her canvas and rigging were in good shape, though. Odin had primary responsibility for those.

Evening had come at last, and the doctor had produced a somewhat edible chicken stew. Tellam was keeping below. No one else was eager to approach Spider and Ezra, but every now and then Spider would see Weatherall or toothless Dobbin or the doctor staring at them. Others stared, too, but eyes always averted quickly.

Men talked quietly. Spider could catch none of what they said, but he could guess most of it. Jenkins was mentioned more than once.

"Perhaps we should have a scuffle between us two," Ezra said, keeping his voice low. "So these gents don't think you are a curse, too. I won't hurt you."

"You won't even touch me," Spider answered. "But, no. No. If they want to fight you, they can fight us both. But storms pass. Perhaps this one will."

"You are a good friend," Ezra said. "You could not debate a donkey, but you are a good friend."

Hob rushed toward them, with the cat Thomas in his wake. The boy held a long stick, like a broom handle, with a lengthy metal spike protruding from it. Three rats were skewered on that spike.

"I get an extra tot of grog for this," Hob said happily, holding his stick out over the rail and shaking it heartily until his rodent victims slid into the waves. Hob, hooting and hollering, ran off to get his reward.

Thomas stayed behind and seemed vaguely disappointed.

"You'll just have to work faster," Ezra said, stroking the cat's chin. "You were made for rat killing, you know. Shouldn't let a snip of a boy do your work for you."

"The damned cat does not understand you." Spider laughed. "You give beasts too much credit for brains."

"They are better than most people I've known," Ezra replied. "You rate slightly higher than cats, I'd say, maybe not so high as dogs."

Spider rolled his eyes but decided not to press his friend on the matter.

Barlow marched forward and stood before Doctor Boddings, who was drinking from a wooden bowl. "Well, Doctor Cook, that was a rare soup," the captain said. "Rare soup."

Boddings did not rise from the keg he sat upon. "I did my best. Onions were plentiful, if not of the freshest. I do love onions, and they are rather healthful, too. Very good for the digestion."

"Yes, I suppose. We likely won't have any more onions soon, or any other garden delights until we reach Jamaica, but that's as may be." Barlow removed the cane from his shoulder and tapped it against the deck. "Tell me, Doctor. Can you lay eggs?"

"Eh?" The physician looked confused.

"I admit it would be a good and rare quality in a doctor, to have him be able to lay us some eggs," Barlow said. "I doubt you can do it. But circumstances compel me to ask. Can you lay eggs?"

"What in the Lord's name . . . ? Are you drunk, sir? Of course, I do not lay eggs," Boddings mumbled tersely.

"Then stop killing my damned chickens!" The captain punctuated the command with his cane, whacking Boddings soundly on the shoulder. "Boil the eggs, damn you, not the fucking birds!"

Boddings cried out. "Damn, sir! Damn!"

Barlow whacked him again. "You want soup, you catch a fucking fish! Carve a fucking pig! Boil your own fucking leg and balls if you must! But I shall have my fucking boiled fucking eggs, sir. I shall! Idiot college man!"

Barlow stomped off. Laughter lifted from the deck. Boddings stood fuming.

Ezra laughed with the others, but the comedy did little to lift Spider's spirits. Too many evil eyes had been turned their way.

The doctor straightened his jacket and glowered at Ezra.

"Seems you have tempers all stirred up," Boddings said, scowling.

Ezra chuckled. "I did not slaughter the man's fowl, Doctor. How many did you kill, by the way? It's appreciated. Very tasty."

"Do not mock me," Boddings said. "You should be concerned for your own soul." He strode forward with as much dignity as he could muster, muttering something about Jesus. He staggered a bit. Spider wondered if that was because of the captain's blows, or because the physician's bowl had contained more than mere broth.

"It's a pretty night, too pretty for bickering. A tune, maybe," someone said. It was Dowd, the broad-shouldered black man who had charge of the night watch. "How about it, John? I'll fetch yer fiddle."

"Not tonight," Weatherall said. He kept his eyes aimed on the deck, save for a glance at Ezra. "Don't like the comp'ny." He went below.

"Best we get some sleep," Ezra said.

"Aye. Sleep. With an eye open." Spider nodded. "Maybe both eyes."

Spider awoke suddenly.

He'd expected the nightmares. Being surrounded by suspicious men had not made for a restful night, of course, but the nightmares . . . All the talk of witches and burning, all the tension of knives and guns, the death of Jenkins and the body's quick descent into the deep—such things led to a haunted and fitful sleep.

The dreams had been particularly horrible. Fire and smoke. Charnel smells. Shouts and taunts. A woman's face, burnt black, framed by his grandmother's auburn hair. He had never seen his grandmother, of course, but the dreamer knew her face just the same. Now he shuddered at the nightmare memory of the white smile in the charred face, and the dead woman's words: "I love you, Johnny." He still could see her, stretching out arms to him, beckoning him toward her, into the fire.

Spider sat up, shook his head, and wished he had a drink. He had no notion of time; he only sensed that dawn was not yet here. It took him a moment to realize the shouts of his dream could still be heard— they were part of this world, the real world, not the nightmare.

The voices came from up on the deck. Someone climbed the ladder quickly.

"Dead, I say," were the only coherent words Spider could make out.

He rose, took a step toward Ezra's hammock, then noticed his friend was not there.

Spider was up the ladder and on deck in a couple of heartbeats. A couple of hands stood there in the night, and one held a lantern that threw an orange circle of light onto the deck. In the center of that circle, Ezra stared up at the stars, seeing nothing of this world. He was seated awkwardly, against the larboard rail, next to a hip flask that had poured most of its contents onto the bloody deck beside him.

But he was not dead drunk.

He was dead.

Spider leapt forward. "Lord, no!"

A crowd grew around him. "Found him here," someone said. "Must have been drunk and mindless. Hit his head on the damned rail and busted it."

Spider had not seen Ezra go up the ladder, but it was not a rare thing for him to do so. Ezra liked the night stars and slept less than most men.

Now, he was lost in the longest sleep of all.

The wound had bled profusely, and moonlight rippled in the puddle. Spider, no stranger to violence, coughed and choked nonetheless.

"When did he come up top?" Spider asked finally. "Who was with him? Who?" He glanced around but saw no sign of Tellam.

"No one with him," Weatherall said. "We found him thus."

Spider spat and tried to clear his mind. Ezra's forehead was a bloody mess, but his dead eyes were peering skyward. "Did anyone move him?"

"We rolled him over," Peg answered. "Wanted to see who he was, help if we could. We could do nothing for him."

"He hit here," Barlow said, running a finger along the rail above Ezra. "Wet and sticky right here." The captain stared skyward for a moment. "Drunk, he was, no doubt."

"Heard him muttering earlier," Peg said.

Spider shot the one-legged man a glance. "Talking to someone? Who?"

"Didn't hear no other voice. Maybe talking to God, or the devil. About a woman. Said he missed her."

That made no sense to Spider. Ezra had known women, but had never been particularly attached to one. He elevated no one woman above the others, and was never maudlin.

Spider, kneeling now by his friend's side, looked up at Barlow, then back at Ezra. Gently, he closed his friend's eyes and wept. The rum and blood oozing onto the deck seeped into his britches.

He and Ezra had laughed about death, how it lurked nearby always, and how they had no right to expect it to keep away for long. And now, here it was. Victorious, as always.

"Well then," Barlow said. "He's your friend, Spider, so you lay claim first to anything of his you like. The rest, such as it is, we'll sell at bids among the crew, according to the articles. Get it all off him and heave his worthless carcass o'er the side."

"Wait," Spider said, choking a growing rage. "I want to do this proper, say some words. Do we have a Bible aboard?"

Barlow glowered for a moment, then let out a loud sigh. "Words make no matter," he said. "We didn't give Jenkins no words. And I have no use for a Bible."

"I don't give a good goddamn about Jenkins," Spider said through clenched teeth. "This is my friend, and a good man."

"Jesus will sort all that out," Tellam grumbled. Spider had not seen him approach, but he recognized the voice. He turned toward it and glared at Tellam. The tattooed man's eyes were closed, and his lips moved in silent prayer. Spider kept his gaze locked on Tellam until the man opened his eyes again. The latter returned the stare, but his expression was as blank as stone.

"Doctor Boddings has a Bible," Hob piped up. "Least, I think it is a Bible."

"I, indeed, have a New Testament," Doctor Boddings said, "as any decent man should. But I will not lend it to preside over such a wretch as this, this spawn of demons."

Spider huffed. "This is my friend."

"Your friend, not mine," Boddings growled. "Nor is he the Lord's friend, I should say. His soul, such as may be, is consigned elsewhere, I make no doubt."

"Damn true," said Peg. "He's cursed, he is."

"Cursed, indeed," Boddings agreed. "But bless the Lord for lifting the curse from us, aye? Bless him, gents. Bless him. We no longer sail under Satan's taint."

Spider smelled the alcohol on the doctor's breath even from a yard away. "You need not be involved, if you have no compassion for one of God's own. I'll say the words. Can't read, but I'll say the words. I just want to hold the Bible as I pray."

"No," Boddings said, his forehead wrinkling in deep folds. "No. My Bible is not for this . . ." He waved a hand in Ezra's direction, then stalked off, grumbling.

Odin shut his good eye and laughed quietly.

"High words is a waste of your time, Spider," Barlow said. "Heaven, if it be a real place and not a fucking lie, ain't got no use for such as him. Nor you, nor me, for that matter. But it is your time to waste, I suppose."

"Aye," Spider answered.

"What'll you claim from him? He ain't got much," Barlow noted. "Nice knife. Bone handle, looks like. Boots may serve, but his feet are damned huge. Wind prob'ly will cut right through that fucking mangy coat. Take your choice. Crew can bid on the rest."

"I'll take the flask," Spider said. "That is all." He reached for the leather-bound flask and sniffed deeply. Strong rum. Spider's rage grew, but he willed himself to control it. It would not do to let it show, not here, not now.

"Very well," Barlow said. "See it don't lead you to the same sorry state. Say your damned words, then haul him up and over and into the deep, and out of my sight." Barlow stalked away, cane on his shoulder.

Spider began sobbing quietly as others drew back or headed elsewhere. "Ezra," he said quietly, leaning toward his friend's face. "I'll avenge this, brother. I swear it."

He knew Ezra had not filled himself with liquor and tripped or stumbled into the rail. There was no bloody chance of that.

Ezra would have a daily dose or two of heavily watered wine, for his health. He would sometimes have a bit of highly diluted grog when he ate. Spider had often urged his friend to drink more, to fend off the constant sniffles and stomach bugs that plagued Ezra.

But Ezra did not drink hard liquor, and he did not get drunk.

Ever.

4

Spider seethed. He and Ezra had always known death might ride in any day on a musket ball, or on a sword point, or on a mighty storm. Many times they'd spoken of preferring a swift death, that they might avoid hanging or burning. But this! This was death by a coward's hand, and the more Spider saw, the more certain he was that his friend had been murdered.

The now-empty flask lay on the deck beside him as Spider tended to his friend. Already, Ezra's flesh looked pale in the moonlight. Spider was dying to examine the flask, pewter wrapped in leather, to see if it might provide a clue to the killer's identity.

He did not dare voice his thoughts, though. There were, perhaps, seventy killers aboard *Plymouth Dream*, and not a damned one of them cared about justice for Ezra. No one cared, save for Spider John Rush.

Every one of the suspects already had a past of black deeds, and not one of them was likely to put up with Spider poking around into the circumstances of Ezra's slaying.

Spider's only chance of serving justice on Ezra's murderer was to remain silent, pretend the ruse with the flask had worked, and act as though his friend had been nothing more than the victim of his own foolish, drunken binge.

It would be difficult, and painful, but it was the only way.

Spider's mind filled with images of *Plymouth Dream*'s crew.

Tellam might have done this. Ezra had shown up his friend Jenkins badly, and the man had died at the captain's hand as a result of that fight. Perhaps Tellam had blamed Ezra and sought vengeance. But with all the talk of witches and curses flying about the vessel in the wake

of the fight, any one of the souls aboard might have done the bloody
deed, in a bid to erase the supposed curse. For all Spider knew, the
same culprit might now be whetting a blade intended for his throat,
or waiting in the dark to club him. He was Ezra's friend and, perhaps, a
target because of it.

He certainly would become a target if he began lobbing accusa-
tions and difficult questions.

He did not even consider taking his concerns to Barlow. Despite
his speech about the common good after the fight, the captain likely
considered the loss of Ezra a good thing, something that would hush
the rough talk and prevent more trouble. If Spider stirred things up,
Barlow might well heave him overboard to keep Ezra company.

Even if Barlow did give a damn about a bloody murder on his own
vessel, telling him would only cause a ruckus and alert the crew that
Spider was on the hunt.

No. Spider would not have that. He would keep his head down and
his mouth shut. He would pay heed to what went on around him, listen
to all that was said, and learn who had killed Ezra Coombs.

And then, Spider would cut the goddamned bastard in half.

He could not examine the flask now, but he had a chance to
examine Ezra and the vicinity as he removed his friend's jacket, boots,
and knife, then prepared to stitch him into the shroud. Barlow, when
asked, said he would not waste sailcloth on Ezra, but he allowed for
use of a large and tattered black flag. The ensign was riddled with holes
from moths and chain shot, and had been partially burned. It was
crusted with sweat, salt, and old blood, and would have been an embar-
rassment to fly, even over a pirate vessel.

But it was all Barlow would spare, and it would have to serve.
Spider felt strongly that there should be a shroud, however meager it
might be.

The flag bore Barlow's device of a white skull dripping blood. The
irony of that rattled Spider, because the front of Ezra's head was sharply
dented where something had hammered him, and his face and head
were sticky with blood.

Spider winced and slowly ran his fingers over the wound. No . . . wounds. Two clear, deep impressions could be felt beneath the bloody, matted hair. Spider eyed the gunwale, smeared with blood. It was smooth cedar, and he did not see how it could possibly have caused such a pair of wounds. Certainly, Ezra did not fall and hit his head twice, and Spider doubted such vicious wounds would have resulted even if Ezra had run headlong into the rail at full speed. No, the killer had hit Ezra with something hard and heavy, then hit him once again to be sure, and dragged him against the rail. Spider could see a smear of blood on the deck, darkly wet in the bright moonlight.

Spider's fingers found something else. He thought it was a shard of bone, but looked at it and realized it was a splinter, embedded in Ezra's skull. Applewood, not cedar, or he was no carpenter. He pocketed it for later inspection.

Hob plopped down beside Spider and placed a leather-bound New Testament on the deck, next to the spilt liquor and blood. The book was in sorry condition, its pages frayed and its cover whitened by much exposure to salt spray and sun.

Spider picked it up gently. "Did the doctor change his mind, boy?"

"No," Hob said. "But I helped him stow his stuff and knew right where it was. The doctor is asleep already, deep drunk."

"Thank you, Hob. We'll do this quick, then. I ain't able to read it anyway. After, you can get this back where it belongs." Spider put a hand on Hob's shoulder. "Not sure the Lord would like you stealing a Bible."

"Borrowing," Hob said. "Borrowing a Bible, and for a good cause."

"Aye," Spider agreed. "A good cause."

Spider placed the book beside his dead friend, careful to keep it from the gore and booze, then finished stitching the shroud shut. He did not run the needle through Ezra's nose, as was customary, to assure himself Ezra was truly dead. There was no doubt of it.

Spider closed his eyes, picked up the weather-worn Bible, and began to pray quietly.

"Lord, Ezra don't deserve it, and I've no right to ask it, but if your mercy be what they say, spare some of it, I beg, for my friend Ezra Coombs. He's done some ill in this world, as have I, but not so ill as we might have done, and we'd both of us had picked a better path if one had been open to us. If it be worth anything, he was a friend to me as good as any. A sturdy man, a good sailor, honest among friends.

"God bless his soul, if it please the Lord."

And damn the coward who murdered him, he added silently.

5

Spider would never forget the sight of his friend slipping into the dark waters. He'd watched from the rail a long time, as though he could still see the bloody black flag sinking in the moonbeams that fought to penetrate the waters, even after *Plymouth Dream* had passed far beyond the spot.

He saw nothing but the deepest of graves.

Spider hid out in the lumber hold. He had not bothered trying to sleep. Instead, he sat there, where a swinging lantern fouled the air and provided untrustworthy light as *Dream* rolled. Spider stared at the flask, hoping it might provide a vital clue. A couple of times, he kissed Em's pendant for comfort.

It was a small pewter flask, of the sort hunters sometimes carried, wrapped in a leather harness and small enough to tuck into a pocket. He had not found the cork. Full, the flask might have been heavy enough to strike a fatal blow, especially if swung at the end of a long strap. The harness had fittings for a strap, but there was none attached and Spider had not found one near Ezra's body. He examined the leather harness, which bore old scratches and stains, but no fresh marks.

Spider teased the flask from the harness. He had seen such flasks elaborately engraved; sometimes they bore the name of the owner or the name of a ship or a particular battle. This one showed no signs at all, save for a small maker's mark that meant nothing to Spider.

He sniffed at the empty bottle and again recognized the strong scent of rum.

The flask told him nothing else. He rummaged about, found

a length of leather cord, and fashioned a strap for the harness. He returned flask to leather and hung the damned thing on a lantern hook.

He pulled the splinter from his pocket. He smelled it, peered at it, twirled it in his fingers, and chewed on it. It was applewood, no doubt. Spider wished that fact told him more, but at least it was something.

Almost anybody aboard *Plymouth Dream* might have been the culprit. No one had admitted seeing anything or hearing any sounds of a scuffle. It must have been a surprise attack. Had it been a real fight, Ezra no doubt would have marked his man. No one fought Ezra without getting hurt. Spider determined to eye faces come morning, looking for bruises and scratches, but he knew it likely would be folly. All the signs pointed to a sneak attack.

So, then, who could the culprit be?

Tellam was the obvious suspect. He would bear watching.

Even so, Spider could not accuse the man of murder on the basis of what he knew so far. Tellam likely had mates aboard, and perhaps one of them had struck a blow as a favor. And all the talk of Satan's taint and witch blood . . . anyone might have attacked out of fear. Tellam could have instigated the slaying, convincing someone else to do the bloody deed.

Spider cursed himself for thinking in circles and willed himself to concentrate.

He tried to remember who had been on deck at the time. Men of Dowd's watch, and there were only a few of those. Dowd, of course, a quiet man Barlow deemed worthy to take charge at night. Weatherall, Dobbin, and Peg all were assigned to that late watch, and a few others whose names he had not yet learned. It mattered little who was assigned, though, for watches meant very little aboard *Plymouth Dream*.

On a naval ship, or on a legitimate merchant craft, for that matter, comings and goings were easier to track. Men kept regular watches, with times set for working and for sleeping, and there were ample officers' eyes upon them. Everyone had a particular place to be, and a particular time to be there.

That was not the case on a pirate vessel, and certainly not the case aboard *Plymouth Dream*. Some men had particular tasks, while others seemed only to take up space, with no apparent use until it came time for a fight. Nothing happened on a schedule, and Spider had seen crewmen swap watches freely with little supervision. The men on *Plymouth Dream* frequently traded chores or gambled to foist their duties off on others. All that likely would change if the ship went into battle; he'd already been told that his role in a fight would be boarding party duty unless ordered otherwise. Men would know what to do when bloodshed was in the offing, but they cared little for the day-to-day work of sailing.

As for his own watch, Spider could not narrow anything down there, either. They had been below sleeping, for the most part, but men had gone up top and come back down throughout the night, whether they went up to piss or smoke or drink or just to get away from the stench below, a miasma of sweat, farts, urine, and the odor of boiling whale fat soaked into the wood, plus Elijah's damnable woman scent.

Spider held a saw, momentarily imagining it slicing the neck of Ezra's killer, then placed it into the large bucket, the one he had picked to hold the best tools. The dangling flask threw an odd shadow against the bulkhead, like a man swinging from a gallows. Spider snatched the damned thing off the hook and threw it into a corner.

Who might have had strong reason to kill Ezra?

Captain Barlow, perhaps.

Hell, the captain may have slain Ezra just to shut mouths and end all the talk of curses and witches. He'd made a grand talk after killing Jenkins, but might well have decided the loss of one more able fighter was not so bad a price to pay to quell the bitching during a lengthy voyage.

For all his talk of strength in numbers, Barlow himself was on the wrong end of that equation. He ruled, through guile and strength and terror, but only so long as his crew did not rise up. He had no marines, no Admiralty to enforce his will, and the captain knew it—Spider could see it in his eyes.

The captain had stepped in to stop Ezra and Tellam from killing one another. Had his tough talk and threats been only that? Something to stop a volatile situation from growing worse? Perhaps Barlow, once things had settled down, had carefully arranged an accident in the night. Find Ezra, club him dead, drag him against the rail, and drop a flask of rum. A sad and tragic event, but one that kept fear and anger from fermenting into an uprising, and one that kept Barlow from having to openly kill another member of his crew. Men might balk at the fear of such a thing, but if Barlow turned threat into deed too often he might well touch off a mutinous powder keg. But an accident, God's judgment and not the captain's, might serve.

Once coming to that conclusion, Barlow would not even have to do the bloody job himself. Either Dowd or Addison, the only two Barlow seemed to trust at all, might have arranged the death on Barlow's orders. Or they might have done so on their own initiative.

And what of Doctor Boddings? He had made his disdain for Ezra quite clear. The doctor was no fighter, but it took no fighter to crack a man's skull in a surprise blow. Ezra might not have suspected such a thing at all from the rotund surgeon, and might well have let his guard down. The doctor had been drinking rum, too. Was the flask his?

Why was Boddings aboard this vessel, anyway? He must be sixty years old if he was a day, Spider guessed. Why turn pirate at that age? Boddings had said he wished to reach Jamaica, but he had not really talked of his future or his past, and had done his best to avoid conversation. He kept to himself, and his manner kept others away from him.

Might Boddings have some mysterious agenda? Might Ezra have somehow run afoul of him?

And what in hell was this talk of Ezra muttering about a woman? What woman?

Other men's faces flashed in his mind. Elijah. Dobbin. Crazy Odin. It all made Spider dizzy.

He found an old knife blade in the bucket and began seeking some decent wood or bone to serve as a handle. He searched among the strewn metal and wood and rope and bone for anything he could fashion into small weapons he might conceal. He thanked the Lord he was a carpenter and could go about with sharp things without arousing suspicion.

Spider and Ezra had boarded *Dream* together, and the killer might believe Spider carried the taint of Satan as well.

Spider spat on his hands and rubbed them together rapidly. He had work to do. If it came to a fight, he would give them hell.

6

Shortly after first light, Spider wrapped himself in his pea coat, bound his unkempt blond-brown hair into a black strip of rag, and climbed on deck. A steady wind filled the sail, and *Plymouth Dream* was riding nicely with her larboard side high and a gentle rocking fore and aft. The sky was gray, and the clouds were low. The cold seeped into the earring he wore, and the stud felt like an icicle piercing his lobe.

Hob was carting about a bucket of hardtack, and Spider grabbed a couple. "Fresh water forward," Hob said.

Thomas the cat trailed Hob.

"Did you get the doctor's Bible back where he keeps it, boy?" He did not really care whether Boddings got his book back, but he was tired of silence.

"Yes, sir, I did. He snores and grumbles a good deal in his sleep, but he's dead to the world when he's drunk. There was no trick to it."

"Good. He'd been drinking hard, I'd judge."

"Always seems to," Hob said before rushing aft to distribute biscuits.

Spider's bucket contained mallets, a file, pliers, calipers, a couple of rulers—and the long knife, its new handle conspicuously white so it could be spotted and plucked free quickly. He had his belt knife, too.

Spider went about inspecting the ship, checking fittings and planking, spars and ratchets, booms and hatches. By an act of will, he made himself start far aft, away from the point amidships where Ezra had been killed. He did not want anyone to think he was on the hunt.

There was endless work for any carpenter on any ship, even one in excellent condition, and Spider saw many things that needed attention, but none that needed immediate work. As he stooped by a scupper, feeling for rot and finding none, he was aware of the gazes that followed him. He had lost a friend, but there would be little sympathy shown among this crew. Pirate lives were easily lost, and he was not among old acquaintances here.

Men turned away quickly whenever he looked at them, but Spider made a point of studying faces, looking for fresh cuts or bruises, signs to show perhaps Ezra had been able to fight back after all. He saw none. All the scratches, cuts, and scrapes he spotted had been there for days, at least.

There was not a man aboard who did not have bloodstains somewhere on his clothes, but Spider saw none that looked fresh.

No one spoke to him, and most hands went silent when he came nearby. A couple of times he tried to strike up a conversation, hoping to nail down who had been up on deck at the time of Ezra's death. He got little but shrugs and stares in return.

The one exception was the strange cuss they called Odin. When Spider studied his gruesome face, the man stared back at him with his one good eye. Odin laughed quietly before turning and climbing into the hold.

Spider shuddered and looked for Tellam. He saw no sign of the tattooed bastard—and he reckoned that was a good thing for Tellam.

He heard the tapping of Barlow's cane before he heard the man's voice. "And how do you find our pretty *Plymouth Dream*, sir carpenter?"

"Tools were a righteous mess, but *Dream* seems sound enough. Her boats are horrible. I'll know more after I get around the ship." Spider was in no mood to talk to Barlow, but he forced himself. He wanted a closer look at the pistol tucked into Barlow's belt.

Barlow stared off into the sky. "It is good, Spider, good to get on with your work. Addy did good with you, I think. You may be worth keeping around."

"I keep busy, sir." The grip of Barlow's gun might be applewood, Spider thought. He'd have given much to get his hands on it, to see if it had recently splintered or been stained with blood. But Barlow was in constant motion, and Spider never got a clear look at the gun for long.

The captain tapped a spot on the taffrail with his cane. "There, I think. A swivel gun would be useful there. Blast at anyone trying to rake us. We have one below. I will tell Addy to have it fetched up. You can mount it."

"Aye, sir."

Barlow glanced about at men tossing coins and dice, eating hard-tack, idiotically attempting to juggle knives on a rolling deck, or dozing against a gun mount. Pirate vessels needed many hands for thievery at sea, but *Dream* did not require so many hands to sail her. Life on the account was largely an endless search for diversion.

"Initiative such as yours is sorely lacking, I should say." Barlow smiled. "Hell, it's no matter. They're hungry, wanting for something, too idle. We'll likely find us some prey as we get farther south. A little profit, hey? And a little hard work to earn it? And then a sunny place in the Caribbean to spend it all, and a rendezvous with friends. We've a small fleet, Spider, a small but mighty fleet."

"Aye," Spider said.

Barlow left abruptly, and Spider continued working his way about the vessel. The masts and booms were sound, and the deck was in good shape, if in need of a good scrape with the holystones. There'd be some work to keep these lazy hands busy, he thought, but he decided against saying anything to Barlow. The man knew his deck was filthy, and he could decide for himself whether that needed correcting.

Finally, with the sun a bit higher and the wind easing off, Spider came to the spot he sorely wished to inspect. Bloodstains on the deck showed where Ezra had fallen, and a smear indicated he'd been dragged a short distance to the rail.

He looked around for a cork but found none. It bothered him that the cork should be missing; no one wandered about with an uncorked flask. He looked this way and that, imagined the damned thing rolling about, and realized that the tossing deck might have sent it anywhere. Seeking it was useless.

Spider ran his fingers across the bloody wood, then wiped away a tear. A familiar scent arrested his attention, and he sniffed his finger again. Gunpowder. He eyed the deck more closely and knelt until his nose almost touched it. Gunpowder, grains scattered here and there, some of them stuck in the bloody stains.

Spider closed his eyes and tried to envision the murder. Ezra, staring at the sky or off to sea. A half-dozen men, maybe, on deck because of duty, and who knows how many there just because there was nowhere else to be? Privacy was scarce on a crowded ship.

Had the killer tried to shoot Ezra, and perhaps suffered a misfire, then used the butt of the gun as a club?

No, Spider decided. That made no sense. A shot would have drawn a dozen eyes instantly, and the ruse with the flask indicated an attempt at deception. Also, a misfire would have given Ezra a chance to bloody the son of a bitch.

No, the killer had not tried to shoot Ezra, but that did not rule out the butt of a blunderbuss as a convenient club. Only Barlow and Addison carried guns aboard *Dream*. Or, perhaps, a belaying pin had served as a weapon; the presence of gunpowder did not prove a gun had been used. Powder was no surprise on a ship like this, and these decks were rarely cleaned. That gunpowder might have been there long before Ezra was killed.

Spider imagined the killer skulking toward his prey, perhaps creeping beneath the boom. The man would have had almost no time to do the bloody deed before being seen, so he would have struck quickly. One sudden blow, and another to make certain.

What would follow the clubbing?

Drag the body toward the rail. Had the killer intended to heave Ezra overboard? Probably. That would have made Ezra just another damned sailor who vanished in the night.

But Ezra was a big fellow. *Dream* had many strong, stout men among her crew, but lifting Ezra would not be easy, nor would it be something that could be done quickly.

So, the attempt failed. Perhaps someone approached, or the killer grew nervous. In any event, here was a dead body on the deck of a captain who might react badly—unless he was the killer himself. So improvise. Drag the dead man against the rail, drop the flask, smear some blood on the gunwale, duck out of sight, emerge with the crowd once the body was discovered.

Spider looked around and tried to decide where he might dash if he had to vanish in an instant. He might have rolled to starboard under the mainsail boom, or dodged behind a ship's boat. He might have scurried into the hold, for the hatch was not far away. There were shadows, too. On a night vessel with no real routine, it might be done.

Vanishing may well have been the simplest part of the crime, even for a killer with nowhere to run.

Damn! Spider tried to recall who was on deck when he came up top, but it was a blur. He remembered Weatherall and Dowd were close by the body, and Barlow showed up quickly, but there were others milling about. And Spider had gotten there slowly, groggy from a bad sleep.

Trying to remember faces and voices from that dark night would get him nowhere. He had to focus on the evidence at hand, scant though it may be.

7

*B*y late afternoon the lack of sleep finally caught up to Spider. Having cut away part of the taffrail and mounted the swivel gun as a stern chaser, with the help of five men who had said hardly a thing during the labor, there was no other immediate carpentry work to be done. The worst problem he'd seen was the figurehead—the "figureheadless," perfumed Elijah had dubbed it. A cannonball had long ago decapitated the poor wench, leaving only a savagely torn and splintered neck above her naked torso. It seemed a bad omen to Spider, but Addison said she'd been that way almost a year, so Spider saw no need to hurry in making repairs.

Odin and Elijah sat on a hatch cover, playing dice. Spider nodded at them, and they both grunted in return. Odin's long, unruly hair was pulled back from his face and held by hairpins that looked like brass. The pins provided a better view of the ugly scars where his eye had been, and lent him an even more sinister visage.

Elijah rolled the bones and shouted, "Six!" He scooped up the dice, and quicker than a wink Odin whipped a hairpin from his head and stabbed Elijah's forearm.

"Damn! Bastard!" Elijah jerked his injured arm back, prompting a small shower of blood in the hairpin's wake. The dice clattered away across the deck to vanish through a scupper.

"Do not snatch them up before I see them," Odin said. Then he laughed his usual dry chuckle and replaced the bloody narrow spike in his hair.

Addison, looking around wildly, rushed forth. "Confound, gents, what do you do here? If Cap'n should see this, one of you or both would die quick, and you know it."

"Ha!" Odin barked. "I am not scared of Barlow."

"We've lost enough hands," Addy said tersely but quietly. "Elijah, can you work?"

"He stuck me good, sir, but I will recover." He held up his arm, his hand clasped over the hole, and glared at the crazy coot who'd stabbed him.

"No vengeance, do you heed?" Addison moved in close to Elijah, until the black man returned his gaze. "You know Odin does this sort of thing. You should not grab at the dice. See the fat surgeon," Addison ordered. "And if you be wise at all, you'll both keep your mouths closed and you'll not draw any more blood over a damned game."

"Lost my bones," Odin said.

"I will make you a new pair," Spider said as Addison retreated.

"Ha!" Odin exclaimed.

A friendly gesture such as making a new set of bones might give Spider an inroad to the crew, he thought, although Odin's quick violence had him wondering whether the coot could have clubbed Ezra. Odin was old—hell, ancient—for a pirate, but his thin arms were roped with muscle, and he had just shown himself to be as quick as a barracuda on the pounce.

Spider headed toward the forward hold, reached the bottom of the ladder, and stopped short. Sitting on a low hammock, whetting a knife against an oiled stone, Tellam flashed a cheerless grin that looked gray in the faint light streaming down the hatchway. As *Dream* rolled, that light faded and brightened, lending Tellam an almost spectral aspect as his face vanished, reappeared, and vanished again.

"They tell me you spent a lot of time sniffing your friend's blood on the deck," the man said.

"I stopped there to say farewell again, yes," Spider answered. He tried to make it sound civil, but was fairly certain he'd failed.

"Sad thing, him getting all drunk like that." Tellam inhaled deeply, then whispered his next words. "Satan leads a man into dark ways."

"So I've heard." Spider walked toward the hatch to the lower hold. He steeled himself as he passed Tellam, alert for any sudden move, and keenly aware of the sharp blade in Tellam's hands. Spider placed his own hand on the hilt of the knife in his bucket. Other men snored nearby. Spider wondered if he'd walked into an ambush.

He walked three steps beyond Tellam and pulled his own knife free. He figured the bucket itself might make a good weapon or shield. But there was no need for that. Tellam remained seated.

"You think I killed your friend, Spider John?"

Spider exhaled slowly, and turned even more slowly. He kept the knife concealed behind the bucket. "Did you?"

Tellam shrugged. "Maybe his curse just laid him out. Witch blood, you know. Can't be good for a body." Spider could not make out the man's features in the uncertain light, but he could hear the mockery in his voice. He could hear other men rustling about in their hammocks. He willed himself to be calm and still.

"I wouldn't know anything about that," Spider said.

"It's best he's gone, I say." Tellam resumed sharpening his blade. "Better him than the rest of us."

Spider resisted the temptation to strike. His throat felt as taut as a hawser towing a heavy prize, but he managed to spit and get his voice under control.

"I'll pray for a safe voyage," Spider said. "But first I'll pray for some sleep."

"If you think I murdered your friend, Spider John," Tellam said quietly, "I will be happy to discuss it with you, swords in hand, anytime you want."

"I have made no accusation," Spider answered. He had meant to add, "and vengeance belongs to the Lord," but had not been able to get the words out. He was not going to leave that work to the Lord.

"See that you don't," Tellam said. "And you'd best hope that curse is truly lifted, because you brought that devil spawn aboard, didn't you?"

By the time Spider climbed into the lower hold, he was shaking with anger—and more than a little fear. Staring down Tellam was like staring down a rattlesnake.

8

It was dark when Spider emerged again on deck. Clouds obscured stars and moon, and a chilly wind rocked the lanterns swinging from ratlines. Weatherall scratched something resembling a tune from a sadly worn fiddle, while Peg danced nimbly about and hopped higher on one leg than many men could on two. Thomas the cat cavorted, seeming to be playing a game in which he got underneath Peg at each leap, then darted to safety just before the man's wooden leg thumped the hard deck.

Around them, men clapped or jeered.

Spider worked his way through the men toward a large kettle and the aroma of pork. Smoke curled from the kettle, swinging on a metal stand to keep it level as the ship pitched and yawed. Boddings lifted the heavy lid and poked a fork in. He yanked out a small slab of burnt meat and slammed the kettle lid down. "Say no word of complaint, sailor," Boddings said, thrusting the pork toward Spider as if he were aiming a rapier at his heart. "It is horrible, but it is hot. Cold salt pork will not do in weather such as this, I dare say, although it seems effort goes unappreciated among pirates."

Spider grabbed a plank of wood from the pile near the kettle and a wooden cup from the barrel next to it. "I can eat anything, Doctor," he said. "Often have had to." He recalled the surgeon's holier-than-all harshness after Ezra's death and wanted to shove the fool's head into his damn kettle, but he would never solve the murder puzzle that way. He willed himself to be calm and civil.

Boddings snarled. "The boy Hob has hardtack, and they've tapped a terribly sour wine yonder." He aimed his thumb over his shoulder, and Spider went to fill his cup. He drained it, filled it again, and then found himself a spot against a hatch cover and sat down to eat.

Odin ate, grinned, and laughed in his own spot, leaning against a gun carriage. Spider dug into his pocket, withdrew the pair of oak cubes he'd cut and painted, and rolled them across the deck toward Odin. Spider had found the distraction comforting after his encounter with Peter Tellam.

The one-eyed man scooped the bones up and smiled.

"Better than what I lost," he said. "Tobacco in trade?"

Spider nodded. "Aye. I'll appreciate that."

Hob came forth, smiling and holding out the bread bucket as though it were a gift from God. "Biscuit, Spider John?"

"Aye. If you have a bit without something crawling about in it, that would be nice."

"All infested, I fear, but the rats ain't been in it," Hob said. "This one is not too bad, I suppose."

Spider eyed the bread, and the bugs swirling within it, and shrugged. He had certainly eaten worse.

"Sit and eat with me, boy," Spider said. "I have questions."

Spider placed the bread on his slab of wood, tore it into chunks, and crushed weevils in his fingers before flicking them dead on the deck. Then he speared his knife into the pork and bit into it. Salt pork, burned in a black kettle full of smoke, and not much of it. Oh well, he thought. Starving would not help matters. He took another bite.

Hob seemed intrigued. "What sort of questions, sir?"

Spider chewed a long time, waving a finger to let Hob know he'd heard him. He also pondered how much he could safely say. Hob seemed innocent enough, but the boy had been aboard the ship before Spider arrived. Spider had no idea what allegiances the lad may have formed among this murderous crew.

Finally, he dug the holstered pewter flask from his coat pocket. "I did not see in the dark, but this is not Ezra's flask," he said.

"You think he stole it?"

"I don't know," Spider said. "Perhaps it was borrowed, like Doctor

Boddings's Bible." He winked at the boy, who grinned. "In any event, it
is not Ezra's and I should not like to keep it. It should go to its rightful
owner. You are a bright lad. Have you seen it before? Know who it
belongs to?"

Hob took it, turned it over in his hands, removed it from the
leather harness, and even sniffed it. "I don't know anyone's got something nice as this."

"Yes, it is a good flask," Spider said. "You certain you don't know
whose it is?"

"Sorry. No. I can ask about, if you like."

"I can do that m'self," Spider said. "Thanks."

Odin stood, laughing, and tossed his plank and cup into a barrel
before wandering off.

"What is that man's story?" Spider wondered aloud.

"Odin? He sailed with Blackbeard."

"He sailed with Edward Teach?" Blackbeard was the notorious
pirate of legend, as dread and frightening a figure as piracy had ever
produced. Tales of his crimes and murders rolled like wind across the
Spanish Main and up and down the colonial coast.

"Aye," Hob said in a tone of quiet awe. "He seen Blackbeard himself
kill a dozen men at once, with his beard on fire and a sword in each hand."

Spider spat away some gristle. "Edward Teach is dead, you know. It
might surprise you to learn this, but he bled like anyone else."

"After being cut fifty times and shot a hundred," Hob said.

"Tales, Hobgoblin. Just stories."

"They cut off his head, to keep him dead, and tossed his body
overboard. And his headless corpse swam around the ship three times
before it disappeared. Odin told me all about it."

"Was Odin there?"

"No, but he knew Teach and he heard it all."

"I got my doubts, boy."

"Blackbeard will rise up from the deep someday," Hob said.
"Lookin' for his head."

"We should look for your head, Hob. You ain't using it."

Weatherall stopped fiddling, bent low to acknowledge the jeers from the crowd, then walked toward Spider and Hob. He dropped his bow and fished around in Hob's bucket for a biscuit. "Can't say it is bad to have your friend gone," he said without looking Spider in the eye. "Curse and all that. But I suppose you feel the loss, eh?"

"Aye," Spider said. He clenched a fist and thought about breaking Weatherall's nose, but decided against it.

Weatherall didn't seem to notice the fist. "Did you know his past?"

"Ezra didn't talk much."

"Well, then." Weatherall chewed his bread, spat out a wriggling weevil. "Curses and deaths. A bad thing. A bad thing, but, well. May we all have a more pleasant voyage now." He looked at Spider and sighed.

"A bad thing," Weatherall said, scratching at the still-young beard on his cheek.

Spider took the flask from Hob and showed it to the fiddler. "Do you know who owns this? I thought it was Ezra's but mistook it in the dark. It is not his."

Weatherall looked at it, scrunched up his eyes, and tilted his head in thought. "I've not seen it before, as far as I reckon. Ain't been aboard much longer than you, though."

"I'll ask about," Spider answered with a nod. "It is a good flask, and I suppose the man would like to have it back."

Weatherall leaned forward and picked up his bow. "Might just wave it about here and ask," he suggested.

"Not a bad thought," Spider said as Weatherall moved on. Peg and Tellam watched from the rail, sneering. Spider rose, tucked his knife into his belt, and walked into the brightest lantern light he could find. He held up the flask.

"This," he said loudly, "is a decent flask, as decent as an empty flask can be, anyway. It was found with Ezra Coombs, and I apologize to the owner he, um, borrowed it from." Spider silently asked the Lord, and Ezra, to forgive him for that bit of slander. "In the dark, I thought it was his own, but when I got a better look I realized it was not." He turned in a slow circle as men gathered closely around him.

"If it be yours, you may have it back. I ask no price for it." Spider looked closely at the ship's company, gauging reactions, but learned nothing. No one claimed the item.

"Well then," he said. "I'll ask about below, too, and you all pass the word. If any be missing a good flask, come see me." He tucked it into his pocket and headed aft.

Word would pass quickly aboard the vessel. Boredom meant men seized on the least of things for conversation. All would be asking about the flask, pondering who owned it. Someone might recall something, and say so, even if the killer himself was too clever to give himself away. All he needed was for one man to say to another, "Isn't that yours?"

Spider hoped any talk about the flask would force a killer out of hiding.

9

Another night brought nightmares and fitful sleep. He had seen Ezra, his face peering out from the bloody black flag, fading into a deep sea lit by hellfire below. Spider's gram had been there to welcome Ezra into hell, and she had waved and smiled to beckon him, too. "Come, Johnny, come."

That had forced him awake in the deep of the night, and Elijah had growled at him to stay quiet. Spider wondered if he had been talking in his sleep; if so, had he said anything that might alert Ezra's killer that Spider was on the hunt? Had he blurted out enough for someone to deduce his own bewitched bloodline?

Spider had a devil of a time returning to sleep after that.

Someone whistled, and he thought he made out the words "bugger the king."

He donned his pea coat and climbed up on deck. Sails were going up and catching wind, and the sharp snap of filling canvas could be heard even over the shouts and jeers. Peg stood nearby, laughing.

Spider tapped Peg's shoulder. "Why such a din?"

The one-legged man spoke without turning to look at Spider. "Our friend from the Admiralty is back," he said. "Three masts, acres of sail, and slow as hell. Turns like a boulder."

Spider did not bother to fight through the crowd looking aft. Instead, he climbed a ratline and looked over their heads. There in the distance astern stood a frigate under English colors, bow aimed precisely at *Plymouth Dream*. She would carry twenty-eight guns at the least, Spider thought, far outgunning Barlow's ship. He looked skyward, felt the wind on his cheek. Steady, and in the frigate's favor. *Dream* was built for sturdiness and cargo, not for speed, and Spider figured the frigate ought to be able to run her down with ease.

The crew disagreed with that assessment. They jeered and cat-called. Weatherall stood in the ropes, above the crowd, waving a dirty white sheet wildly back and forth. "Fuck all kings and admirals! Fuck them all!"

Spider did not join in the shouting. "Seen her before, I take it?" He had to raise his voice to be heard over the commotion.

"Aye," Peg answered. "This is the third time in a month. Haunting us, she is, but she ain't catching us."

"Bring 'er about, lads, south by southeast," Barlow called. "Look alive, damn ye! If you let these pigs catch you, I shall hang you my damn self, I will! Haul now!" Barlow ranged amidships like a caged cougar, eager to pounce on something.

Hoots emanated from the men around him as *Dream* swung around and her sails filled again with a series of sharp snaps. Spider watched the pursuer, and it seemed Peg's assessment was true. The frigate certainly looked like a sweet dancer, but she apparently was crewed by pressed men and layabouts. She came around slowly in pursuit, and the distance between hunter and hunted grew accordingly. Old Lieutenant Bentley, Spider's nemesis of old, surely would be knocking some heads if he were over there, Spider supposed. It was not as though *Dream*'s crew was made up of God's finest-made sailors, but they'd managed to outmaneuver the navy lads.

"As I said, she ain't catching us," Peg yelled.

"Not today, she won't," Spider said. He dropped to the deck.

Weatherall shouted, "Bugger the royals!" and lobbed a few more choice words for the king before heading toward the hatch leading below.

"Addison! Carry your lard over here, if you please," Barlow roared, pulling at his own beard.

The burly first mate answered the captain's call. "Here I be, Cap'n, fit to fight for all my somewhat excessive weight. What is your pleasure?"

"I have in mind a ruse," Barlow said. "I want to feint toward

Bermuda. We shall dance, of course, tack as need be, but keep us on a southeasterly way, and let yonder frigate see us before we leave her behind. If she thinks we are Bermuda-bound, we might throw the hound off our scent."

"Aye, sir, a sound plan, and a few extra days will not cost us, I agree. Our friend will wait. I shall make it so."

"Good man, I rely upon it. Carry on, mate."

"Aye, sir."

Barlow headed aft toward the officers' bay in the hold before the poop deck.

With excitement among the men fading, Spider headed below again. No one had claimed the flask or pointed out its owner—nor did anyone seem concerned that he was asking about it. *Whichever of these sons of bitches killed Ezra*, Spider thought, *he's got balls of oak.*

Spider dropped into the crew hold. Weatherall was returning the filthy white sheet to his hammock.

"You certainly have no love for our navy friends," Spider said.

"None at all," Weatherall growled. "Got pressed once, whipped twice, no good reason other than some officer wanted to maintain discipline, as they say. To hell with that."

Weatherall started back up the ladder. Spider rolled into his own hammock and closed his eyes. He did not intend to fall asleep, but he did. Images of Ezra sinking in his black shroud soon filled his mind. It would be another night of haunted dreams.

10

Spider's investigation had not progressed a bit. Another day of subtle questions elicited only evasions and grunts. Small talk ended when he came around.

Today might well offer chances for talk, though, for it was Sunday.

While *Plymouth Dream* failed to observe many nautical traditions, such as decks scrubbed clean and keeping hands busy with routine maintenance chores, there was one tradition Barlow had insisted upon—duff to eat on Sundays. On naval and merchant vessels, Sunday was a day of rest and a day to enjoy the flour pudding flavored with molasses. It was considered a treat by seamen fed on cold salt meat and bug-ridden bread the rest of the week, and a Sunday without duff was considered sacrilege.

Spider stood in a slow line behind Peg, holding a wooden bowl, a wooden spoon, and a leather mug. The one-legged man, who had been at least a tad courteous toward Spider as compared to many, turned to him and asked, "Anyone claimed that flask?"

"No," Spider said. "Is it yours?"

"No," Peg said. "I think Weatherall had one like it, maybe, but if it ain't his, I would maybe buy it from you."

"He says it ain't his," Spider answered.

"Then might I buy it? I got some tobacco, and an extra shirt, you can have in barter. I've never had so fine a flask as that one."

"Let me see," Spider said, "if its owner comes forward. If not, I suppose we can trade."

"Very well."

They moved up in line. Doctor Boddings, huffing like a grave digger under a hot sun, tried to push a ladle down into a deep pan of extraordinarily thick duff. Cursing under his breath, he grabbed a knife and dug into the stuff. As Spider and Peg watched in a mix of amusement and horror, the surgeon used his knife to lift a thick brick of supposed pudding from the pan. Spider could see salt cubes in its surface, glinting with diamond brightness.

Boddings dropped the duff into Spider's bowl. Spider sniffed it. It smelled like a wet dog. "What is this?"

"It is duff, damn you, and if you think you can do better, then the galley is yours!" Doctor Boddings set to digging out a portion for Peg and continued grumbling. "Men sit on their arses all day while I, a man with degrees from not one, but two, reputable institutions of higher learning, toil in a kitchen on behalf of a damned fool captain who despises men of more education than himself, which I deem includes almost everyone on this ship!"

Peg looked at the duff Boddings dropped in his bowl and sighed with disappointment.

Spider used his fingers to pinch a portion of duff from the bowl and put it in his mouth. He swirled the tasteless mass about on his tongue, chewed it with difficulty—he'd once eaten a raw slab of shark skin that was not nearly so difficult to chew—and reluctantly swallowed it. "Can we have some molasses for this, Doctor?"

"Get thee away!" Boddings waved his ladle like a sword, pointing toward a tin cup of molasses swinging from a boom. "Fetch your own molasses. I am a surgeon, damn you, not a slop cook!"

Spider nodded, poured some molasses on his duff, and walked toward the keg to fill his mug. Sunday meant wine, but it generally was watered down to the point of uselessness.

Spider sat against the gunwale, near Weatherall, who stared at his duff as though it were a woman who had spurned him.

"Peg says you had a pewter flask," Spider said. "Are you sure you are not missing one?"

Weatherall, his mouth filled with the doctor's ridiculous duff, reached to his belt and pulled away a pewter flask. He held it up, shook it, and handed it to Spider. Then he swallowed and spoke. "Never lost mine. It has some whiskey in it still. Have a swig if you like."

Spider popped the cork and drank deep. "Thankee." He handed the flask back to its owner and wondered if Peg had simply been mistaken, or if he had some other purpose. Spider's questioning about the flask certainly could have alerted the killer that Spider was on the hunt. Could Peg have been trying to cast suspicion on Weatherall to divert it from himself, or from someone else? Was he that clever?

A call coming down from the mainmast cut Spider's line of thinking short. "Sail ho!"

Men began scurrying up the lines, calling out lusty battle cries. The pirates had spotted potential prey, and there would be hunting. Odin, in charge of the crews handling sails aloft, began barking orders and reminding everyone he had sailed with Blackbeard. Barlow's eyes gleamed, and he called for his spyglass. Weatherall tossed the remainder of his duff overboard and pointed across the rolling sea.

The rising sun was still low on the horizon. Spider looked off the starboard bow, where Weatherall was pointing. A brig rode the easterly wind on a converging course with *Plymouth Dream.* The distance was too great to make out much, but she was flying England's colors and had not, so far, altered course to make a run for it.

Up top, *Dream* was mounting the king's flag as well. Barlow had banners from France, Spain, and other nations in his stores, to be used as he saw fit. His own banner, a field of black sporting a bleeding white skull, was not waving above. The captain was not going to play fair and raise his battle flag.

"Peg, take a glass up the mast with you and keep watch for that navy shadow of ours," Barlow said. "This beauty on our horizon could well be bait."

Peg headed up the ladder with remarkable speed for a man with a wooden leg, Spider thought.

Spider had also wondered if the interloper was a lure, designed to entice *Dream* into pouncing into a trap. It certainly was a possibility. She also could be a brig full of bandits not so different from *Dream*'s crew; perhaps her captain was moving in with thoughts of plundering Barlow's ship. You often could not tell the nature of things on an outlaw sea until it was too late.

The sea was rather calm, with *Dream* making about ten knots under a cloudless sky painted pink by the rising sun. They already had ranged far enough south to enjoy much warmer temperatures, and the sailors had left their coats lying below.

Spider judged the other ship to be making about ten knots as well, cutting a nice wake. She was still too distant to make out many details. It would be a while before the ships met, assuming one or the other did not break away and attempt to run. *Dream*, with three masts of sail opposed to the brig's two, would have the advantage of more canvas, but the brig likely had a narrower hull. A race could get interesting, Spider thought, even though neither captain, so far, had decided to run. The brig likely could sail much closer to the wind than *Dream*, so if maneuverability became a factor, Barlow's ship could be in trouble.

Barlow peered through his spyglass. "She's got gun ports open," he said. "I count six of them. We may be outgunned here, gents."

Spider, with his naked eyes, also saw gun ports on the brig's hull, but they didn't look quite right. He worked his way aft, where Barlow barked orders to the men in the rigging and assailed one man for lifting a rifle above his head.

"Do you want them to see that, you fucking fuck?" Barlow punctuated his words by spitting overboard. "I swear to you by God or devil, if they show sign of expecting an attack, I will blow your fucking brains out of your fucking head."

"Cap'n," Spider said quietly once Barlow had finished spewing venom. "Might I borrow your glass?"

"Why?"

"Something ain't right about yonder vessel," Spider answered.

"Very well," Barlow said, handing over his scope.

Spider walked to the starboard rail and spied through the glass. Once he had the other ship in focus, he was certain. "Cap'n Barlow, those gun ports are naught but black paint."

Barlow smiled wide. "Are you certain, Spider?"

"Aye," Spider said. "She ain't as deadly as she looks. Those ports are fake, painted on. But they ain't been retouched in a while. Edges ain't smooth. She hasn't got any guns below, not on her port side, in any case."

"Well, I'll be damned." Barlow grinned. "We may not need to run today after all. She's got real guns on her main deck, though. I saw a couple. I'll lay odds those are full of nasty shit."

Spider handed him the glass and headed forward. He hoped the fakery meant *Dream* was rendezvousing with a merchant vessel, with a crew more disposed to surrender than fight. But the sneer on Barlow's face, and the man's deep inhalations and fierce exhalations through the nose, told him the captain was planning carnage whether the target vessel put up a real fight or not.

"She ain't making a move," Barlow said to Addison. "Looks like we'll have a nice slow dance. Maybe they think they'll take us, or maybe they think we'll have a nice little fucking church picnic and exchange news and such." Barlow laughed. "All I know is it would be nice to take another vessel with us to add to our little fleet. Let us load up our guns, Addy, slow and quiet before she gets close enough to see what we are doing."

"Aye, sir," Addison said, raising a telescope to his eye. "She seems a beauty. I am not seeing a lot of hands on deck, but that could be a ruse." Addison ordered gun crews to go to work. Men scurried toward the forecastle, where powder was stored. Others moved to the gun carriages and opened chests containing four-pound balls. The chests near the swivel guns held grapeshot, which would scatter like pellets from a shotgun and wreak holy hell upon the crew fired upon.

Barlow screamed upward. "Peg! Any sign of our fucking Royal Navy friend?"

"No, sir."

"His Majesty's lazy crew of layabouts has not deigned to grace us with their presence, Cap'n," Addison said. "It's just us and that brig on the whole damned sea."

"Excellent," Barlow replied, twirling his cane. "Addy, grab a couple of fellows and break out our weapons, if you please. I think we shall have work today. No damned hurrying or rushing about, though. Keep it all out of sight. We have time aplenty, and we'll go on letting them think we're just eager to have ourselves a little floating tea party."

"Aye, sir," Addison said with a leer that indicated he looked forward to the action to come.

Spider did not look forward to it, and he muttered a very quiet prayer. "Let them choose surrender over fighting," he whispered. "Let them give us no cause to slit throats and fire our guns. Let this end peaceful, if it can, Lord."

Spider had been through this drama more times than he could remember, and he did not want to go through it again. But if it came to a fight, he would swing his sword for all he was worth, because the last thing he wanted to do was die. If the world would not let him live in peace, he would try to live anyway, and hate himself afterward for whatever sins he had to commit to make that happen. He had heard Jesus forgives, and he fervently hoped it was true.

He reminded himself he needed to live so he could avenge Ezra and so he could one day return home.

He kissed the pendant he'd carved for Em.

Weatherall appeared by Spider's side, looking nervous. "This wretched sword is yours, I'm told."

Spider eyed the beaten scabbard, the frayed leather on the hilt, the ridiculous long thread of rope that served as a shoulder strap. He grasped the sword and took a deep breath, surprised at how good it felt to have a weapon again. He had been walking about unarmed in a nest of vipers.

"It is," he answered. "Many thanks. Not as fine as yours, it seems. Looks as though you got a proper naval officer's sword there."

"Took it from a properly dead naval officer," Weatherall answered, sneering.

While the boarding party members armed themselves, others prepared ropes and grappling hooks. When the time came, they would crouch out of sight below the rail, awaiting word to snap the trap shut.

Hob came running up to Spider. "Take a brace of these," he said, proffering a wooden bucket filled with flintlock pistols. Spider took a couple.

"Doctor Boddings has the powder and balls and flints and wadding, all by the mizzenmast," Hob said before running off elsewhere.

Spider strapped the cutlass over his shoulder, tucked the pistols into his belt, and prayed he would not have to use any of them. He headed toward the mizzenmast to get powder and ammunition, and doubted very much his prayer would come true.

Barlow clapped an iron hand on Spider's shoulder as Spider waited his turn in line.

"I hope you fight like your friend," Barlow said. "I was sad to lose him after seeing him in a scuffle. May you show a good account of yourself today."

"I fight damned hard when I must, Cap'n," Spider assured him.

"See that you do," Barlow said, leering and swishing his cane violently through the air. "See that you do."

Neither *Plymouth Dream* nor the interloper had hoisted a black flag, which would have signaled piratical intent and an offer to spare survivors in case of surrender. *Dream* continued the charade of seeking a peaceful encounter. Spider suspected the other vessel was pretending, too.

Spider got his gunpowder, wadding, and balls and moved to the rail to load his guns. He looked to starboard, where the target vessel was larger now. It still seemed bent on a simple rendezvous with *Dream*. "Just fucking surrender," he whispered to himself. "Don't let it become kill or be killed. Give Barlow what he wants. Don't make him take it."

Then he tucked his loaded guns into his belt and tried to prepare himself for the probable carnage to come.

The prey was closer now, and Spider could make out men moving on her deck. No one was brandishing weapons, of course, and neither ship was putting on sail. Everything pointed to a casual meeting at sea, an exchange of news, drinks all around, a welcome interruption of a dull routine.

Spider was certain this would be anything but that.

Crewmen looked at one another with rapacious smiles.

Spider spotted Weatherall farther ahead, staring at the target. The man seemed lost in thought. "Be nice if they just handed over their ship and all joined our merry little band, I say," Spider said.

Weatherall grunted. "Aye." Then he turned and walked away.

"Still no sign of naval sail," Peg hollered from above.

"The sea is all ours today, by thunder!" Barlow clapped his hands. "And that bitch is headed right into our jaws, lads! Be she a merchant or a ship of wolves like us, we're taking her today! You know your jobs, men! New lads, you are with the boarding party. Let's make them bleed until they be empty!"

Then he turned his attention to the rigging. "Odin! You lads reef sails, smartly now!"

The oncoming vessel loomed ahead, and it, too, reduced sail to a minimum. Closer she drew, her fake gun ports now obvious to the naked, experienced eye, and her crew waving and calling across the waves. *Dream*'s murderous lot waved back and hailed the other vessel, but kept guns and blades hidden behind backs or behind the rail.

The vessels were now within hailing distance of each other.

"*Plymouth Dream*, bound for Africa," Barlow bellowed, waving his tricorn. He spaced out his words to make them understandable. "We've a fair fiddler aboard, if you'd like to celebrate this chance encounter!"

"*Loon*, our ship is, bound for Boston," replied a cadaverously thin man with long blond hair falling in sloppy curls on his shoulders beneath a ridiculous black hat. "Captain Joshua Horncastle, at your service. We can spare some excellent French wine to share with our new friends."

"Come alongside, then, if you please!"

The voice of *Loon*'s captain sounded strained, and Spider suspected Horncastle and crew had plundering thoughts in mind. He tugged Em's pendant from beneath his shirt and gave it a another quick kiss.

"Tie these on your arms, sir," Hob said, tugging on Spider's sleeve and proffering a wooden bucket filled with scraps of deep-blue cloth.

"What the devil is this?" Spider lifted one of the lengthy scraps from the bucket.

"Cap'n says it'll make it easier to tell who is who once the balls and blood fly," Hob said. The eagerness in the boy's voice told Spider that Hob wanted very much to tie blue ribbons around his own biceps and lurch into battle. Spider grabbed two ribbons from the bucket and said, "Hob, you pass these out and then you get the hell belowdecks and stay there."

"I ain't no coward," Hob said, turning to hand a pair of ribbons to Weatherall, who had circled back and resumed his spot near Spider. Then the boy ran off as Spider yelled, "You do as I say, Hob!"

Disgusted, Spider spat overboard for luck and felt his stomach tighten. He tied the damned blue ribbons around his arms. It would not be long now before Barlow tipped his hand. *Dream* would come alongside the brig, and Barlow would give the call to action. And if the Lord heeded Spider's prayers, the fellows on the other ship would drop their guns and beg for mercy rather than show fight.

But the expressions staring back at him across the water told him the Lord was not heeding prayers on this Sabbath.

The ships slowly drew closer and closer on their convergent paths. The dance proceeded at an agonizingly slow pace as Spider and the rest of *Dream*'s crew waved and whistled in a friendly manner while keeping careful eye for any sign of treachery. The men on *Loon* waved back and yelled greetings—and Spider noted numerous hands hidden below the rail, or behind backs, in postures no different from those aboard *Dream*. Spider wondered how many men over there were crouching behind the rail, or waiting below with guns and steel.

Weatherall, looking grim and holding a knife behind his own back, whispered, "Mother of God."

"It's looking less and less like a pack of vestal virgins over there," Addison replied quietly.

"Aye," Weatherall said. "It is my hope we vastly outnumber them, and they will see that and just surrender."

Any hope of that was lost in the next breath as a rifle shot from the approaching vessel sent a ball across the waters to thunk into the mainmast.

"Fuck them, lads! It's a fight!" Barlow lifted his cane high and pointed at the brig. "Fire!"

The gun crews struck matches and lit fuses. Aiming was not necessary at this close range. The four-pounders roared thunder and belched their black clouds of smoke, and the swivel guns unleashed their devastating grapeshot across *Loon*'s deck. The small pellets ripped sails and sent blood flying.

Grapples flew, muskets fired, and blasphemous curses lifted from both vessels.

A swivel gun on the target ship replied, and the rail near Spider splintered. Flying wood and gun smoke streaked across his face, and he recoiled in pain and uttered a new silent prayer.

A handful of *Loon*'s guns—Spider had not counted them—flashed fire in the smoky haze. *Dream*'s rail exploded in places, and a man standing next to Spider flew backward and vanished beyond the mizzenmast. A trail of blood marked the path of his flight.

"Hard over!" Barlow fired a pistol, and *Dream*'s grapplers heaved on their lines. *Loon*'s grapplers did the same, and the hulls of the two vessels thunked together in a jarring collision. "Free-for-all, lads! Cut them down, one and all!"

Horrifying screams lifted from both ships as brigands raised their voices in hopes of creating fear and panic in their enemies.

Spider cursed inwardly, but it was kill or be killed, no matter where he wished he was at this moment. He could cast aside his humanity, and his conscience, or he could die. Survival instinct prevailed.

A pistol in each hand, he ran toward the starboard rail and leapt upon it, then launched himself toward *Loon*.

Others did the same. *Dream* sat a bit higher in the water than *Loon*, so Barlow's marauders had the advantage of height and speed, but still more than a couple of leaping Dreamers collided with men swinging on lines from the enemy ship.

As Spider leapt through the air, a late-firing four-pounder on *Loon* took a direct hit from one of its counterparts on *Dream*. *Loon*'s suddenly crippled gun lurched off its carriage, tilted crazily upward, and launched its own ball skyward.

Shouts and gunshots filled the air, and the sound of balls whizzing through space to either side of him filled Spider's ears.

Spider did not land on his feet, but he rolled and rose quickly. A man he did not recognize rushed him. The bastard could have belonged to either crew, but Spider did not see any blue ribbon on the man's arms so he fired his right-hand blunderbuss, and the man's forehead and cheek opened up in red gore.

The man fell at Spider's feet, dropping a saber. Spider knelt, tossed his empty gun aside, and took up the other man's blade. He spun, found an enemy—for that was what they were now, despite his earlier prayers—and slashed a throat. That vanquished man fell, and behind him Spider saw Addison thrust a knife upward into another man's chin. Addison's foe stared with bulging, dying eyes, and Addison kissed the man before spitting on him and shoving him aside.

Odin, Peg, and others up in the rigging rained withering musket fire down on *Loon*'s deck, and Spider hoped like hell they could see those blue ribbons on his arms.

The deck below Spider's feet lurched crazily, and a glance upward told him the rigging above was fouled. Spars and lines were all tangled after the collision, but it would not get straightened out until one side vanquished the other. For now, the two crews were locked into a struggle to the death.

For a brief, surreal moment, Spider imagined everyone from both crews dying in this battle, and imagined some other vessel coming upon the conjoined ships in the future, the passengers gawking at all the dead men lying on the decks.

Then a man plummeted like a meteor onto the hard deck nearby and died in a wet, red thunk. Spider could not determine in a glance whether the man was part of his crew or part of the enemy's crew, and in that precise moment he wondered whether God himself gave a damn about that matter.

Gun smoke assailed Spider's nostrils, and a musket ball zinged by with a bizarre bumblebee sound.

Near the target ship's mainmast, Weatherall crossed blades with two men. Spider pressed his left-hand gun against the spine of one of Weatherall's foes and shot him in the back; Weatherall sliced the remaining man's leg and kicked him in the groin.

Spider tossed aside the second empty gun and took up his own sword in his left hand. Then he ducked low, in hopes of being able to see underneath the gun smoke wafting across the deck, and spotted a scuffle aft. He rushed to the aid of the man with blue fabric on his arms. Spider slashed, stabbed, got his back against the rail, and fought for all he was worth.

Smoke burned his eyes, gunshots rang in his ears, and every breath he took tasted of blood and fire. A musket fell near his feet, and Spider glanced above to see men clambering like monkeys across the interlocked spars, sticking one another with knives.

Around him, wood splintered as musket balls raked masts and yardarms. An unholy din of shouts and curses and gunshots and blades ringing off one another made any sort of communication impossible. The only thing to do was fight until there was no one left to kill—or until he himself was dead.

And so he did, and he lost count of the bellies he cut wide open and the necks he hacked. The tilted deck under his boots grew slippery with gore, and he stumbled against a corpse more than once.

Tellam, bare-chested and with blood streaked across his wild tattoos, emerged from a waft of smoke. He grinned like a man demented, muttered quietly, and stared at Spider while approaching with a cutlass upraised. Spider squared in defense, but Tellam veered away and drew steel across another man's back.

Coughing from smoke and wiping sweat and blood from his eyes, Spider felt a lancing fire across the back of his right thigh. He whirled, lashing wildly with both blades, but there was no one there. A musket ball, not a sword, must have done the damage, he decided, hoping he would live long enough to have Doctor Boddings look at the wound. He nearly fell but staggered against the mast and remained upright.

"Oh Lord, oh Lord, oh Lord," said a man who sounded Irish and did not sport the blue armbands of *Plymouth Dream*. He lumbered across the deck, a sword dangling in one hand and his guts trying to spill out around his other hand. Spider took two steps, drove his blade through the man's neck, and figured he'd done the poor son of a bitch a favor.

Black clouds of smoke, the flares of guns, the shouts of men in indescribable fear or in rapturous bloodlust, the stench of vomit and burnt powder—all these assailed Spider's senses, and it was only the knowledge he'd lived through such blasphemies in the past that helped him get through the present.

Spider wished like hell that Ezra was here. Ezra could fight like a demon, and Ezra would have stood side by side with Spider, offering his protection and making sure that, whatever else happened, he would do what he could to help his friend survive. He and Ezra had always looked out for one another, above all else.

God, how Spider missed Ezra right then.

The wind caught a scrap of sail shredded by musketry and grape-shot, and it whipped across Spider's face and blocked his vision. He ducked low, rolled, came up in a low crouch, and found himself face-to-face with a man he did not recognize. Spider slashed the stranger's throat.

A mighty roar sounded above all the other din, and Spider looked in that direction to see Captain Barlow leap aboard the enemy ship. "Fuck and bugger!" Barlow screamed as his feet found the deck, and his pistol fired point-blank into a man's forehead. Barlow threw his emptied pistol aside and then grabbed the handle of his ever-present cane, and Spider noted the quick twist that allowed the captain to pull the handle away from the cane's stem and reveal a rapier blade within. Spider also noted the cool efficiency with which Barlow slipped the newly revealed blade into an opponent's throat. "Now that I have slain you," Barlow screamed while turning to whip his blade across another man's eyes, "I will find your mother and sister, and I will diddle them both! Diddle-dee-dee, diddle-dee-doo, I just might bugger you, too!"

A man putting fire to the touchhole on one of *Loon*'s swivel guns, in hopes of blowing the marksmen above to hell, took a musket shot to the head. He fell across his weapon, and the damned gun swung wildly and thundered. Spider dove to the deck as grapeshot riddled the chests and backs of men around him.

Spider rose as Barlow stabbed another foe, this time through the heart, and laughed like a maniac. His mad, foul, singsong banter continued as the currents of the pitched battle mercifully forced Barlow and Spider away from one another. Spider had never seen anyone take such joy in killing, and it made him feel a bit sick inside.

He had no time to ponder such things, though. Spider jumped back to avoid a cutlass slash, then stabbed the man who had tried to kill him. Meanwhile, he thought he heard Hob shouting.

Spider looked in the direction he thought had produced that voice, but all he saw was a stranger's face. Spider spat on that face before stabbing the body below it. Then he heard Hob again.

"*Plymouth Dream*!"

Spider spun toward the sound. It was Hob, indeed, with fire in his eyes, a pistol in each hand and blue ribbons on each arm, leaping across the rails and landing on the enemy deck.

Spider cursed. "I told you to hide below, Hob!" But if the boy heard him, he showed no sign, and then a thick, bright, fiery orange flash nearby beat all of Spider's senses into submission. He fell to his knees and wondered what exactly the hell was going on.

Hob moved on, and Spider lost track of him as enemy crewmen rushed him. Spider desperately wished to be somewhere else, but that did not happen, so he jumped up and slashed and stabbed, kicked and slashed, stabbed and kicked.

It seemed the tumult would never end, and Spider watched man after man fall dead while the deck lurched maniacally under his feet. A frightened chicken flapped wildly and fell from the larboard rail, and the target vessel must have had swine aboard, because Spider could hear the animals grunting in fear below in the hold.

The fight raged on, with smoke and ripped sails and blood flying, and all the anger Spider had tried to conceal since Ezra's death slowly swelled up in him, until he swung his rusty blade with what felt like demonic force and wished every man he hacked was his friend's killer. He had fought many times before, but he'd never slaughtered like this. He both hated it and found it freeing.

A flash of green-and-yellow plumage flashed in front of Spider's face—a cockatiel or parrot, he could not be sure—and he lashed at it with both swords. An explosion of feathers and blood erupted. God, how Spider hated those damned birds.

Somewhere along the line, after a wicked blow to the head, Spider decided he'd already died and gone to hell and that this madness would just go on forever, and ever, and ever.

Eventually, though, the eternity of battle gave way to Barlow's booming voice. "The bitch is ours, Dreamers! We've won!"

Spider found himself bloodied and sweat-soaked, but finally with no one standing in front of him to fight. The other men nearby wore blue armbands and familiar, weary faces, while a few dozen living strangers knelt on the bloody deck with their hands laced atop their heads in submission.

"Thank you, Lord," Spider muttered. "Thank you, thank you."

"Well done, well done, lads!" Barlow twirled his cane and brandished a pistol. "Victory and spoils are ours, gents!"

Spider sank onto his ass and covered his face with both hands. His shirt and breeches bore the rips and tears of enemy blades, and his arms and hands had more than a few scrapes. He alternatively praised Jesus for preserving him and begged Jesus to forgive him, then noticed a few others doing the same. One of those was Weatherall, who held his right hand over a viciously bleeding gash on his thigh, but who otherwise seemed to be all right. Weatherall uttered a prayer Spider could barely hear, but he heard enough to know it was an echo of his own.

Spider's heart danced when he saw Hob, alive and well. The boy stepped toward the rail and flung something out upon the waters, and Spider's throat seized up as though in irons when he realized the boy had tossed someone's arm into the deep.

Spider prayed that Hob would not become just another pirate on the account and wondered if God listened to a pirate's prayers.

Barlow laughed like a madman and spun about slowly. "It is our day, gents! Our day!"

Then Barlow's eyes went wide. "Is that the captain?" Barlow pointed his sword at a scrawny, long-haired man being dragged toward him by two *Dream* crewmen.

"Aye, I am Captain Joshua Horncastle, commander of the *Loon*, and I want to know what the bloody hell . . ."

Barlow, glaring wildly, pulled a pistol from his belt and stuck the barrel into Horncastle's mouth. Barlow pulled the trigger, a rain of gore flew in the wind, and the man fell dead onto the deck. "Enough of your goddamned nonsense," Barlow said. Then the captain laughed again.

"Overboard with him," Barlow yelled, "and with the rest of his cursed lot, alive or dead, unless they are useful. Addy!"

Addison rushed to Barlow's side. "Aye, sir."

"Get in the cabin and down below and discover what we've fucking won, aside from this fine vessel. And have someone gather our own dead, so we can treat them decently."

"Aye, Cap'n."

Barlow then turned his attention aloft. "Peg! What goddamned news? Is our escort from the Royal Navy skulking about?"

"Nothing else out there, Cap'n!" Peg seemed enraptured to Spider's eyes despite the fact that a cannonball or something had removed more than half of his wooden leg. He sat upon a yardarm over on *Plymouth Dream*, the broken hunk of wood dangling beneath him next to his good leg.

"Ha!" Barlow spun in triumph. "Bless us, I say! The devil may already own our souls, but we, blessed above all other mortals, live another day to fight and love and count our fucking blessings! We are the most free of men, ruling all within range of our guns and our blades! Let any fool who might stand in defiance of us bend over for the devil's buggery, for we are masters of our own fates!"

Weatherall handed the captain the stem of his cane, and Barlow wiped his slender blade on a dead man's chest, then locked the sword back into its housing.

"Good show, John Weatherall. You're a man, you are. Glad to have you aboard. Now go see that idiot Boddings about your wounded leg, and let us all hope he is a better fucking surgeon than he is a fucking cook."

Weatherall departed, and the captain addressed Spider. "You fight like a man who has done it a few times, Spider John, that slash on your leg be damned. You are earning your keep. Now go see Boddings, then get up top, part these vessels, fix what needs fixed," he said. "Peg's fucking broken leg can wait until the important work is done. Grab a couple of sure hands to help you up top. And Hob! Where are you, little cock? Grab some buckets and start filling them with guns. Gather up the swords, too, boy. Anyone besides Addy or myself holding a weapon had best turn it in now, or get shot in the balls."

Addison's voice lifted over the crowd. "Cap'n, I do not ken what treasures await us below, but surely there is none so fine as this."

Addison stood in front of the aft cabin, grinning, with his right hand clamped on the arm of a stunningly beautiful black woman. She wore a gray muslin shirt, untucked, and a dark skirt that fell to her knees. Her sleeves were rolled high on slender, yet well-muscled, arms, and her feet were bare. Her wide eyes, framed by long, dark curls, flashed white defiance at Barlow.

Spider, like all the other crewmen, stood and gawked. The captain, looking perplexed for once, stammered something inaudible.

"She was hiding in the cabin, Cap'n," Addison said. "Bit of sport for the former commander of this brig, I dare say."

Spider figured her age to be around fifteen, maybe older, maybe younger.

"I am Captain Horncastle's wife," the woman said, without parting her clenched white teeth. Her accent was born on some island somewhere, no doubt, but Spider could not place it.

"Unfortunate, that," Addison said, pointing to the captain's remains being carted toward the rail.

Her mouth fell open, and her lower jaw shook. Then she grabbed a knife from Addison's belt and slashed at his neck.

Addison was taken by surprise, but he was still able to step back and raise an arm in defense. A wicked sweep that might have cut his throat sliced some skin from his left forearm instead. The woman spun with the force of her blow, and Addison drove a fist into the back of her skull. She fell hard, and the dirk slid across the bloody deck.

"Bloody bitch!" Addison drew his blade and stepped toward the woman.

"No," Barlow said.

Addison stopped and stared at the captain. "No?"

"No."

Barlow stepped toward the woman. His dark eyes, normally hard as glass, were soft, and he ran a hand slowly through his dark beard. "What is your name, girl?"

"May," she answered, propping herself up on an elbow. Blood from the deck clung to her shirt.

"You have spirit, girl," Barlow said. "That bastard ought not have brought you out here. I am glad I shot him, I dare say."

May's eyes widened, but she said nothing.

"If you wish," Barlow continued, "you may join my crew. No man aboard will touch you."

That brought some jeers from the men.

"No man aboard, I say!" Barlow, back to his familiar bellowing form, spun, swinging his cane hard and forcing Spider and a couple of other men to jump backward to avoid a thwack. After a tense pause, the captain turned back to address the girl, his demeanor once more soft as a kitten's.

"What do you say, lass? Will you sign the articles and join my crew, with equal share in all so long as you pull your weight and abide by our laws?"

May rose slowly, her lip quivering and her eyes lowered. Then she dove forward, hard, toward a spot below Dobbin's feet. Spider caught sight of a flintlock pistol there, and May snatched it. She rolled quickly, got to her feet, and strode toward Barlow before anyone in the stunned crowd could react.

She put the barrel against Barlow's forehead and fired.

Nothing happened. The pistol had already fired its lone shot and had been cast aside by its previous wielder.

May glared at Barlow, who returned her gaze with a rather sad expression. "Spirit ye have, for certain," he said quietly. Then he turned and walked away. "Addy, bind her well and find her a spot in *Dream's* forecastle. Set guards on her. Then get back to assessing the plunder. Men! Elect three, per the articles, to help with the count and see none are cheated."

Barlow returned to *Plymouth Dream* without looking back.

Addison, surprised and pissed, nonetheless complied.

Spider handed his sword to Hob—and suddenly felt very exposed—then turned away and cringed. The girl's courage and determination moved him greatly, and it reminded him again of the grim duty he needed to perform on Ezra's behalf. In a way, he envied her, for she had no need to mask her hatred. She knew who had killed her husband, and she had nothing to gain by hiding her feelings. Spider, on the other hand, had to swallow his anger and move about a vessel full of suspects. He looked about at the carnage on *Loon's* deck. He would create some carnage of his own when the time came for his bloody vengeance.

That revenge had just become less likely, though, for Spider knew what would come next. Barlow had won a new vessel for his brigand fleet, and he would have to assign a prize crew. That meant dividing *Dream's* crew, and that meant Ezra's killer might go aboard one vessel while Spider was on the other. Both ships were damaged, and both would likely need a carpenter's touch, but dividing his investigative efforts would be a huge hurdle.

Spider spat in contempt of the forces arrayed against him and furiously bit his tongue.

11

"So, there, lad," Doctor Boddings told the man rising from the hammock. The common area surrounded by the officers' small bunks had been converted into a temporary surgery, and Boddings had just finished wrapping a bandage around a man's torn tricep. "You shall be able to work, I dare say, and this mess will mend nicely. A tot of rum might help with the pain a bit, I should think."

Spider, aboard *Plymouth Dream* again, waited at the top of the ladder with Weatherall and a couple of other wounded men while Boddings uncorked a small jug and poured a stingy shot of rum into a pewter cup. The patient took the cup, nodded appreciatively, swigged down the liquor, and then headed up the ladder.

"Glad to see the surgeon prescribes rum," Spider said. "Although I suspect most of his prescribing is done for himself."

Weatherall looked at Spider as though he was unsure whether to talk. "Aye, perhaps. Might be Boddings is helping himself a bit more often than the captain would like."

"I do not think Cap'n would appreciate that," Spider said.

"No." Weatherall laughed.

"What do you think he plans for the girl?"

"I do not know," Weatherall said, his tone growing more serious. "Perhaps he is just saving her for himself, as captains are wont to do, or perhaps he thinks he can sell her, or compel a ransom. Addison seems to have more immediate plans."

"Aye," Spider said. "Think Barlow and Addison might come to blows?"

Weatherall's eyebrows lifted, but he shrugged, saying nothing.

Elijah came by bearing two buckets sloshing with water. The slender man was entirely naked and dripping wet. "Cap'n has five sisters," he said. "I have never yet heard him say a foul thing 'bout a woman, nor seen him hurt one."

"The devil you say," Spider answered.

"Truth. I think that is why he spared her," Elijah said, "and I'll bet a tenth of my share against a tenth of yours he does not allow her to come to harm."

"Genteel manners in a pirate captain," Weatherall mumbled. "The Lord doth move in mysterious ways, or so we are told."

"I think I will not take your bet," Spider said. "I have seen stranger things upon the Spanish Main."

Elijah winked. "If you'd be clean, here's your opportunity, gents," he said, setting down his burden of buckets. Spider ripped off his own tattered shirt and the sweat-soaked kerchief from his head, and decided to leave his britches and boots on. He tossed aside shirt and kerchief, then used his hands to cup water from one of the buckets and splash his face, shoulders, arms, and chest.

Beside him, Weatherall stripped off his own long-sleeved shirt and draped it over his arm. Weatherall's shirt was covered in blood—most of it the blood of other men—but otherwise was in much better condition than Spider's.

"You handle that blade of yours well," Spider said. "Seems nary a sword got through your guard, except that devilish one that sliced up your leg."

"My father knew how to fight, taught me well," Weatherall said, lifting a bucket and turning it upside down over his head. Spider grabbed the other bucket and did likewise. The soaking felt good, as it was the closest thing to a bath Spider had enjoyed in weeks. The goddamned decks could use a good soaking and scraping, too, Spider thought, but he doubted that was going to happen. No captain in Spider's experience would have tolerated the bloody mess that coated *Dream*'s decks, but Barlow apparently did not give a damn.

The next man in the medical line headed below. Spider nodded at the ugly rip across Weatherall's thigh. "That is a painful sight."

"I will be fine," Weatherall said, then pointed over Spider's shoulder. "He will not be."

Spider looked where Weatherall had pointed and saw two men cradling a third in their arms. The fellow they carried bled profusely at the belly, and the men carrying him cried for the doctor.

"He fell into a boat," said one of the couriers, a malcontent named Bartleman. "We just found him moaning. God, he's in a bad way." They laid him at the feet of Spider and Weatherall.

"This man's hurt worse than any of us," Spider called down into the hold.

"We thought him dead," said the other man accompanying the wounded man. "Guts are all ripped. But he breathes yet."

Boddings, cursing, climbed up the ladder. "I will take a look, damn ye." He did not clamber entirely out of the hatch, but instead froze with his head and shoulders peeping out from below. He looked at the wounded man and muttered, "Wasted time, gents, wasted time." The doctor called to his patient below. "Hand me up that black bottle there, from my kit. No, that one, ye lout! The bottle tucked into the strap. Yes, that one, damn ye. Hand it up, smart now. Waste not a moment."

Boddings received the small black bottle and handed it to Weatherall. "Have the poor wretch drink this, right away. Then take him somewhere, as peaceful a spot as you can find. He will not live long. Shouldn't waste the medicine, frankly, but ... I am a Christian man. This won't save him, but it will kill the pain, most of it, anyway."

Then the doctor clambered back down, cursing.

Spider held the man's mouth open while Weatherall poured the thick fluid. It smelled horrible. "What do you think ... ?"

Weatherall shook his head. "I have no idea what this is."

The man was moaning, and trying to shake his head back and forth in agony, but clearly was not swallowing. The thick blue fluid welled up in his mouth and oozed down his cheeks. Spider felt the man's forehead and could not recall ever touching flesh so hot. Spider smacked the man's cheek in hopes of inducing him to swallow; the patient gagged and convulsed violently but swallowed the medicine. Then a gasp ripped from his chest, and Spider thought the man's life likely flew out upon it.

Spider struggled to remember the man's name, or anything about him.

"See to him," Weatherall told the men who had brought the wretch. "Soak a rag, mop his brow, try to make him comfortable. May he rest in peace."

"I don't even know his name," Spider said.

"Tallmadge," Weatherall said. "Works aloft, mostly. Quiet man."

Spider and Weatherall were lost in thought when a shout broke the silence. "Cap'n! We've done well, indeed, sir!"

It was Addison, hollering from atop *Loon's* forecastle.

Barlow replied. "And how well might that be, Addy?"

"Three chests, full to the brim with silver bars, a couple thousand pounds sterling silver by my estimation," Addison said, his words eliciting a round of loud cheers. "Also, she carries a wealth of timber and chilies, tobacco by the ton, six hogs, plus other food and water aplenty. And lots of hogsheads of wine, sir! I took the liberty, as they say, and judge it to be very fine. French, unless I miss my mark, and I seldom do with wine. Fit to celebrate with the Frenchman when we meet, I dare say!"

"You dare say?" Barlow yanked a gun from his belt and fired at Addison, but the ball struck the mast behind the captain's intended victim. "You have had enough wine, damn ye! Enough, I say, you loose-tongued son of a mermaid whore!"

The distance was enough to render the shot an unlikely success, but still a flying ball of lead was a danger not to be discounted. Nonetheless, Addison showed no fear, nor even a twitch; indeed, he gave what Spider considered to be a rather courtly bow. "Admonishment deserved, my dear cap'n, admonishment deserved. 'Tis thirsty work, killing and thieving and counting, and it wearies the brain, sir, it truly does, but I should have awaited your pleasure, sir, before saying so much. I will bring you a more exhaustive accounting of our new belongings as soon as may be. It shall be some time."

Addison rose from his bow and stumbled backward a step. Spider judged the first mate had sampled the fine French wine several times.

Barlow stuck his empty pistol back into his belt. "You're my good right hand, Addy. See that you remain so!" The captain then began climbing into the rigging. "Have those chests of silver hauled over here. Find a goddamn boat over there that doesn't leak like a fucking wicker basket and get that over here, too. And butcher a hog or two for tonight. We shall celebrate in high fashion, lads! High fashion, indeed! Leave the rest aboard *Loon* for the moment."

"Aye, Cap'n," Addison said, turning back toward *Loon*'s hold.

"Quick to anger, that one," Spider said, nodding toward Barlow.

"Yes," Weatherall answered. "Any spark will do, it seems. And any drink'll do for Addison."

"Who is the Frenchman?"

"Some bastard they want to sell something," Weatherall said, shrugging. "They have said little, Barlow and Addison, and they shush when anyone catches them talking about it. Gossip is they have something of rare worth, and a Frenchman intending to purchase it for a handsome price." Weatherall's expression said he hoped Spider might shed some light on that mystery, but Spider knew nothing.

"I hope we all get to share in that," Spider said.

"We shall see. We shall see."

The current patient lifted himself from the hold. "Doctor says whoever is bleeding the most should go down next."

Spider indicated Weatherall should climb down. "I do not think my wound will slow me down at all," Spider said.

"Thank you." Weatherall bowed. "You are a good man."

12

A couple of hours later, with a chilly wind out of the west and a blazing orange sun an hour or so from vanishing below the horizon, Spider sat high on the mizzenmast, secured by a safety line and hauling up a new spar to replace a damaged one that had to be cut away. His shirt had been dunked in a bucket and hung on a line to dry, so he was naked to the waist and shivering a bit despite the hard work. Peg worked just above him, explaining how his false leg had broken. He asked about the flask again, and Spider asked for time to think about it. He wasn't certain he wanted to part with the only physical clue he had to Ezra's death, but he wasn't sure what further use he could make of it.

Odin, across the way on the mainmast, inspected rigging repairs and chortled softly. Strange man that he was, Odin seemed to be as fine a rigger as Spider had ever seen and supervised the younger men with a sense of pride and only the occasional reminder that he had sailed with the most notorious pirate who had ever lived.

Below, men who had won dice rolls to push duties off on others or who had simply decided not to work took advantage of Addison's labors aboard *Loon* and the captain's trip belowdecks to keep an eye on stowage of the silver chests. They had already been at the wine, and some rum had been brought up as well.

Spider cursed them and wished someone would motivate these ruffians. Several of them could use a knotted rope against the skull, in Spider's estimation.

Peg seemed not to notice the party below and went on about his leg.

"Same ball as took out the spar," Peg said. "I was sitting in the trees, m'legs hanging down, aiming a musket at some scalawag over there on *Loon*, and the damned ball ripped up through m'wooden leg and through the damn spar. Lost me leg and damn near me ass! Fell at least five feet, straight down, until I got tangled in a ratline. Spent most of the rest of the fight hangin' from a fuckin' rope."

It had to have been the four-pounder that got pounded by one of *Plymouth Dream*'s guns. Spider recalled how the barrel had tilted upward after its carriage shattered; it was a stern reminder there simply was no safe place on a ship when it went into action. Spider had heard Peg's tale three times now, but laughed all the same even though he was in an ill humor. For all he knew, Ezra's killer was among *Plymouth Dream*'s battle dead, or about to be assigned to *Loon*, and the thought that the son of a bitch might elude him boiled his gut.

He also had some suspicions about Peg. He could not forget the man's mention of the flask and his connecting it to Weatherall. Peg deserved a closer look as the suspect in Ezra's murder.

But Peg's story was a good one, and the sea battle had eased the way a bit for Spider among *Dream*'s crew. Shared danger, and Spider's demonstrated willingness and ability to take part in the bloody work, had created a camaraderie of sorts. He had seen the situation many times before; until crewmates saw a man in action, and knew he could be relied upon to carry his share of battle and risk, he remained a question mark.

For the sake of a chance to learn more about Ezra's murder, Spider made himself laugh at the tale one more time. He wondered how many years Peg would live to tell it.

Not even one if he turned out to be the killer, Spider thought.

"So my damned leg splintered like a rotted mast in a hurricane," Peg said.

Spider's own leg wound had turned out to be a mere grazing; Boddings had almost deemed it unworthy of a tot of rum. An ointment, a bandage, and a drink, and now the pain was mostly a memory.

"That's a fine tale, Peg," Spider said. "Fine tale." He made sure the new spar was snug, with help from some fellows hauling on the other side of the mast. "That is the kind of crazy thing that often happened to my friend Ezra."

Peg lowered his head a moment. "May he rest in peace."

"Aye," Spider said. "May he." He eyed Peg, looking for signs of sincerity and noting none.

They worked in silence, securing the lumber into its place, then going to work to rig it. Spider looked at Peg's broken, wooden leg. The peg was attached to a leather holster that fitted over the stump where Peg's knee used to be. Leather straps tightened it to the man's leg. "That will be but a few moments to fix, I dare say."

Peg laughed. "Appreciate it, I will. Lost m'spare. Lost it, or some bloke stole it. Prob'ly someone thinking he's funny, or I pissed someone off."

Spider pondered. A man's wooden leg seemed an unlikely item for theft. "What was the spare made of? Oak, like this?"

"Nah. It was an ugly chunk of applewood. First stump I got after losing the genuine article. Kept it as a spare, but I liked this one what got broke a sight better."

Spider had found applewood splinters in Ezra's skull.

"I will make sure the new one is at least as good," Spider said. They worked a bit more in silence, and then Spider decided to push his luck as Peg seemed to be in a mood to converse.

"You said Ezra was talking the night he died," Spider said. "Something about a woman. Did you hear any more, a name or anything? And are you certain he was alone?"

"Did not hear another voice nor see another soul, damn me if I did," Peg answered. "All I heard was your friend saying he missed her, or more proper, 'I miss her.'"

"Hmm," Spider said, then wished he hadn't.

"Why?" Peg asked.

"It is just that he never told me of a woman, not once," Spider said.

"Never met a pirate what didn't have his secrets." Peg chuckled.

"I suppose you have the truth of it," Spider said, although he was far from convinced.

"Not so tight, there," Odin hollered across the empty space between masts and pointed to Spider's work with the hawsers.

"Aye," Spider said, paying more attention.

"Ha!" Odin barked.

As they worked, Spider ran the facts of Ezra's murder through his mind and tried to picture what must have unfolded.

Ezra had gone up on the deck. Someone had attacked him, clubbed him over the head, and then tossed that pewter flask at the body to make it seem as though Ezra had been drunk and fallen. That had been a fatal mistake, of course, because that flask convinced Spider that murder had been done.

Spider had seen Ezra fight a hundred times and knew the man lived by a code of sobriety and caution among strangers. He tried to envision someone getting close enough to Ezra to land a sneak blow— because he could not imagine Ezra being unable to fend off a blow he saw coming. That had never happened in all the time Spider and Ezra had been friends.

So . . . had Ezra gone on deck to meet someone? The only man aboard *Dream* who had a history with Ezra—aside from Spider himself, of course—was Peter Tellam. And that tattooed bastard had a motive, a deeply ingrained fear of witchcraft. But Spider could not see Tellam being able to get so close to Ezra without his friend raising his guard. A surprise punch did not seem to be Tellam's style, nor did it seem likely Ezra would be fool enough to let it happen.

So . . . who? Why?

"Reckon we are finished here, carpenter?"

"Aye, Peg, I think we be done." Spider checked once more that the rigging was secure. "Let's repair that stump of yours, and we'll tell Boddings it will hurt you like hell and see if we can get him to prescribe some rum."

13

I t was decided that Addison would command *Loon* and sail her to the rendezvous point, where the rest of Barlow's fleet would gather, after both ships sailed around Bermuda in hopes of thwarting the naval frigate. Afterward, they would beat hard for Jamaica.

Several *Loon* survivors had signed Barlow's articles, so only a handful of Dreamers were needed to fill out the minimal crew. Addison chose Peg, who loved his polished new oak stump, and a black fellow named Oscar to serve him aboard the other ship. Spider sighed in relief; the bulk of his suspects would remain aboard *Plymouth Dream* where he could get his knife into a throat once he determined who had killed Ezra.

There was more cause for relief as well. The skeleton crew for *Loon* told Spider that Barlow intended to keep the vessels together. That meant Addison, Peg, and Oscar would remain close by. Spider might still be able to avenge Ezra if one of those three turned out to be the killer.

Spider was relieved that *Loon* was not to be sent off ranging. He had been keeping an eye on Peg and would not want to see the bastard move beyond his reach. Would a man with a wooden leg prompt Ezra to drop his guard? It seemed possible, and Peg seemed a rather friendly sort compared to many other members of the crew. He just might be the type of man to get near enough to Ezra to land a murderous surprise blow, the type to mask murderous intent with friendly manner.

If Barlow had sent *Loon* off in search of prey, Spider would have been separated from Peg, and it was even possible he would never see the man again. Spider had not eliminated Addison as a suspect, either, so he was doubly glad.

Before the prize crew went aboard *Loon*, however, there would be a celebration. Addison, with the elected help of Dobbin, Weatherall, and Elijah as representatives of the crew, chosen because they could read and write a little, had assessed most of the booty from *Loon*, and it was substantial. The silver bars' value surpassed Addison's estimate by half, and most everything else could easily be sold around the Caribbean, in the colonies, or in Africa or England. There remained some goods to count on the morrow, but even if that all turned out to be useless, *Loon* had been good prey. The ship itself would prove to be a valuable asset to Barlow and his pirate fleet.

Along with all that, of course, there was the woman May, bound in the forecastle. Spider figured Weatherall was correct, and that she was destined to be sold as a slave. She may have been Horncastle's slave, for all he knew, although she had seemed fiercely devoted to him. Spider wondered if she would be mentioned in the assessment of booty, which Addison was reading aloud now.

Weatherall broke out his fiddle, and Barlow ordered some more of the fine wine hauled from *Loon* to be shared among the crewmen, and the brigands drank hard and danced beneath diamond-sharp stars in a cloudless sky. The weather had warmed considerably as they had sailed farther south, and the men were ready to loosen up after all the killing, the burials at sea, and the auctioning off of men's worldly goods. Spider had acquired a silver earring and now had a ring on each ear.

All that business done, it was time to live. Pirate grief typically was a fleeting thing. When there was time to drink and dance and enjoy this short life, that was what one did.

"Freedom, I say, is mighty sweet," Elijah opined, with Dobbin nodding drunkenly nearby and adding an incomprehensible, scarcely audible commentary. Elijah went on. "Do you know where I might be tonight, if not here?"

Dobbin opened his eyes wide, as though Elijah had asked him to name the capital of every European nation. "How the hell should I know?" At least that was what Spider thought toothless Dobbin had said.

"On a plantation, no doubt," Elijah said, "shoveling holes, toiling in fields, or serving tea to a man who thinks himself my master, or breeding him a batch of new slaves, my babies to become his property." His eyes blazed in his handsome face, and the sweat of alcohol and passion rolled down his ebon cheeks as he took a deep swig of rum. "No, sir. No, sir. No, sir. That is not the life for a man, and that is not the life I choose."

"Preach the gospel according to Elijah," Peg shouted. "Testify!"

"I choose the sea, and the waves, and the risk, and the bloodshed, and the rewards," Elijah said. "Come what may, I make my choices here and live or die by my own hand. I am a man. Hear me, Lord? Hear me, gents? I am a man!"

"And a crack shot," Peg said, pointing sort of randomly upward. "Perching up there, musket in his hand, powder and balls hanging from his neck, he's as deadly a bastard as any."

Peg staggered drunkenly up to Elijah and put an arm around the man's shoulders. "Deadly bastard as any."

"You smell like a grave," Elijah said, erupting in laughter. Then he took the one-legged man by the arm and spun him in a country dance.

The survivors from *Loon* danced and sang, too. They already seemed part of *Dream*'s crew. What else could they do? Having already sailed under a pirate flag with Horncastle, they lacked any notion of loyalty. It mattered little that they sailed and fought under a new captain. They could accept Barlow's terms and sign the articles, or be shot and tossed overboard. There was no choice, really.

Spider remembered having made that damnable choice himself, long ago. Too many years and too many deaths had passed since then.

He spat and shook his head hard to rid it of such maudlin thoughts. He had work to do. It was time to find out if wine and rum had loosened any tongues.

Spider had a million questions, and a rowdy crew might just be the place to find answers. He endeavored to partake slowly, in hopes of commanding his wits while others imbibed deeply. That was his plan, anyway. But tension tied him in knots, and he was both happy and surprised to still be alive, and he found himself drinking a bit more than he intended. He could hear Ezra laughing at him and see the big man shaking his head.

Weatherall scratched a country dance tune he called "Bartholomew Fair" from his fiddle, accompanied by much clapping of hands and stomping of feet. Captain Barlow and Addison smoked pipes aft, and the scent wafted to Spider and made him wish he had more tobacco. Thinking hard had made him go through it at a furious pace.

He walked up to a comrade and bowed.

"Oscar," Spider said, banging his cup against the black man's. "*Loon* looks a sweet little ship. I don't think you'll have to work too much to keep her afloat."

"Aye," Oscar said before drinking deeply.

"*Dream* is no worse than she was after repairs," Spider continued, lifting his cup. "I have to replace some planks in the rail, mind you, but she'll be fine. *Loon* fared a might worse, but we all shall meet up with the Frenchman safely enough, I dare say."

Oscar lowered his cup quickly, looked around wide-eyed, and then got the hell away from Spider in a hurry.

Spider kept his head down and tried to feel whether anyone was staring at him. He wondered if a ball was about to come flying from Barlow's gun. He had judged the captain was too far away to hear him with all the music and merrymaking, and considered the calculated risk to have been worthwhile, but Oscar's instant fright had Spider worried.

No gunshot roared into the night, no ball tore through his head or back, and Spider eventually relaxed. He wandered about, stole a lit pipe someone had carelessly left sitting on a four-pounder, and tried to work up the nerve to ask more questions.

Odin sat on a keg, his head on his chest, snoring. A chicken settled in at his feet, as though nesting.

Hob passed by with a platter of jacks, spilling rum as the boy tried to adjust his gait to *Dream*'s gentle rolling motion. Spider grabbed a tankard. He drank greedily and imagined Ezra's rolling eyes. *Damn it*, he thought, *you haunt me, my friend. I will avenge you, by God or devil.*

The staccato drumming of Peg's wooden leg grew louder, and the aroma of pork filled Spider's head. He dearly hoped Doctor Boddings would not find a way to render fresh pork inedible.

Peg approached bearing a harpoon upon which slabs of roasted pork had been skewered. "Have one," Peg said. "Courtesy of *Loon's* larder and the doctor's kitchen skills."

"Ah, yes," Spider cried. "Spoils to the victor."

"They ain't spoiled," Peg said. "Hell, we just killed the damn pig today."

"I apologize," Spider answered, lifting a slab of meat from the harpoon. "I am certain the pork is fine." He took a bite, and juice dripped down his chin. "Indeed, a fine dinner," he said, somewhat surprised. It seemed Doctor Boddings had even glazed the pig with honey.

Peg grinned. "Aye," he said, heading away. Then he pivoted and pointed at Elijah. "Deadly a bastard as any!"

Peg seemed not at all bothered by his new peg leg, and Spider took a bit of satisfaction in seeing that. He ate the rest of the pork, tossed the bone into the sea, then resumed his smoking.

Spider's pipe billowed out a cloud that stung his eyes, and he gazed out over the quiet ocean and ran the suspects through his mind once again.

Captain Barlow. Spider earlier had mostly dismissed him as a suspect, but that episode with Addison had him thinking things over again. Barlow was a calculating man and seemingly loath to waste a good seaman and fighter, but he had demonstrated more than once that he might do any damned thing in a sudden fit of anger. If he was willing to fire his weapon at Addison, he surely would not balk at clubbing Ezra to death.

But what could Ezra have done to piss off Barlow? Spider had trouble imagining it, for Ezra was a cautious fellow. Only talk of witches and such could prompt his friend to throw caution aside and throw an unwise punch, and Barlow had made clear more than once that he set no real store in what he called superstitious nonsense. It seemed unlikely that Barlow had said something to set Ezra off and spark a fight.

Peter Tellam. That tattooed devil thought of himself as God's executioner, and despite his life as a sea reaver he seemed convinced that the Lord would forgive all that, but his every word and action was at odds with the idea of a stealthy attack. Tellam enjoyed causing fear. Tellam enjoyed confrontation. He would not attempt an attack by stealth, and Ezra would never, under any circumstances, let Tellam get close enough to bash in his head. It was unthinkable.

Doctor Boddings. The surgeon had made his feelings about witches and their spawn well known. Spider tried to imagine Boddings strolling toward Ezra on the moonlit deck. Would Ezra see the chubby old man as any kind of threat? Probably not, Spider decided, and that could have provided the surgeon with opportunity. Was Boddings a man to act so boldly as to murder another man? Spider decided to keep a close eye on the surgeon.

Addison. The first mate was a mystery. The bossy son of a bitch seemed just a little bit drunk most of the time, but nonetheless had shown himself to be a capable seaman and fighter. Spider recalled the utter fearlessness Addison had displayed when Barlow shot at him. He followed Barlow's orders, but he clearly did not fear him. Such a man might do anything. But could he get close enough to Ezra to land a surprise blow? Perhaps. If he could keep calm as Barlow's blunderbuss ball whizzed past his head, he might well disguise his intentions enough to catch Ezra off guard.

Peg. The man was surprisingly agile for one who had a wooden leg, and so he could not be written off as a suspect just because of his injury. Also, he had tried to direct attention to Weatherall. No one else aboard *Dream* had mentioned the flask at all. The flask was the one physical clue that might be tied to the killer, the one physical clue that proved beyond a ghost of doubt that Ezra Coombs had been murdered as opposed to dying in a drunken accident. Spider had mentioned it aloud, hoping to provoke a reaction, and only Peg had reacted.

Peg had brought up the topic twice. Did he need to retrieve the flask for some reason?

One other fact had anchored itself in Spider's mind. Peg's missing spare wooden leg was made of applewood, like the splinters in Ezra's crushed skull.

John Weatherall. The man was a hell of a fighter, judging from what Spider had seen during the taking of *Loon*. Weatherall, perhaps, could have stood up to Ezra in a fight. But could he have gotten close enough to Ezra to land a surprise blow? Spider doubted it.

Weatherall, despite his battle prowess, had seemed reluctant to fight before *Dream* and *Loon* joined battle. He struck Spider as a man who knew how to fight, but who would prefer to avoid it. A decent sort, not a murderer. Plus, he was relatively new to *Dream*, having come aboard not long before Spider and Ezra, so he was an unlikely recruit for someone else's machinations.

Spider spat and dumped the burnt remnants of his pipe tobacco into the sea. Given the fuss about witchcraft raised by the confrontation between Tellam and Ezra, almost anyone aboard might have killed Ezra. *Damn me*, Spider thought. *Even bloody Hob might have killed him for all I know.*

As soon as he had that thought, he had another. As bitter as Spider was, he honestly could not see Hob as a killer—but he could see him as an ally. Hob darted all over the vessel on chore after chore, worked a great deal with Doctor Boddings, and carried messages to and fro for Barlow and Addison. Few of the crewmen paid much attention to the boy. Hob might very well prove a valuable ally, and so Spider resolved to recruit him.

He spun slowly, in search of the boy, only to see Tellam's tattooed face emerge from the shadows. Tellam stopped in front of Spider, grinning wickedly.

"You look about you as though you are always seeking something," Tellam said, sneering. "Your friend's ghost, maybe? Or someone besides the Lord to blame for his death?"

Spider thought long and hard about disemboweling the man before him. He stared into Tellam's frozen eyes and imagined his knife plunging into the bastard's gut, twisting into his intestine and jerking free with a bloody rip. He wanted to show them all who was as deadly a bastard as any.

But Spider had already felt the imagined impact of Barlow's bullet once this night, and so reined in his violent emotions.

"I keep my thoughts to myself, Peter," Spider finally said. "It is an admirable trait, you see." He pushed his way past Tellam.

"Coward," Tellam growled in a low voice.

Spider kept walking.

"You heard me, I know," Tellam said. "You always listen and watch. Always lurking about."

"Aye," Spider growled, turning. "But your thoughts amount to shit, so I ignore them."

The men stared one another down for several seconds, each aware of the knife tucked into the other's belt, and Spider, at least, wondering whether Barlow was taking notice of the confrontation.

Odin awoke suddenly and laughed.

Tellam made no move. He simply leered, his hand near his knife handle. Spider eventually turned and headed for the hold. He felt Tellam's eyes digging into the back of his skull.

He would have to talk to Hob later. Right now, he could not stand to be on the deck.

Spider grabbed a swinging lantern from a brace and took it with him below. With everyone drinking and dancing above, he had an opportunity to search the crewmen's chests and sacks. Perhaps he could find a mate to that pewter flask, or a possible murder weapon of applewood. Any sort of clue would be welcome at this point, for he felt himself adrift.

Spider hung the lantern on a hook and started with the oak case for Weatherall's violin. The man had left it open on his hammock. Weatherall had the instrument and the bow up on deck, scratching away at dance tunes while the men wailed in song, but the case included a small compartment within. Spider tugged it open, but it contained nothing but some small tuning wrenches and some rags used for wiping the fiddle down after performing.

He found Peg's rucksack and rifled through it to find it held naught but clothes and a pouch of tobacco. Spider stole that.

Tellam kept his belongings in a small oak chest, protected by a padlock. Spider pulled down the lantern and tried to peer into the keyhole. It seemed it would be easy enough to pick. He glanced up the ladder and saw no one coming down. The ruckus from above had grown louder, and the celebration was still young. No one was likely to go below as long as the booze was flowing freely above. Spider decided to risk it.

He hung up the lantern again and pulled one of Weatherall's tuning wrenches from the fiddle case. This he used as an improvised key. Sweating, and constantly looking toward the ladder, he fiddled with the padlock. It took forever, and sweat beaded on his brow, but at last it came open with a loud clack.

Spider tossed the wrench back into the fiddle case and then plundered Tellam's chest. Grimy clothing, a tricorn hat that time had reduced almost to a rag and—*well, damn me*, Spider thought—a machete, with a blade as long as Spider's forearm and a handle of carved applewood.

The weapon was tucked into a heavy leather sheath and wrapped in a shirt. No doubt the captain knew nothing of this, and Tellam was wise to keep it hidden and locked away. Had he taken the weapon up on deck with him that bloody night and used it to break Ezra's skull?

Spider held the weapon up to the lantern and examined the handle. It was heavily beaten by time, full of dings and chinks, none of which stood out as fresh in the lantern light. It bore no sign of bloodstains, but it certainly was heavy enough to have caused Ezra's wounds. Tellam might have held it by the leather sheath and wielded it like a club. That way, he could kill without leaving telltale incisions in his victim.

Was Tellam that clever? Spider wondered.

He arranged Tellam's belongings back in the chest and closed it up. Once the padlock was in place, Spider started going through other sacks and boxes, but found nothing as damning as that weapon of Tellam's.

He wanted to lie down and think but talked himself out of it. He did not want anyone coming down the ladder to find him alone in the hold. That would not do if anyone noticed some of the goods had been tossed about.

Hatchways gave access to the lower hold and to the giant main hold amidships, so he could easily search belowdecks thoroughly, but Spider deemed it unwise to disappear for too long.

Reluctantly, Spider went above and rejoined the revelry, resolving to take the next opportunity to poke around below. Peg, pissing over the rail, raised a leather jack and shouted a heigh-ho. "Where have you been, Spider John? We tapped another keg!"

"I was having a smoke, away from the cat scratching at the fiddle."

"Oh, Weatherall plays well enough," Peg said. "You are a harsh critic, Spider, a harsh critic." Drunk, Peg managed to cram most of those sentences into about ten syllables. "And deadly a bastard as any!"

"I suppose I can be pure hell when I need to be," Spider said. "Where is the keg?"

14

*I*t was morning before Spider got an opportunity to speak to Hob in relative privacy. Spider was mounting a swivel gun brought over from *Loon* to serve *Plymouth Dream* as another stern chaser. He'd asked for Hob as an assistant, and once the gun was hoisted into place, Spider had dismissed the fellows who had done the heavy lifting but kept Hob at hand while he tightened everything down.

Plymouth Dream sailed easily now, making at least twelve knots with *Loon* trailing a mile or so off the port stern. South of them in the distance, Bermuda rose like a dark mountain from the sea. Spider could make out a few of her sister islands as well, and he thought Barlow's ruse was well considered. There were many places in these waters where a ship might lay up and hide a while, and if their frigate pursuer spent time checking out even a few of them, *Dream* might be well on her way to Jamaica before the hunters realized she was nowhere in sight.

"Don't see why as we can't lay over a day or two," said the helmsman, a tobacco-chewing ape known as Simmons who smelled like death and spat brown goo all over *Dream*'s decks because he didn't notice there was an entire ocean to spit into instead. "Could use a bit of a cuddle, is all I am saying. And maybe some booze that ain't watered down like fish piss."

Spider had heard similar grumbles from men who wanted to lay over in a Bermuda port, thinking they'd earned a bit of good, non-watered rum and some wenches, but he was glad Barlow had decided against that. Once *Dream* dropped anchor in a harbor, there was an opportunity for Ezra's killer to run away or join another vessel. Hell, that was what Spider would do if he did not have a murder to avenge.

Spider decided he would rather never set foot on solid ground again than let Ezra's murderer elude justice.

Spider spent a few seconds envisioning his dirk plunging into the killer's throat, then remembered he had a plan. He ignored Simmons, who now muttered softly to himself with one hand in his pants. Spider blinked, then looked at Hob.

"I like you, Hob," Spider said in a low voice. "You are a good lad."

"Thankee," Hob said in a quiet tone that matched Spider's.

Spider chuckled. "You're a sharp one, too, I must say. Can I trust you, boy?"

"Will you stop ordering me about like a child when there's action?"

Spider laughed softly. "I shall try. I cannot promise you more than that, I am afraid."

"I am not a child."

"I know that. In fact, I am depending upon that very thing." Spider tightened the last of the heavy screws. "I believe you to be a man, Hob, and I could use your help. Walk with me."

Spider heaved his tool bucket and headed forward, down the ladder and hugging the starboard rail, with Hob beside him. Behind them, Simmons breathed hard, with one hand on the wheel and the other still in his britches, and Spider wondered if it might not be best to put the son of a bitch in a boat and let him row to Bermuda and find a woman.

Hob laughed. "He ought to do that below."

"Ignore him, boy," Spider answered.

They talked quietly, taking advantage of small gaps between clumps of crewmen who were either working or slacking. South of them, the island of Bermuda was a dark, jagged shape drawn across the horizon, close enough to distinguish but too far away to be distinct. Barlow had decided to sweep beyond it on the north, within sight, then round it and continue farther south and east before breaking southwest toward Jamaica. He hoped the tailing frigate would stop at the port there and ask questions, wasting time while *Dream* went her merry way.

That plan suited Spider, for it gave him a few more days to unveil Ezra's killer. Once they reached Jamaica, there was a chance the crew would be divided among Barlow's other ships, and a good chance a few men would desert altogether once paid off. Spider guessed Barlow's Bermuda ruse gave him about two weeks, maybe a few days more if the captain decided to scour the colonial coast in search of prey.

"I want to tell you something," Spider said to Hob, "but I wish you to promise me my words will go no further. Promise me."

"I swear it," Hob said quietly, his chest swelled and his head tilted up like that of a soldier at attention.

Spider inhaled deeply. Confiding in someone felt like diving into the deep, bloody sea.

"I do not believe my friend's death was an accident," he finally said. "I believe someone murdered him."

"Why?" Hob stopped in his tracks, and Spider kept walking. Hob caught up quickly. "Why?"

"That flask," Spider answered. "Ezra was not a drinker. He had rather strong feelings about it, because his old man was a drunkard. Ezra used to tease me about my drinking, he did."

Spider paused while a man passed them by, then continued. "So, I am certain someone clubbed him on the head and tossed that flask on the corpse to make it seem he'd drunk himself silly and fallen."

"What a goddamned cowardly thing to do," Hob whispered.

"Right," Spider said. "It was a goddamned cowardly thing to do, and I mean to avenge my friend, or die in the attempt."

They had arrived at the tool chest, and Spider set his tool bucket down and opened up the chest. "I mean to find out who did the deed, and I mean to cut him up."

"Barlow will kill you," Hob said as casually as someone pointing out it might rain.

Spider sighed. "If I avenge my friend first, what happens next is of no account." He gulped after saying that, because he realized he had been thinking that way, and had shoved thoughts of Em and his son out of his mind. He closed his eyes, took a deep breath, and berated himself. He owed more allegiance to more people than he could track in his thoughts, and he silently vowed to do better.

Spider looked into Hob's eyes, seeking an ally. "Will you help me solve this mystery?"

Hob held out his left hand, then pulled his dirk from his belt. He cut his palm and held out his hand for Spider to grasp.

Spider lifted a blade from the tool chest, then made an incision just below the stump of his missing digit. He grasped Hob's bloody hand with his own. "God bless you, boy."

"I dare say it is far too late for that," Hob answered. "But what I can do for you, I will do."

"Very well, my friend, very well." Spider blinked against tears and managed to stop them just before they could go rolling down his face. "All right. Most everyone on board thought Ezra a witch spawn, so anyone could have thought they had reason to kill him. Have you heard any loose talk?"

"Most everyone seems to think it best that he's dead—I'm sorry, Spider, I am. They feel a curse is off us with his death. I've heard no one taking credit nor casting blame. They all seem to think he got drunk and busted his own head open."

"Aye," Spider said. He decided to try a new course. "I know that is not the case. Do you know of this bloody Frenchman we're off to see?"

Hob looked about quickly. "You know about that?"

"Not even Barlow can control every damn wagging tongue on a pirate vessel," Spider said. "What do you know? Barlow and Addison seem very secretive about it, and I think it might have something to do with the murder."

Hob seemed reluctant to speak.

"Go on," Spider said, "no one is paying us any attention." For once, Spider was glad to be aboard an undisciplined vessel. He could not imagine a pair of hands being able to stop working and talk so under a good commander's ever-watchful eyes, but under the loose governance of *Plymouth Dream*, they had only to keep their voices low.

"I know little," Hob whispered. "I know that the cap'n and Addison got their hands on something, and they think the Frenchman—I do not know who he is—will pay them an extraordinary price for it. I heard Barlow say it would be a king's ransom, and Addison talked of buying himself a colony in the New World. But they do not speak of it to us. I only hear things because no one pays me any mind."

"And that's what will make you a good spy, my boy," Spider said. "Perchance Ezra overheard something about this Frenchman, or saw something he was not meant to see, and it got him killed."

"Perhaps," Hob said. "I know the cap'n sent *Blowfish* sailing ahead to arrange a rendezvous with the Frenchman while *Dream* stocked up on recruits and other needs, but that was before you and your friend came aboard. But I have no idea what it is they have got, or why a Frenchman would pay handsomely for it."

"Hmm," Spider said. "Well, then. Let me think on this. Keep your eyes and ears open for me, boy, and let me know if you learn of anything. In the meantime, have you noticed anyone changing since the murder?"

"Changing?"

"Aye, like changing their ways. Maybe a fellow used to talk a lot, and suddenly he don't, or fellows gathering together who didn't used to, or some other odd change."

"Ah," Hob said. "No. It all seems normal, as normal can be on a ship like this, anyway. Wait! Peter Tellam and Doctor Boddings, they confer a lot, quietly."

"What do they discuss?"

"The Bible, Doctor Boddings says. But they don't seem to want anyone else at the meeting. They lean close together, peering at the doctor's New Testament, and whispering together."

"Does Barlow know they're doing that?"

"He scoffs, tells them Jesus ain't the cap'n of this damned boat."

"Odd pairing, Boddings and Tellam, but they do both profess to love the Bible," Spider said. "Could be innocent, could be they're plotting, could be they're looking into the Good Book for words to absolve themselves of a murder."

"Damn," Hob whispered.

"You have got to be quiet, boy," Spider warned. "Watch and listen, but don't say nothing and don't ask a bunch of foolish questions. You'll stir up the kind of trouble that'll get your throat slit. Mark me?"

"Aye."

"Well, then, maybe that's something, what you told me," Spider said, scratching his bearded chin. "Maybe that's something, I say. Now, get yourself to wherever it is you should be. I have some thinking to do."

15

*M*ore days passed, and the weather grew steadily warmer. *Plymouth Dream* had broken southwest at last. Spider estimated her speed at seven knots or so, but as they poked along south they would pick up the trade winds and ride them, making much better headway toward Jamaica.

It was one of those days when the sea just went on forever, and one wondered if the rest of the world had simply vanished.

Men worked up a sweat and smiled and drank in the morning sunshine.

Spider, however, could not share in their fine mood. It felt good to have a confidant, but Hob thus far had not turned up anything of value in Spider's investigation. Even the apparent conspiracy between Tellam and Doctor Boddings had not produced a real clue. Spider had spent days watching and listening, and never saw nor heard a damned thing to indicate the two were doing anything more than discussing theology, with Tellam generally seeming confused and the doctor constantly defining terms such as "theodicy" and "exegesis." Spider wondered if perhaps "love thy neighbor" might be sufficient, and whether that simple admonition might be more than most people could handle, anyway.

Spider went to his hammock each night in a state of frustration and slept only in fits. His dreams were filled with vengeance, and he slaughtered crewman after crewman in nightmare after nightmare, but each morning he awoke with the realization that he was not one goddamned inch closer to unmasking Ezra's killer. Some mornings, he imagined himself setting a fuse to the powder magazine below and killing every soul aboard. At least that way, he'd know he'd slain the bastard who'd killed his friend.

Unless, of course, Ezra's murderer was over there aboard *Loon*, sailing in tandem with *Plymouth Dream*. The sheer unfairness of it all haunted Spider and sent his thoughts spiraling into a very ungodly place.

He splashed water over his bearded face and sneezed away whatever goddamned hair or dust had invaded his nose during the night. An indeterminate ruckus aft slowly resolved itself into intelligible sentences. "She's back!" "Bugger the King!" "Fuck the Royal Navy!"

The mysterious pursuer had appeared again. Spider, deciding it was already too goddamned hot to keep his shirt, doffed the garment and tossed it down the hatch. Then he headed toward the noise.

"Fucking George, I fucking scoff at thee!" Weatherall stood at the rail, silhouetted in the dawn light, whipping his sheet to and fro and shouting at the top of his lungs. Gathered around him, *Plymouth Dream*'s crew shouted taunts and screamed catcalls. Barlow, pacing the poop deck, snarled and spat, swooshing his cane back and forth like a scythe. "Odin! Peg! You men look alive up there; we'll be dancing here. Helm, steady for now."

"Aye, aye," came the response from the helm. Above, Peg and Odin growled as men spread along the yards.

"Peg! Signal *Loon*, tighten up aft of us. Let's remind our friends they'll be fighting both of us."

"Aye, aye!"

Thomas patrolled the deck, snarling and hissing, but whether the cat's taunts were aimed at the king's men or merely urging *Dream*'s crew to quiet down, Spider could not tell.

Spider wandered toward the poop deck and, deciding there was enough room up there, climbed the ladder. "Bloody bastard is following us rather doggedly, I'd say."

Barlow strode toward the top of the ladder and snarled. "Of course, he's fucking following us," he bellowed. "Do you honestly believe, for one bloody goddamned second, that I don't know yonder English vessel is following us? Do you?"

"No, Cap'n," Spider said, reaching the top of the ladder and standing before Barlow. "I just thought out loud, sir. Surprised he ain't lost hope by now, is all."

"Well fucking stop thinking out loud!" Barlow's hand went to the pistol tucked into his belt, but he did not draw it. "I will think. You obey!"

"Aye, sir."

The pursuer, well aft and on the opposite tack, had not yet turned in pursuit. Her sails were mere scraps of white in the distance, far beyond the range of any gunshot or taunts from the pirates. Spider was not much of a navigator, but even he could see that the English captain had already squandered his best opportunity to close the gap. The distance between vessels was still growing.

Barlow grimaced and scratched his beard. He watched Spider intently, while a chorus of boos and jeers continued around them on the poop and below on the main deck. "You do not follow the mob, do you, Spider John? Think for yourself, aye? Well then, deep thinker, I shall ask your thoughts, after all. What do you make of this frigate that plagues us?"

"I believe yonder vessel to be captained by an idiot," Spider said, "else it is crewed by idiots. I have seen press gangs bend sail more smartly than that. We won't even need to load a stern chaser."

"Aye," Barlow said. "It seems we are pursued by the dregs of the Royal Navy, by fucking ignoramuses who could catch us only if we cut away our sails and dropped all of our shot into the fucking sea."

Spider stared at the captain, trying to discern whether he was pleased or disappointed. Then Barlow growled deeply. "But they keep finding us, nonetheless."

Barlow spat overboard in contempt. "Fuck the bastards," the captain said as the frigate finally, slowly came about in chase. "Helm! Hard to starboard! Dowd! All sail, goddamn it! All sail!"

Spider watched as *Dream*'s crew put Barlow's orders into action. The men, who struck Spider as useless layabouts most of the time, did an outstanding job and altered course as smartly as he had seen done on any Royal Navy vessel. Booms swung, lines tightened, canvas slacked and swelled anew. Spider peered into the distance aft and noted the sailors on the pursuing ship were far less efficient. The rules of wind and wave would soon put ample distance between hunter and prey. *Dream* had not a damned thing to worry about.

Despite the outcome, Spider could not help wondering how the goddamned ghost ship kept appearing behind them. "It is like they know where we are going," he said aloud to no one in particular. "How the hell else could they hound us like this?"

"Aye," Barlow growled. "Her captain thinks he knows where we are bound, anyway. I agree. That makes sense." He stared at Spider long and hard. "Still, his crew cannot seem to answer smartly, aye? Pressed men, or malcontents, or fucking lobcocks who prefer not to risk their fucking necks in a confrontation with us. Aye? Cowards, I say, or lubbers unable to tell a hawser from an anchor. Fuck them. We slip away time after time. And we shall do so again."

Spider peered aft. "Aye, Cap'n. The distance between us and them grows. Her cap'n must be timid, indeed."

Barlow spun about, his ever-present cane perched on his shoulder. "If this is the best George has got, I dare say we shall rule the seas! Damn Roberts! Damn Blackbeard! Barlow will be the name they all remember, because Barlow will be the one to endure!"

Spider, unsure of how to respond to such demented conceit, turned and headed forward, happy to know that this day *Dream* would outpace her hunter. And he took hope in that fact, because it gave him more time to avenge Ezra.

16

Morning was announced with angry shouts from Barlow. "Furl the sails! Let no canvas remain. We shall drift, by God and devil! Then get the bloody hell on deck, every goddamned one of you!"

The ship's bell rang out in a frenzied cadence, and shouts went up. Men let down the sails in rapid fashion, under Odin's snarly guidance, then began hustling down the ratlines as *Plymouth Dream* slowly came to drift.

Spider was already on deck, replacing oar locks on one of the ship's new boats pilfered from *Loon*. He dropped his tools at Barlow's call and strode aft where the crowd was gathering. The captain stood above on the poop, silhouetted by the early-morning sun and holding his blunderbuss in one hand and his cane in the other.

Three days had passed since the phantom frigate had been sighted astern—and the nights had been haunted by nightmares. Ezra on fire, Spider's gram on fire, witch chants. Lack of sleep, and fear of talking aloud if he did fall asleep, had Spider's nerves unraveling like bad rope. Barlow's fierce demeanor and the spittle on his beard pulled on those nerves.

Spider cast a hard glance across the water in all directions, but saw nothing to justify the all-hands call. *Loon* trailed quietly behind, and those were the only sails he saw.

Thomas the cat seemed to sense Barlow's agitation and sprang toward the closest hatch.

Barlow was as livid as Spider had ever seen him. "Elijah! Keep your goddamned ass aloft and signal *Loon*! I want Addison aboard now! He's got no time to piss nor shit!"

"Aye," Elijah said in a tone that suggested such an order should have been given before his descent. He reversed course and climbed back up the ratlines, graceful as a ballerina and ascending at a speed that made Spider gasp.

The light morning breeze could not dispel the tension. *Loon* drifted ever closer while *Dream's* crew waited in silence. Spider watched Barlow pace back and forth, brandishing his flintlock pistol wildly and cursing to no one in particular, or perhaps to God or the devil.

Spider heard shouts from beyond the rail and saw a handful of crewmen rushing to help Addison clamber aboard. Peg and Oscar followed him over the rail. He'd brought an oar boat over from *Loon* and now strutted defiantly across *Dream's* deck. Spider noted a brace of pistols in Addison's belt. "Do you miss my counsel already, Captain Barlow?"

"I miss your guns, Addy. Pray me, draw them and shoot the first of these bastards who gives you the least reason."

Addison laughed, as though he'd been looking forward to shooting someone for a month. He drew the two pistols from his belt. "I will gladly put a ball through the brain of anyone here who displeases me, Cap'n. You may rely on it."

"God help me."

The whispered words came from behind Spider, and he turned to see Doctor Boddings clutching his Bible.

"Mister Dowd! Go below and search every goddamn nook and cranny," Barlow bellowed. "If there be room enough for a fucking shadow, you fucking feel it out. You know what I seek!"

"Aye, sir." The muscular black man headed toward the ladder and quickly disappeared below.

"While he does that," Barlow continued, "every mother's son of you will strip, naked as the day your whore of a mother brought you into this world. Hesitate, and I will put a ball through your fucking brain, I swear it!"

Spider looked about him. Everyone seemed surprised by this, but everyone was complying, even crazy, one-eyed Odin, although the long-haired man chuckled quietly as he did so. Weatherall snarled while removing his shirt. "Someone stole a damned expensive wine or something," he said. "Just confess, and save us some effort."

"Amen," Peg whispered.

Tellam stripped, revealing his numerous tattoos. "This is not going to end well, lads."

Spider whipped his own shirt off, then removed the kerchief from his head. "What do you think he's seeking?" He followed the question with a glance at Weatherall.

"I will be damned if I know."

"I do not recall ordering you bastards to talk!" Barlow seemed unhinged, on the edge of hysteria.

Spider, already barefoot, tugged off his britches. He silently prayed that whatever came next would provide a clue to Ezra's murder. Days had passed in boring routine, nights had passed in frightening dreams, and Spider was no closer to solving the mystery of Ezra's death than he had been that first night.

"Addy! Walk among them. Stick a goddamn finger up their asses if you have to. You know what we are seeking."

Addison spat. "Do you mean to tell me . . . ?"

"Yes, curse you!" Barlow brought his cane down hard on the rail with a whack that cracked like lightning. "I do fucking tell you, and I order you to search every throat and bunghole on these men until you fucking find it!"

"Aye," Addison said, spitting and returning one of his guns to his belt. "Well enough, then. Lads, I will be poking about, as it were. I can do it while you live, or I can do it after I shoot you in the head. The choice is yours, I dare say."

"Goddamn this all to hell," toothless Dobbin muttered. "What in bloody hell do they seek?" It was a garble, of course, but Spider had no trouble understanding most of it.

"Damn me if I know," Weatherall whispered. He stood naked, save for a bandage around his left forearm and one on his leg. Spider started to speak, but the captain's harsh curse of "Damn ye, Doctor!" halted his question before he could ask it.

Doctor Boddings, attired in britches, boots, and a decent linen shirt, had not yet moved to doff any clothing. Barlow stared at him. "Do ye balk at observing my orders, Doctor?"

"Captain, I dare say whatever thievery you believe has taken place here, I am well above it. I do not steal from the larders, dip into the kegs, or otherwise behave in the manner of a common criminal. Surely, sir . . ."

Barlow's pistol thundered, and the ball grazed the doctor's shoulder before burying itself in the mizzenmast. "God curse you, for an educated man you are miserably stupid! Get your clothes off, man, damn ye!"

Boddings, eyes wide and his jaw working up and down in panic, began stripping. Spider, already naked himself, eyed the doctor's wound and decided he would live.

Barlow paced, tossed aside his fired gun, and drew another from his belt.

Addison walked among the men, kicking clothes about, turning boots upside down, and stopping behind each crewman. The first mate leered as he conducted the search of each man. Men winced, some cursed, but Addison found nothing. Spider felt especially bad for Hob, but noticed the boy bore the indignity without wincing.

"I will be damned, I will," Addison said, standing before Peter Tellam. "Your bloody pecker is tattooed!"

That drew a few soft laughs and a loud "Ha!" from Odin, but most of the men remained quiet.

Spider's mind raced, and he clenched his fists. They had to be seeking whatever it was that Barlow planned to sell to the Frenchman.

"Goddamn ye to hell, sir," Weatherall muttered, rearing up on his toes as Addison moved behind him.

"It must be done, lad," Addison said. "So long as I find naught but shit up there, you've naught to fear." Addison felt the bandages on Weatherall's arm and thigh to assure himself nothing had been tucked beneath them.

After that, it was Spider's turn. Spider ground his teeth together as Addison's boot kicked at his clothes. Addison then eyed the pendant hanging from Spider's neck and took it in hand. For a moment Spider feared the man was going to crush the fragile piece, but Addison's beefy hand did not close upon the one possession Spider cared about, and the piece fell back to lie against his chest. Spider unclenched his fists and did not strike.

The first mate moved behind him.

Spider braced himself for the invasion and spat as Addison forced his fingers inside. Spider reminded himself he'd been flogged once and had survived that pain and humiliation. This could not be worse than that. "Now, then," Addison whispered, "I take no more joy in this than you do."

Spider stared at Barlow and imagined himself killing the man, and killing Addison, and Tellam, and everyone else. But he remained stoic.

Addison checked the bandage on Spider's leg, and then it was done.

Spider let out a deep breath, with a silent curse upon it. *If there truly be any witch blood in me*, he thought, *let me plague Barlow and Addison with burrowing leeches.*

"Fuck!" one of the new men from *Loon* yelped and turned and slapped Addison's face. Addison laughed and put his pistol against the man's forehead. "Well, then," Addison whispered before pulling the trigger. Wind blew a stream of crimson mist across the deck as the man fell, and Addison drew his second pistol and held it aloft. "Take note, damn ye! I do not bluff. I do not suffer insolence!"

The man's body lay on the deck, spilling blood. It was Larwell, a man Spider did not know well, but he could recall the man smiling while singing a lusty song. That would never happen again.

No one said a word after the shooting, but the tension was unbearable.

Spider calculated the odds, and knew that if everyone revolted at once, Barlow and Addison would be overwhelmed. But Barlow and Addison had weapons, while the crew did not, and every man aboard kept his eyes down and chose not to see the dead man's blood pouring across the deck. Barlow and Addison had stripped *Dream*'s crew of far more than clothing.

Spider spat and tried to calm his mind. What could he learn about Ezra's death from this? How could this indignity lead him to vengeance?

The thing they sought had to be something of extraordinary value, something that would make a Royal Navy vessel track them south all these furlongs along the colonial coast. The pursuing vessel had to know their destination, or else Spider could not explain how it showed up again and again. The frigate had to be chasing after Barlow's mystery item.

So then, he thought. A small object, of immense value, valuable enough to push Barlow and Addison to risk provoking a revolt. And maybe, just maybe, it was the key to Ezra's death. If Ezra had somehow stumbled onto the secret, surely Barlow and Addison would not have hesitated to silence him.

Had Ezra seen someone poking about, in search of the mystery item? Perhaps the thief, whoever he was, had killed Ezra to cover his trail.

"Done!" Addison waved his right hand aloft and kept his pistol level in his left. "I have poked every bum, Cap'n, and I dare say some of these bastards enjoyed it. But I did not find what we seek."

"Very well," Barlow growled. "Have Elijah get his ass down here and search him, and send Peg aloft to look out. Every mother's son stays right where he is, until Dowd is done below. Get yourself another pistol, Addy. Trust no one."

"I assure you of that, Cap'n," Addison said, making a pretentious curtsy. "I trust no one. Not even you."

Barlow glared, and gritted his teeth, but made no answer.

Spider felt himself trembling with anger and fought to control it.

"What is it you seek?" Cooper, one of the sail hands and a man with three daughters in England, had asked the question. Spider closed his eyes and winced at the crack of thunder. He opened his eyes in time to see the man fall dead to the deck, while Barlow tossed aside his now-empty weapon and drew yet another from his belt. Spider said a silent prayer, in hopes that no one else would be so foolish.

"Damn ye all," Barlow said. "Have I not led ye well? Have I not filled our coffers with gold, with silver? Are we not all destined to live out our lives as rich men, if we just hang together a while longer?"

Spider heard men mutter about him and saw them nodding in approval. He could not make out all the words, but he could make out the word "aye" arising from several throats.

"Cast this blasphemous bastard overboard," Barlow said, aiming a pistol at the dead man who had dared question him. "And the other man, too. Gentlemen, know this. I will make ye rich if you just be smart, and I will make ye dead otherwise. You need not know another goddamn thing in this world. Rely on it."

"Bugger," said Odin, chortling.

A handful of men, chosen by Addison, lifted the corpses from the deck and carried them to the rail. Barlow nodded toward Addison, who said, "Toss them."

Spider shuddered when he heard the splashes, echoes of that final splash he'd heard when Ezra's shroud-wrapped corpse plunged into the sea.

"Not a damned thing, Cap'n," Dowd called, peering up from the hatch. "Not a goddamned thing."

"Then search again, goddamn ye, search again!" Barlow raised his cane for emphasis and aimed his blunderbuss at Dowd's head. "It did not fucking disappear! Go search again."

Dowd said nothing and ducked below. Spider felt the breeze against his naked skin and wondered how long Barlow would hold the men here.

Barlow strutted to and fro on the poop deck like a madman and repeatedly pointed his gun at the men below. His eyes were wild, and he spat constantly. Spider convinced himself that Barlow would next cut open bellies and bowels to find what he wanted.

"We ought to search your spirited lass locked up in the forecastle, Cap'n." That was Addison, leering. "She could hide it well, I dare say."

Barlow seethed. "I said no man aboard would lay a hand on her."

"Seems if all the crew is subject to our searching, there be no reason to leave the wench out of it," Addison said quietly, looking about as men nodded in agreement. "The damn thing was fine and secure until she came on board, wasn't it?"

"She could not . . ."

A soft chorus of ayes rose among the men. Barlow, his face red with anger, assessed the situation. Spider assessed it, too. If Addison stirred up the men enough, Barlow could not possibly maintain control of the ship. Every man aboard had been violated, and they would not accept being treated worse than a mere prisoner.

"Well, then," Barlow said, and Spider judged the captain was going to acquiesce in hopes of distracting and placating the crew. "I doubt me the beauty is some talented London thief or a spy in employ of the French crown or some other great world power. It seems a bit far-fetched that she married a fool pirate just to be captured and brought aboard *Plymouth Dream* so she could slip out of her bonds like a fucking magic fairy and steal our precious cargo. Under the very snotty noses of our fucking guards, even. Probably naked when she did it, no less, or fucking invisible."

Captain Barlow stared at Addison the whole time he talked.

"But she is fair to look upon, aye, and if you think she may be our thief, Addy, well, then." He paused, then nodded. "Very well. We shall all have us a look."

Barlow tucked his gun into his belt, came down from the poop deck, and removed a key from a cord on his neck. He walked through the crowd on the deck, without a single indication he feared a mutiny, and strode confidently to the forecastle. Men followed him in a flock. The only sounds were the creaking of timber, the waves washing the hull, and their feet upon the deck.

Barlow stopped at the forecastle, pausing dramatically while he stared at Addison. Then he opened a padlock, threw back the hatch, and ducked inside.

He dragged May out and set her down to lay upon the deck. She was dripping with sweat and looking tired, but her eyes were wide with defiance. Her hands were tied behind her back, and her ankles were tied together. Spider noted the bonds were tight, and the knots were good. Her wrists and ankles were scarred where she had struggled.

The captain drew a knife and bent to cut her bonds.

"Stand up," Barlow said quietly.

She complied, with difficulty and with a bit of help from Barlow. She glared at him but said nothing.

"My first mate thinks you are a thief," Barlow said. Again, his manner was 180 degrees from that which he used toward his crew. "A magical thief, at that. I am sorry, but it is necessary to prove otherwise."

Barlow stepped away and drew his pistol. Addison stepped forward to search the girl.

"Not you," Barlow said calmly.

Addison stopped in his tracks, smiled, and turned away.

"Dobbin, you may have the honors," the captain said. "Strip her. Search her. Eyes only. Gentle as you can, or I will shoot you dead."

Addison grumbled. "So no thorough search, then? Playing favorites, are you?" Others among the crew voiced complaints, too, but in low voices so as to not stand out in the crowd and draw the captain's wrath.

"I will not subject a woman to any more indignity than is fucking necessary, Addison." Barlow twirled his cane. "We shall have her stripped, and her clothes searched, and search her as thoroughly as can be with eyes alone."

He glared at Addison. "That is my final word on the matter."

Addison made no reply.

"Stripping this woman is not a Christian act, Captain," Doctor Boddings said tersely. Tellam added an amen.

"It is far too late for me to worry about my un-Christian acts, Doctor," Barlow said. "If you please, Dobbin."

May snarled ferociously and lunged awkwardly at Barlow. She aimed to bury her teeth in his neck, but he knocked her aside with little effort. She stumbled into a crewman, who shoved her back toward Dobbin. She fell in a heap.

"If you please, Dobbin," Barlow repeated.

Dobbin, knees shaking, complied. The crew, on the cusp of rebellion moments ago, watched lasciviously as Dobbin tore away her clothes. Spider felt sorry for May and wished she'd left a mark on Barlow's throat.

May bore the search with as much dignity as possible, but her eyes said Barlow would die one day by her hand.

"Nothing, Cap'n," Dobbin said, after gawking at every exposed inch of her.

"Of course," Barlow replied. "Are ye satisfied, Addy?"

"Not so much as I might have been," Addison said. "But I believe she does not have our prize tucked away."

"Go help Dowd search, Addy. Dobbin, give the woman her clothes, replace her bindings, and lock her away again."

Dobbin picked up May's shirt. She snatched it from his hands, whipped it at Barlow's face, then stormed off toward the forecastle. Dobbin followed with her skirt, and Barlow signaled a man to help him. "She may be more than any one of us can handle," Barlow said quietly.

All the searching so far had turned up nothing. Spider had already done a great deal of fruitless searching below for clues to Ezra's death and tried now to imagine where he might hide such an object as the one Barlow sought. It could be tucked into a roll of sail, buried in a keg of powder, sunk in beer, or even hidden somewhere above in the rigging; a clever man might devise a means of doing that. Unless the thief was an idiot, poking about below in the crew's chests and sacks was pointless. It was not likely to be found by anything less than an all-hands search.

They remained there, with no sail mounted and *Loon* drifting nearby, until near sunset. Spider's legs grew weary, and his calves knotted in pain. Barlow, Addison, and Dowd had taken turns covering the men and searching the ship. No one had eaten, but at least Barlow had permitted Hob to pass watered-down rum about.

The three officers, each holding pistols as though some bastard might need to be shot at any moment, conferred on the poop deck. They tried to do so quietly, but Barlow's curses ripped the air and his arms flailed wildly. Spider worried that the man might fire an accidental shot and kill yet another member of his crew.

They had a sticky problem, Spider surmised. Somewhere on board, their precious item had been hidden, but it could take the entire crew days to search the vessel thoroughly for a small object. And the officers could not, or at least would not, trust the men to do the searching.

Spider's fear grew. Barlow was demented, and there was no telling what he might do.

"Blast it!" Barlow stepped away from the others and pointed his cane at the gathered men below.

"One of you stole from me," he growled. "One of you has taken upon himself an item that will make all of us very, very rich men. It is a brass shaft, about the size of my finger, with metal bands that spin about on it. The bands are marked with symbols in black.

"One of you has it. And one of you can find it and bring it to me. When I hold it in my hand, I will reward the man who gave it to me. I say I will fucking greatly reward the man who gave it to me, I say—and I will devise the most ungodly fucking tortures for the man he took it from. I will disembowel him, slowly, and feed him his own guts while I scrape his balls with a holystone. I will, I will!"

Barlow leapt over the poop deck rail and landed before his naked crew. "Mark me, while I wait for one of you to find the goddamned thing, I will kill men left and right. And I will keep killing men until I have my prize back, or until I have killed every mother's son of you!"

He fiddled with a key on a chain around his neck, opened a padlock, and clambered into the cabin below the poop deck, slamming the hatch closed.

"You heard him," Addison said, "and you know he will do it. If you are hiding that precious jewel in hopes of selling it yourself, such a thing will not happen. Barlow will rendezvous with his buyer with the thing in hand, or he will sail into port with no one alive but him and me and Dowd. Mark me.

"You'd be better served to kill one of your mates, peg the blame on him, and claim you found the bloody thing in his belly. You'd be better off doing that than trying to keep it for yourself."

Addison climbed down from the poop. "Oscar, you and Peg stay over here. Cap'n needs men he can rely upon. Weatherall, gather me two more rowers. I am going back to *Loon*. And all of you put your damned clothes back on. You look a disgrace."

"Cold meat and some cheese," Doctor Boddings said, stuttering while pulling his britches up over his pale legs and shaking visibly. His grazed shoulder was no longer bleeding. "I will carve some meat and cheese, and that's bloody it. No cooking. Hob, boy, come help me." The doctor picked up his remaining clothes and headed toward the galley, muttering, with a hastily clothed Hob scurrying behind.

Addison climbed over the rail and down to his boat. Spider dressed slowly.

"Silly bastard Barlow thinks he's Blackbeard," Odin said to himself. "He ain't Blackbeard. He ain't up to Blackbeard's knees."

"Watch that talk," Weatherall warned. "Cap'n hears any talk like that and he'll shoot you, depend upon it."

"Ha!" Odin smacked his hands together. "And the inevitable comes a might sooner, then? Ha!"

Weatherall turned to Spider, who shrugged.

"I do not cower for William Barlow," Odin said. "He ain't Edward Teach. I shipped with Teach. I saw Teach fight. I saw Teach drink flaming rum and breath fire. I saw the devil, and his name was Ed Teach.

"Barlow wants to be Teach, but he ain't," Odin continued. "I ain't scared of Barlow, and he knows it. Ha!"

After snatching up his clothes from the hot deck, Odin sauntered off, laughing loudly.

"I wonder if that man is demon-haunted," Spider asked of no one in particular, "or if he just sees too much to take any of it seriously?"

Weatherall spat. "If this situation is funny, I swear I do not see it."

Spider answered, "Amen."

The sun was touching the horizon, everyone was hungry and angry, the sails were all furled, and no one had set a course or ordered anything.

If ever a vessel was cursed, Spider thought, *this is surely it.*

17

*F*ew men slept. Spider heard one man snoring in the dark and crowded hold, but the others sighed audibly or muttered to themselves, indicating prayer or deep thought. No one knew where to turn, or how to keep from being Barlow's next victim.

Plymouth Dream had become a ship of the damned.

Thunder grumbled somewhere in the distance, and the ship rolled with the swells. Spider could tell the ship was underway at last, even though he'd never heard Barlow bellow any orders or set a course. Addison likely had signaled from *Loon* to move on before the threat of storm.

Spider wondered whether drifting idly so long would allow the phantom frigate to catch up to them again. *Dream* had eluded the frigate before, but it was unwise to push that kind of luck. It was good to be riding the wind at last, and the ship's rhythm told him she was picking up speed.

Above, listening at the hatch, Dowd alternatively crouched and paced, guns in hand. Barlow had told him to arm himself and to kill any man who strayed from the hold, or who seemed to be plotting with others.

Spider hung motionless in his hammock, trying to see a way forward and trying to ignore the stench of men and Elijah's ungodly perfume spray. Barlow's madness had cast a pall on an already bleak voyage, and while shared danger had opened the way for Spider to glean information from other crewmen about Ezra's death, he could no longer profit from that. Quiet conversations now would be seen as whispered conspiracies, and the captain likely would shoot on sight—

and every damned man aboard knew it. No one was going to tell Spider anything.

As for Barlow being Ezra's murderer, Spider was now quite convinced that was impossible. Barlow lived by impulse and did not care a fart for what any man thought of him. If Barlow had seen a reason to kill Ezra, he'd have simply shot him and been done with it. He would not have walked up to him and clubbed him by surprise, nor would he have tried to conceal the deed. He would have claimed the act and used it to instill more fear and obedience in his crewmen.

Spider could not let go of the notion that the captain's missing bauble might somehow be at the heart of Ezra's killing, though. The rumor of Ezra's witch blood seemed a very likely motive, but here was another. Perhaps Ezra had somehow seen or heard something related to the thievery.

So, Spider thought, *what can I deduce about the theft?* The person who took it had to have known its worth, and thus probably knew what it actually was. Spider had heard Barlow's description—a small brass cylinder with revolving marked rings—and still had no idea what the bloody thing might be. The description sounded like a navigational device, perhaps, but he could not imagine such a thing being of any real value. Whatever it was, the thief likely knew it.

That put Addison and Dowd at the top of the list of theft suspects. Barlow had said they knew what to look for, and so they presumably knew its value. Did that make them key suspects in Ezra's death as well? Spider wondered.

Of the two, Addison seemed a more likely murderer than Dowd. Addison had balls of steel and seemed to show no fear of Barlow. Dowd shared a spot in Barlow's trust, but did not take part in nearly as many conversations with the captain, nor did he join Barlow and Addison in all their private talks. Dowd seemed deferential, whereas Addison often gave the impression he should be in command.

There were points in favor of Dowd as a suspect, though. Addison carried pistols at all times, and Dowd did not. Addison, if Ezra gave him reason, could simply have shot his man and no doubt could have devised a ruse to justify the killing. The man who had calmly smiled as Barlow's pistol ball whizzed past him likely would not balk at improvising a lie or two.

Dowd, with no pistol, would have been compelled to use a knife, or a handy chunk of wood such as a belaying pin, if he'd decided to slay Ezra. Dowd might fear Barlow's wrath in a way Addison did not, and thus feel the need to make the death seem accidental.

One more point against Addison as the killer and the thief who'd taken Barlow's mystery item—Addison had been aboard *Loon* when the theft was discovered. How long could the thing have been missing before Barlow noticed? Was it likely that it could have been absent for days? Probably not, Spider decided. Given the thing's apparent value and Barlow's mistrust of his men, he'd likely have checked on the mystery cargo several times a day. That meant it had been stolen in the night, while Addison had been in command of *Loon*.

Dowd, on the other hand, led the overnight watch on *Dream*. He could order men about and clear a path between himself and the object; Dowd would have an easy time sneaking around the ship in the dark of night.

Spider tried to envision possibilities in his mind, Addison slowly rowing across the night-shrouded waters, stealing aboard *Dream*, and absconding with the precious brass cylinder. Bold as Addison seemed to be, Spider could not imagine him pulling off such an enterprise, not without help, anyway. Dowd stealing across the night-shrouded deck seemed simpler, more plausible.

Could Addison and Dowd be working together, plotting to overthrow Barlow and usurp his prize? Could Ezra perhaps have heard the two men colluding?

No, no, no, Spider told himself, covering his eyes and berating himself for being a fool. The biggest obstacle Addison and Dowd would face if they wanted to supplant Barlow was the captain himself. It would be far easier to simply murder Barlow in his sleep than to steal his damned cylinder. If Addison or Dowd was making a play to rule this floating den of brigands, there was no need to steal the thing and leave Barlow alive.

Damn! Each time Spider's mind charted a course, he ran aground. It seemed unlikely he could avenge Ezra at all unless he simply burned both ships, killing everyone aboard.

That plan was no good, of course; it would deprive him of the one thing he wanted most. He would look Ezra's killer in the eye and make sure the bastard knew Ezra was being avenged. Spider would not land a surprise blow on his target. He would not burn the son of a bitch in his sleep. He would kill him face-to-face and tell him why.

It would be the closest thing to justice Ezra Coombs could possibly receive on an outlaw sea.

Somewhere in the darkness of the hold, Odin told a tale to no one in particular. "It was a shark, an ungodly large shark, thirty foot if it was an inch," he said. "Come up on to larboard of our boat, bearing down on us, and us out of musket balls. It came at us like a comet, blazing in the water, would've shattered us, certain. Ed Teach stood up, pissed on it and cursed it, and damned if it didn't sink. Never saw it again. Ha!"

Spider envied Odin whatever fantasy world he was living in.

Spider flicked an insect out of his hair and scratched his chest. His fingers snagged on the leather cord under his shirt. He pulled Em's pendant free. It was dark in the hold, but his mind could see it well enough; he'd looked at it a million times.

What would she think of his cold-blooded intent? What would she think of the many bloody deeds he'd done merely to survive in a world of thieves and outlaws? Perhaps, he decided, it was merciful that she did not know.

And though he knew himself unworthy, and doubted he'd be heard on that account, Spider uttered a quiet prayer.

18

The storm threatening in the night never materialized, but gray clouds clamped a lid over the sea and gentle rain fell across *Plymouth Dream*. Bloody, muddy trickles worked their way across the tilted deck to the starboard scuppers. Hob found Spider a decent hat, which now sat atop the kerchief on his head and kept the rain from his eyes. *Plymouth Dream* was under topgallants and catching a decent breeze out of the east, and the ship rolled and rocked on big swells.

It looked to Spider as though the rain would be with them for most of the morning, but no gale seemed to be brewing.

Spider thanked Hob for the hat, then asked quietly, "Cap'n give you any trouble last night?" Hob slept on the floor in the officers' cabin, where he could serve Barlow at his whim.

"He just sat and drank through the night," Hob said. "Glowering at nothing and saying not a word. It was more frightening than his rants, I swear. Doctor was afraid to move, just laid there praying quiet."

"Aye," Spider said, watching Barlow brood near the wheel on the poop deck. The captain stared off into the sea, watching *Dream*'s wake, no doubt thinking murderous thoughts.

"I saw something, night before last," Hob whispered. "I don't know if it means much, but . . ."

"This is not the time," Spider said, mindful of Barlow's every move. "Cap'n may see us. Run along, lad, and don't stop to talk to anyone too long. Cap'n will see that as conspiracy, do you see? We shall meet up once he goes below."

"Aye, Spider," Hob said before running off.

Spider strolled across the rolling deck and sat on the tool chest, wishing he had not used up all of his pipe tobacco. Men around him worked, or pretended to work, without talking or singing. *Loon* strayed behind *Dream*, off her port stern, just beyond shouting distance. A bleary-eyed seaman flipped the hourglass and rang the ship's bell, then trotted off to head below.

"Come about, south by southwest, smartly now," Barlow grumbled, and the men of the watch slowly put his command into action. *Loon* followed suit shortly after, and the gap between the vessels grew a bit.

Amidships, where the mainsail blocked some of the rain, Doctor Boddings stood with Tellam, and the two of them peered at the surgeon's open New Testament. Both men held their heads bowed as Boddings intoned in a low voice, "Jesus, our Lord and Savior, do lift from this vessel the curse upon it and deliver these, your poor souls, to safe harbor, if it be thy good intent."

"Amen," Tellam said softly. "Amen." Then the tattooed man looked upward, his eyes locked fiercely on Spider.

Spider whispered his own amen and glanced skyward, determined not to let Tellam's menacing glare bother him.

Spider wondered how long it would be before they reached Jamaica. They had to be fairly close, but he was no navigator, and Barlow was not one to tell his crew much of anything. They had been sailing about two weeks, he reckoned, more than ample time for the journey, but Barlow's Bermuda ruse and all the tacking aimed at throwing off the frigate's pursuit had added days to the voyage. They had never been becalmed, but seldom had they seen a ripping good wind, either. *Dream*, thus far, seemed to have plodded along on most of her accursed trip.

Spider was ready for it to end.

He wanted to unveil Ezra's killer and kill the bastard in time to jump ship and find a new berth in Jamaica. He would leave life beneath a bloody black flag behind. Hop aboard a northbound vessel, work his way back to Nantucket and Em and little Johnny. To hell with being scared of law officers and jailers. To hell with being afraid of the noose, or the stake of fire. He would live ashore and enjoy peace and quiet and love and good meals for as long as he possibly could, and he would deal with danger if and when it came. The worries of a former pirate on land could not possibly be as terrifying as this damned life, and he would have Em, at least for a while, if she would have him.

Would she? He didn't know.

Barlow clambered down to the main deck, cane perched on his right shoulder. He turned slowly and looked with wild eyes at the men around him. Spider stood and stepped slightly to his left, where a boom and the mizzenmast sails would give him partial cover.

"Well, lads, I see no one has seen fit to bring me my fucking prize." He held out his left hand, palm up. "Is it here?"

No one said a word.

"Is it here? Is it in my fucking hand?"

Barlow whirled and stuck his empty palm near Weatherall's face. "Do you see a goddamned fucking brass cylinder in my fucking hand, fiddler? Do ye?" The captain's dark irises looked small, surrounded by the whites of his eyes, and there was a fat gob of spit hanging in his brown beard.

For a moment, Spider thought Weatherall was going to strike the man, but the sailor remained calm. "No, sir."

"No?" Barlow turned swiftly to confront toothless Dobbin. "I say, do you see my fucking pretty sitting here on my fucking hand?" Raindrops spattered on his empty palm.

Dobbin shook his head slowly and trembled. Spider thought the man might be crying, but it was difficult to be certain in the rain.

"Well, I do not see it, either. Damn me if I do." Barlow whipped the cane from his shoulder and raised it above his head to point toward the sky. He spun it in slow circles, clockwise, while he turned his body widdershins. He held his empty palm forward.

"Would any of you sons of whores like to produce my pretty brass device, and place it right here in my empty hand, while we still have enough fucking men aboard to fight and sail this fucking ship? Would you?"

Barlow spun faster and whipped the cane about in a bizarre dance. "Would you?" He was screaming now, his words almost incomprehensible, spit flying from his mouth. "Would you?"

Then he stopped.

"Well, then," Barlow said quietly. He pointed at someone at random; it was a young man named Smith, who had uttered nary a word since Spider had come aboard. "Seize him up, if you please."

A handful of men responded, as Spider knew they would. Men who feared that the lash might land on their own backs would not dawdle if another might bear the whip instead. Smith tried to fight them off, but it was a futile gesture.

"Bind him to the shrouds, lads. Hob, fetch me my cat." The captain pulled a gun free from his belt.

Hob ran off to comply. Spider winced as Smith was tied to the ropes and his shirt was ripped from him. Spider had seen this before, had endured it before, and he never wanted to see it happen again.

By the time Smith had been secured—without a curse or even an indignant glance at Barlow—Hob had returned with the cat-o'-nine-tails, a short oak handle with nine whips dangling from it. Barlow returned the gun to his belt, hung the cane from his forearm, and took the dread whip from the cabin boy. Barlow looked at it, leered at it, and ran the thick, knotted cords of it through his fingers. He whipped it through the air, laughing. The horrible device whisked the air and cracked with a chorus of wicked snaps.

"Well then, let us see if the cat can persuade anyone on this ship to render unto me what is mine."

Barlow whipped the lashes against Smith's back. Every man aboard blinked at the lightning snaps of the cords against flesh. Red welts appeared and bled, but Smith clenched his jaws and said nothing.

"Tell me, Smith. Where is my precious booty?"

Smith made no sound, but his lips were drawn back from his yellow teeth. He closed his eyes tightly, and Spider knew the man was trying, and failing, to erect a mental wall against the pain.

Barlow cracked the cat against Smith's shoulders, opening a row of new cuts. Smith cried out in pain as bright red blood ran down his dark back.

Before Smith's first cry died out, Barlow landed his third and fourth blows. Blood streamed now.

Spider heard a soft rumble among the men. Barlow heard it, too.

The captain tossed the cat into the air and yanked a pistol from his belt. "Think, lads. Think hard."

If anyone had been thinking of mutiny at that moment, the prospect of a lead ball through the brain stayed his hand.

"Are ye so stupid, lads?" Barlow raged now, his bellowing voice drowning out Smith's heavy gasps of pain. "Are ye not going to fetch up the goddamned thing that might make us all rich?"

Barlow swirled, his eyes blazing.

No one answered.

"Well, then," Barlow said. "More needless death."

Barlow leveled his pistol and fired. Spider watched in horror as Hob spun and fell, his left shoulder torn in a red ribbon.

"Goddamn!" Spider ran forward and drove his shoulder into the captain's gut even as Barlow tugged free his second gun. The smell of gunpowder filled Spider's head. Prudence be damned now, Spider thought. He drove Barlow back into the bulkhead and tugged his work knife from his belt. He ripped the dirk upward, intending to stab Barlow in the balls, but the captain whacked Spider's skull with the handle of his cane and sent Spider reeling backward with a shove.

"Fairies! Ants! Shit lickers!" The captain's eyes blazed madly. He got to his feet quickly, squared for battle.

Spider hit the deck and rolled hard. He heard the thunder of Barlow's second gun, but no ball ripped through him. Instead, it burrowed into the deck in a rain of splinters. Spider rolled onto to his feet, ready to fend off a lunge if necessary, but there was no need.

Spider's reaction had lit a very short fuse.

Other crewmen swarmed Barlow, who fended them off with demonic fury. The captain kicked Weatherall in the stomach and whipped his long sword free from its housing in the cane, cursing and laughing as though killing was the only joy he had ever known.

"I will kill every damned one! Every damned one!" He sliced at Weatherall, who parried with his bandaged left arm and earned himself a new red cut. Then Barlow stabbed a man through the stomach.

"Fucking fairies! Little fucking fairies!"

Barlow spun, opened a man's throat with his blade, and produced a third pistol from behind him, from beneath his shirt. He shoved the barrel into a man's crotch and fired, spitting on the bastard as he fell. "Come then, fairies! There's just me! Just me!"

Spider could not comprehend how a man who had poured liquor down his throat all night could fight with such fury, or bellow so while those combatting him breathed in ragged gulps. Men tried to close in on Barlow, but he held them at bay with great sweeps of his razor-sharp sword. Spider wished to hell he had a gun.

Dowd. He had guns. Spider whirled about and spotted the big black man on the poop deck, commanding the high ground and holding a flintlock pistol in each hand. He held the weapons at the ready, but did not take aim and fire. Spider wondered whether Dowd was still trying to decide which side he would take, or was merely holding his pistols at the ready in case the crew's violence turned his way. It didn't really matter, Spider supposed, as there was no way he would be able to get to Dowd and grab his guns. The man was too alert and too far away.

Weatherall tried to tackle Barlow low and instead took a savage kick to the jaw. Peg used the opportunity to leap high and kick the captain in the face with his oak leg. It was a vicious, well-placed blow, and for a moment Spider thought the battle might be ended.

It wasn't.

Barlow reeled backward, spitting teeth and blood, his torrent of cursing silenced for the moment. He whipped his sword back and readied a wicked swipe. Peg, who had landed in a crouch, did not see the blow coming. Spider knew Peg would never evade it.

Spider threw his dirk, and even as it spun toward Barlow's throat, he could hear Ezra admonishing him: "Never throw away your blade, fool! Always, always, always keep it in your hand!"

It had long been Ezra's contention that Spider relied too damn much on his ability to throw a knife. Spider had countered many a time by throwing his knife into one ridiculous target or another, and had collected many a handful of coins from his friend. No matter how many times Ezra lost that bet, he insisted it was foolish for Spider to launch the knife in a fight with his life on the line. "Someday, you'll throw that knife away and suddenly wish you hadn't," Ezra would say.

Spider missed Ezra very much in that moment.

This time, the knife spun in a clean whirl and plunged into Barlow's throat. The captain stared, wide eyes seeing eternity ready to engulf him, and Spider could swear the man was trying to curse.

Mingled spit and blood oozed from the corners of Barlow's mouth, running into his beard and flowing with the rain down onto his shirt. The captain slumped, fell onto his ass, and died.

Peg grabbed his work knife and stabbed Barlow's chest. Weatherall stepped back and sat, exhausted. Others crowded the captain, attacking and screaming, venting their long-pent fury at last. But they stood back when Spider approached and watched as he pulled his dirk out of the dead captain's throat. Once Spider turned and walked away, they started cutting Barlow to pieces.

"Ha! He ain't Ed Teach." Odin pointed at the captain's corpse, tossed his dirk into the air, and laughed when it thunked into the deck.

Spider slumped to his knees, thanked God he still lived, and pulled Em's pendant to his lips. Then he looked toward the spot where Hob had fallen.

Doctor Boddings was there, waving his arms anxiously in an attempt to draw help. "The boy lives," Boddings croaked, "and will live yet if you fools will stop killing a dead man!"

Spider crawled to Hob's side, and Weatherall joined him. Others ignored the surgeon's pleas and continued abusing and dismembering the captain's corpse. Some had brought forth axes from tool chests. Others searched the dead men, presumably for the mystery item.

The physician, a small case open on the deck beside him, held a ragged shirt hard against Hob's wounded shoulder, and Spider gasped at all the dark red blood seeping into it. "And cut that man down, for God's sake," Doctor Boddings said, pointing quickly at Smith. "He'll need a look, too."

"Jesus," Spider said quietly. Smith was slumped, his legs limp, and would have been lying on the deck if not for the bonds holding his wrists to the shrouds. The man sobbed quietly as deckhands cut at the ropes binding him.

A pair of crewmen set Smith down on his stomach, next to Hob. Boddings eyed the crimson gashes. "He hurts, bad, but he will live. Get him to the surgery, lower him down gently, and wash down his back with fresh water—fresh and clean, mind you! And get him drunk, damn you."

The men lugging Smith took him away, and Boddings went back to work on Hob.

"Jesus," Spider muttered again at the sight of the crimson rows etching Smith's back.

"Aye, we shall need his divine assistance," Doctor Boddings said. "But trust in me, too, Spider John. I may be naught but a middling ship's cook, but I am a fine surgeon for all that."

Spider caught a heavy scent of rum from Boddings's breath and silently prayed that a drunken surgeon was better than no surgeon at all. He knew there was nothing he could do himself to keep Hob alive. The boy's face looked like wet clay.

"We won't be able to get him to the surgery," Boddings said, referring to the common area between the officers' bunks that served as a place for meals until *Plymouth Dream* went into action. "I need a tarp, or sail, or something to keep this damned rain off me while I work! Do it now!"

Tarps were rolled tight against the rail. Spider leapt to cut one loose, and noted *Loon* had come closer in the interim. He wondered if Addison would bring new mayhem to *Dream* when he surmised what had happened. He cast a glance toward the forecastle and suspected May would now become Addison's prize.

Spider gave Dowd a sharp look. "Addison heard the gunshots, and he's coming. Don't know if that's good or bad."

"Back sails," Dowd bellowed. "Let him come to us." He seemed relieved to see men move to put his orders into action and lowered the guns he had been holding at chest height.

Spider took the tarp to the doctor, and Weatherall, Peg, and a couple of others helped him stretch it over Hob.

"Good lads," Boddings said. "That is good; that is good."

Spider held his portion of the tarp with shaking hands and looked down at the bleeding boy. "Hold on, lad, I beg you."

Boddings noted Weatherall's wounded arm, where the sliced bandage was soaked with a crimson ribbon. The torn bandage revealed a nasty gash through the top of a tattoo. "I dare say that will have to keep for a moment while I tend to the boy."

"I will be fine," Weatherall said. "I have suffered worse."

"Perhaps," Doctor Boddings answered. "Try to halt the bleeding on your own, if you can, and do it now. Fetch someone to spell you here, but for God's sake come to me later. That is a poor job of wrapping you did the first time, and God knows what the new gash might have done to whatever you had under that bandage to begin with. You've a medical man aboard, for God's sake! Avail yourself of my services."

"Aye," Weatherall said. He walked away, and another man took his post at the tarp.

A chorus of cheers went up into the cloudy sky, and Spider looked over his shoulder to see Barlow's corpse being hoisted over the rail. It was his torso, at least. A head and an arm soon followed, streaming red drops behind them. More loud cheers went up.

"Good goddamned sight to see," Spider muttered. "May he rot in hell."

"No doubt he will," Boddings said as he dug a ball out of Hob's shoulder. The boy, unconscious, did not notice. "No doubt he will. And he shall eventually see many familiar faces there," the doctor added, taking a quick glance about. "Many familiar faces, I dare say."

Then the surgeon glanced at the spot where Barlow's corpse had vanished over the rail. "And I will stew your bloody chickens this night, you son of a whore!"

19

By the time Addison had climbed the ladder to stand upon *Plymouth Dream*'s deck, the fever of violence and mutiny had cooled a bit. The men had seen many bloody deeds in their lives, but this was different. This time, they'd turned on one of their own. They had mutinied. A few of them wore ashen guilt on their faces, despite the depraved nature of Barlow's command.

Spider felt no guilt. Barlow was entirely at fault. If Spider had not set a match to the powder, something else certainly would have before long. In trying to control his men through murder and fear, Captain Barlow had created the beast that consumed him.

Boddings had patched Hob's wound and moved the boy to the surgery. They'd installed Hob in Barlow's bunk, on the very sound logic that Barlow would never again need it. Smith had Dowd's bunk, for now. Boddings seemed to think Smith would be back to duty in no time; fortunately, he'd taken only a few swipes from the horrid cat-o'-nine-tails. "Best he not sit below and dwell on it," the doctor had said. "Many times, getting right back to work and showing the men that you are none the worse for the flogging is as good a medicine as any. His dignity needs as much attention as his skin, I dare say."

From the hatch above, Spider had watched the surgeon work until Boddings, exasperated, had chased him away. Now Spider stood among the gathered men and wondered what the hell this cursed voyage would bring next. He remembered that Hob had tried to tell him something and wondered whether the boy would live long enough to divulge whatever he knew. Spider cursed himself for sending the boy away, even though he'd done it to protect Hob.

Hob had been shot anyway, and Spider wondered for a moment if God was mocking him.

Then he thought about the son he had in Nantucket and felt guilty because he was worrying about failing a boy he barely knew, instead of being with the boy he'd fathered. His eyes stung, and he blinked against tears.

Somewhere in the midst of all that, the rain stopped.

Addison spoke quietly with Dowd, then grinned greedily. *Plymouth Dream*'s men drew close around him, save for those up in the trees working the sails. Addison removed his wide-brimmed hat and stared upward where the clouds had finally begun to dissipate and make way for bright sun. He rubbed his bald pate, pointed at a rainbow, and said, "I suppose it would be too much presumption on my part to take that as a sign that the good Lord will never let such bloodshed foul our decks again, aye?" He laughed.

"As it stands, gents, you are now a lot of mutineers." Addison clasped his hands behind his back. "I dare say, however, that the only soul who might be in favor of prosecuting said murderous crime is, alas, drifting below in the briny deep, feeding sharks, perhaps. Eh? Or nose-to-nose with the dread kraken, hey, Odin? You said you saw that damned beast once, didn't you? Heh."

"Saw it with Blackbeard. He killed it," Odin said. "Ha!"

Addison ignored Odin. He lowered his eyes, mustered his thoughts, then spoke again.

"Gather, lads, and heed m'words," he said. "I know what happened here, and I dare say I do not cast blame upon a soul of you. I do not. Barlow had his ways, and they was hard ways, and men can only endure such travails as that for a limited time. He was angry, and pushed you too hard, and you pushed back. So be it."

Spider held his breath, waiting for someone to point out that he had opened the battle against Barlow, and that he had finished it with a knife in the man's throat. The men, however, remained silent.

Addison continued, hat in hand, smiling all the while. "Ye all signed our articles, and ye all know that circumstances such as the present convey to me the mantle of command. Agreed? Is there any among you thinks we should have ourselves a little caucus and vote on the matter?"

No one spoke up.

"Is there anyone else aboard what knows how to navigate a ship? No? I thought not."

A few murmurs moved through the hands on deck.

"Very well then, lads," Captain Addison continued, taking them all in with his steady blue eyes. "I value your confidence in me, I truly do. So, let us examine our predicament—shall we?—and determine what course might be best so that our enterprises might turn to success."

The man paced, and the sunlight glinted off his sweaty forehead. "Somewhere upon this vessel, there is hidden a device of great value to several of the political powers. It must be aboard, for surely anyone who knew its value enough to risk stealing it would be too bloody goddamned smart to heave it overboard, fear for his life though he may. No, the bold rascal who stole it from beneath our departed cap'n's nose would not toss it away after a mere threat. So it is here, on this ship, and unless one of the newly deceased stole it and hid it away, one of you knows where it is. Tell me, lads, did you have the sense to search the carcasses of those who fell in battle before you heaved them into the sea?"

"Aye," Weatherall said.

"Even the cap'n?"

"Aye," Weatherall repeated. "There was some . . . urgency in getting rid of him, but, um, he took a sword up his backside, and there was no object there to, um, obstruct . . ."

"Enough," Addison said. "I saw he went overboard in chunks."

Some men laughed, others cursed.

"Aye, blast him," Addison said, "and I do not believe Captain Barlow knew where the precious commodity was hidden, and surely he did not have it on him. No, no, no. So then, did any of the others have it shoved up their bums, or tucked into their girlie girdles?"

"No," Weatherall said. "We searched thoroughly."

"Of course you did." Addison nodded. "Greedy bastards that you are, and an item of immense worth hidden somewhere aboard, I have no doubt you searched most thoroughly, indeed. Well then, not having found it, and doubting some fool tossed it overboard, we must conclude it is on this ship. Correct?"

A chorus of ayes went up. The men seemed uncertain of Addison, but they were obviously relieved that he had not come aboard in a rage. Still, they kept their eyes on the guns tucked into his belt.

"Well then, we find ourselves at an interesting juncture, do we not, lads? One or more of you know where the commodity is, but I alone know where the buyer is going to meet us and when he will be there. The Frenchman. You've all heard the whispered rumors, I know. I have eyes and ears. I alone know who he is, and where he is. Hell, lads, not even Barlow could have sold the bloody thing without me."

Addison grinned wildly, letting his words sink in. "Do you understand? Do you, gents? You may have the precious cargo, but you cannot profit from it without me. I promise you that. You may kill me if you please, throw my bloody carcass to join Barlow's, but you will not profit from it. That item is desired by people far more powerful than any of us. People who command fleets, and armies, and networks of spies. Show up anywhere in the world trying to sell it, and you will draw down upon yourselves a relentless and deadly attention. You'll have your throats slit, your skulls bashed, your bellies filled with musket balls, and you won't have a single shiny bit of remuneration for your troubles. You have not the slightest idea of how to walk among such people without getting yourself killed. You don't.

"Whereas I have the weather gauge on this touchy situation, for I do not have to risk m'neck shopping this little jewel around. I already know a gentleman, whom I've done many an enterprise with in past adventures, and I know damned well he will pay handsomely for our prize. Trust me, I know my trade, lads. I am more than a pirate, more than a man to fetch whatever William Barlow wanted. I am the key, the connection. The Frenchman awaits us now with chests of pure, shiny gold in exchange for that tiny device, that damned valuable trinket."

Spider drew his eyes across the crew, looking to see if Addison's words had made anyone particularly nervous. They all seemed to be listening intently, and no one reaction stood out as unusual. They were criminals, discussing criminal business, and they had traded a maniacal, randomly homicidal captain for one who, at least for now, seemed to be willing to parley.

Addison sighed heavily, strolling as he talked. He stopped to pick up Barlow's abandoned sword and examined it with glee, then picked up the cane housing and rammed the blade home.

"I am not William Barlow. He was my cap'n, and I followed his orders because I agreed to and because, as far as this damned lifestyle will allow, I will deal honestly when I can. But I am not William Barlow, and his ways are not my ways. I understand how one of you, or perhaps a group of you, might have come to the conclusion that Cap'n Barlow would not share the profits from the Frenchman. It was not accounted for in our booty, correct? No one had seen it, or heard a value attached to it. He was secretive, and he asked you to trust him. I do not blame you if you did not. I wondered myself if I might have to, shall we say, make an earnest case to receive my honest pay, and I at least knew what the prize in question was."

He laughed quietly. "I assure you, lads, that I will share, for I must, aye? I need your goodwill. I need the item you have secreted away. I know that I need you all, even if Barlow forgot it. So you have my assurance, and my assurance is the best deal you are going to get—because unless we deal together, we do not deal at all. Thwart me on this, and no one makes any coin. This I promise."

Addison's wanderings had taken him to the tool chest. He sat upon it. "And there it is, lads. My cards are on the table. My thoughts, my intentions are there naked before you all, and you will see the sense of it if you just think a moment. This godforsaken voyage can end with us all selling a much-ballyhooed governmental gadget to the Frenchman for an unholy amount of money that we all can share, that will let us all get off the account for good and live whatever life of ease we choose, or it can end in frustration, with us missing the opportunity of our lives and left to survive on the pickings we can scrape together on an outlaw sea.

I know my choice; you tell me yours. I'm of no mind to avenge William Barlow. I did not like the man. I do not care if you stole from under his nose. I will applaud you for that. Give the bauble up to me, though, and you will share in the reward with everyone else.

"But if you force me to find it, I will not be pleased," he said menacingly, slowly twirling the cane. "I will see that as a breach of the articles, as you not following orders and not working toward the common good of all as what sails aboard this ship. And I will prosecute such a breach of good faith in a most effective, painful, and enduring manner."

He rose. "Think upon it, lads, and use the brains in your skulls. Meanwhile, I need Spider John, right now. Where are ye, carpenter?"

Spider went forward, unsure of what to expect. So far, Addison's reaction to the carnage aboard *Plymouth Dream* had not been anything like what he had anticipated. "Cap'n, sir," Spider said.

Addison grinned. "There is a comely wench yonder on *Loon*, a busty lass with fine tresses and smooth skin. She looks out over the sea. Meanwhile, this damned vessel here makes do with half a figurehead, an ugly, headless creature that surely can bring no luck to her crew."

Spider nodded. "Aye, sir."

"I do not give a farthing for *Loon*," Addison said. "No pirate worth his salt should command a vessel named *Loon*, do you not agree? This shall be my flagship. This shall be my command. And I will not go forth into the fray with half a figurehead. Barlow may have done so, but I will not! So, Spider John, rape yon wooden wench from *Loon* and secure her at the head of my flagship."

"Aye, sir," Spider said, blinking. The figurehead seemed to Spider the least of *Dream*'s worries, but Addison clearly had his own priorities.

"And Peg? Where are ye, lad? Ah, there you are. You shall stay aboard the flagship with me. Gather a work crew and some paint. We are changing the name of this cursed vessel."

Peg blinked. "Is that not to court bad luck, sir?"

Addison laughed. "Do ye consider it possible, Peg, that there is any more bad luck the gods can hurl at this accursed ship, at this crew? Have we not had our share of misfortune, a veritable feast of ill fate, as it were? Do the gods not piss upon us? I believe all the ill luck on these seas has been expended already upon this poor vessel.

"I do not court curses, my boy. I dare to change our luck. And I wish to command a ship whose very name inspires fear in her prey. What sailor, what merchant ever quaked to hear the name *Plymouth Dream*? It is a name such as might be chosen by a bonny lass, flinging rose petals and sipping tea at a goddamned garden party. No, by God and devil, I mean to command a vessel with a fierce name, a name that will live in history, that will endure and strike fear into the minds of any who hear it. Edward Teach commanded *Queen Anne's Revenge*, mark me? Kidd raised hell from the decks of *Adventure Galley*. And here we are, on a blasted ship bearing the meek and mannerly name of *Plymouth Dream*. It should be seen as a mark of shame, I say! I told Barlow so, I did!"

Addison spun in a slow revolution, smiling, his eyes beaming.

"We shall paint over the name *Plymouth Dream* and give this vessel a name worthy of dread sea reavers."

Addison climbed the ladder to the poop deck. "From this day forward, gentlemen, we sail aboard *Red Viper*!"

20

en gawked, and Addison grinned. "You lot know your work. Ship won't sail herself. Dowd, I declare you may be armed at all times now, as commander of yon *Loon*. You may rename her, if you please."

"Ain't courting such luck as that," Dowd said dubiously. "I heard of cap'ns what rechristened their ships, and they all be dead. I will command her under the name she bears."

"Teach changed names on his ships," Odin said. "Ha! But none of you is Ed Teach, by God!"

"Teach is dead, goddamn ye!" Addison roared at Odin, who merely laughed.

Addison calmed himself—it was difficult work, Spider noted—and sighed. "We shall be more wealthy and more famous than ever Teach was if that bauble is turned over to me."

Elijah, up top on the mainmast, began humming a hymn, and other men on the yards took it up. Spider saw Elijah open his shirt to reveal a trinket hanging around his neck. The man took it and clutched it tightly.

Spider tugged free Em's pendant and did the same.

The yellow-and-white cat purred next to Elijah, its tail dangling below the yard and whipping back and forth in time with the music's rhythm. Spider wondered if the cat had climbed up the mast itself, or gone up on someone's shoulder. He'd seen the bloody little beast do both.

Addison drew in a deep breath, expelled it in a rush, and sucked in his gut. "And now, there is one prize aboard that I believe I will inspect more closely."

Addison turned to Weatherall and tossed him a ring of keys from his belt. "That wench, May. Fetch her to me, if you please."

Weatherall stood still a moment, staring at the keys.

Spider winced. He was no angel, and had paid for a few whores, but he had no stomach to see what was about to happen, and he had admired the girl May for her spirit.

Ezra, ever the gentleman where women were concerned, would have felt the same way, Spider was certain. Ezra would be busy hatching some crazy plan to save May from the fate Addison had in mind.

Spider remembered the fire in May's eyes and decided she deserved a shot at revenge every bit as much as he did.

He had to stop this.

"Cap'n," Spider said as Weatherall took his first step toward the forecastle. "That girl has shown some fight, and . . ."

"I believe I can smack her down easily enough, Spider John, without hurting her too much." Addison laughed. "You shall have your turn, worry not."

"You miss my meaning, Cap'n." Spider looked about and raised his voice. "I'm saying she don't deserve to be forced, or hurt. Barlow knew it, Cap'n. He offered her a place and said we'd leave her be."

"Aye, he did," Weatherall said, halting his progress toward the forecastle.

"Amen," Doctor Boddings added, seconded by Tellam, of all people.

Others jeered, of course, but Spider saw more than a few nods of assent. Pirates could admire a courageous fighter, and May had certainly shown herself to be that.

Spider hardened his eyes, for even a little support meant he could raise the specter of Barlow's death and remind Addison just how badly he needed the crew's goodwill. "You should listen to your crew, Cap'n, unlike Barlow. She is a scrappy one, I say, and ought not to be passed about," Spider said. "We should leave her be, sell her in Kingston. She'll fetch a fair price, I say, and a better one if we don't damage her."

A few cheers went up, although not all the men were in agreement. Lust and greed battled in their minds.

Addison said nothing. He was trying to gauge the mood of the men. Spider pressed his case home.

"We're just days from Jamaica, I say. Even ugly old Odin can get a woman in Jamaica." He paused while men laughed.

Odin answered. "Ha!"

Spider continued. "So let us leave our pretty girl untouched, sell her for a better price, and we'll all have more money to spend on more willing wenches in Port Royal. What say you, lads?"

Cheers went up, and hands clapped.

"Articles you all signed don't leave room for democracy on this vessel," Addison said quietly. "And I am not beholden to any promises Barlow made to this wench. I am my own man." He looked about him, meeting men's eyes. "But I see the wisdom of your words, Spider John." Addison's eyes sent a different message, though, and Spider knew he'd made an enemy.

"The business of selling that bauble is our priority, and having our wicks wetted can wait a few more days, if more profit be in the offing. Well enough. Spare the lass for now."

Spider exhaled; he had not realized he had been holding his breath. He probably had not saved May from much. Fetching as she was, the best she could expect was to become someone's sex slave once they reached port. Her husband ought not to have brought her out here, he thought.

But Spider had done what he could.

21

*T*hat evening, as the newly named *Red Viper* listed a bit to starboard and made about eight knots under a bright moon that washed away the stars, men drank, or tended their business, but they did not talk.

It remained to be seen whether Addison and a new name might cleanse away whatever curse this vessel sailed under, Spider thought, but the changes certainly had done nothing to change the mood of the men. Spider watched eyes wander as each and every one of them wondered which of his mates had stolen the precious cargo.

The more Spider thought about it, the more certain he became that Ezra's murder and the theft were linked. He had a healthy suspicion against coincidences.

Ezra's killer had taken deliberate steps to make the crime look like a drunken accident. Spider could easily imagine almost anyone aboard clubbing Ezra to death in a heated moment, but he had a difficult time imagining any of the crew being clever enough to attempt to cover up the crime. No matter which crewman he pictured as the killer, it seemed the most likely move would be to simply run and hide after the deed. Staying about long enough to drop the rum flask and trying to disguise the bloody murder was the mark of a cool hand.

It would likely have taken such a cool hand to find and steal the captain's mystery item, too. Spider was not looking for some uneducated common seaman who got pissed and killed a man.

He was looking for a calculating, cold-blooded bastard—not a superstitious seaman who feared the devil had cursed their ship and that Ezra's presence aboard was the cause of that.

Could the killer be Peg? The man had said a couple of things that made Spider suspicious. He had mentioned Ezra's mysterious words in the night, about missing some woman. Spider could not believe Ezra had been pining for a woman. It made no sense.

Peg also had mentioned the flask and tried to tie it to Weatherall. Peg also had sought to buy the flask. Was he trying to get it back, out of fear that Spider might derive some clue from it?

Peg also previously had a false leg made of applewood, and had shown himself more than capable of leaping high and kicking a man in the head. Could a crippled man have prompted Ezra to misjudge the danger and gotten close enough to land a fatal blow?

Spider vowed then and there to keep an even closer eye on Peg. Addison, upon assuming command, had kept the one-legged man aboard *Red Viper*. Did Addy and Peg share some special relationship? Had they worked together to kill Ezra and cover up the deed?

Addison stood at the bow, staring into the distance. Other than issue a few commands to keep *Viper* on her course, he had said nothing. He had not even menaced Spider over the incident involving May. He merely wandered about, wielding his former captain's cane-sword like a scepter of command, nodding at men here and there, consulting charts and a sextant, but casting no blame. He had not asked how the fight with Barlow started nor how it ended. He simply worked, watched, and waited.

"Damn your eyes, man!"

Spider's gaze went toward the mizzenmast, where two men scuffled. They rolled about under the light of a moon so bright that no one had lit a lantern, a hard white moonlight that made them look like combating ghosts. Spider could not identify the pair but saw no knives. They clutched at one another, threw punches and kicked at groins until Addison called out. "That will be enough, gentlemen!"

The combatants froze, loosed their grips, and slowly separated. Spider noted one was a former *Loon* seaman named Murphy. The other was Peg. "Apologies, Cap'n," Peg said.

Addison stood nearby, his hands showing no weapon save the cane he leaned upon.

Murphy stood, blood dripping from his nose. "He accused me of . . ."

"I think I might surmise his accusation, lad," Addison said. "He perhaps alluded to the possibility you might be the thief who puts our enterprises at risk. Am I correct?"

"I asked him that," Peg said. "We sailed a good while without anyone going after the bloody thing, until these lads came along. I thought it a good notion to ask."

Addison's grin shined in the lunar light. "Perhaps. Are you a thief, boy?"

"I am neither a thief nor a boy," Murphy said. He was maybe in his twenties, muscular, with a shock of wild black hair mussed by the tussle. "Why don't you ask him if he took it?" He pointed at Peg.

"I am asking all of you," Addison said quietly. "I do not care, truly, how I get the bloody thing back in my hands. I am not interested in punishing anyone. The mutiny was, as I consider it, committed against Barlow, not against me. If he'd like to avenge it, let him crawl out of the damned sea and do so! The theft was committed against all of us, and I just want the bloody thing back so I can sell it on our behalf and share with you all a bloody fine goddamned payday."

He headed toward the officers' bay. "So talk it out. Argue it. But the sooner one of you ends this bloody stubborn game, the sooner we can stop going at one another and start spending some serious loot instead. There's whores and fine Portuguese porto in Kingston and Port Royal, do not forget it. Good night, lads. Peg, you are in charge." He climbed down the ladder. Spider could hear Doctor Boddings snoring heavily below.

"Aye, Cap'n," Peg said before heading toward the poop deck. He gave Murphy a little shove. "You are my lookout. Start climbing."

Elijah, sipping at rum, shook his head slightly. He removed the trinket from around his neck and held it dangling in the moonlight. It was a chicken foot, or perhaps a turkey foot, hanging from a strap of leather. The talons clutched at a gray stone that sparkled slightly.

"What the devil is that?" Spider asked.

"It is supposed to ward off evil," Elijah said.

"I do not think it works."

Spider sighed and clenched his fists. He'd seen many bloody things in his life, but never a vessel so plagued as this one. Barlow had claimed to be captain, and Addison claimed to be captain now, but Spider was beginning to think that Satan was truly in command.

22

I n the morning, Addison stood by the hatch as the men of the day watch came up from the hold to the sound of a clanging bell. "Spider, I would have a word with you."

"Aye, sir."

Addison walked aft toward the poop deck, and Spider followed. *Red Viper* was making at least twelve knots, her canvas swelled with wind and her backstays and forestays humming. Addison climbed and nodded at the helmsman.

"Go have a smoke, George, or a drink. I'll handle her for a bit. Return at the next bell."

"Aye, Cap'n." The man ran off, and Thomas the cat, who had been preening on the taffrail, followed him. That left Addison and Spider alone on the poop deck.

Addison took the wheel. Spider stood next to him. The wind pressed at his back, and the ship climbed a swell and dove beyond it, over, and over, and over.

Spider did not speak. He stood, hands behind him, looking down at the deck and waiting for Addison to breach the silence.

Addison lashed the wheel, turned toward him, and put his own nose mere inches away from Spider's.

"You are a good carpenter, Spider John, and a fine man in a fight," he said.

Spider did not answer.

"But I swear it, someday when this cruise is ended and we either have a fortune from selling that fucking decoder or we have to make good with the other plunder we've got, and I am no longer trying to keep a powder keg from blowing among my crew, you and I will cross swords. And I will gut you, make no mistake."

Spider stared Addison in the eye. He had been suppressing anger so long, hiding his vengeful intentions behind a timid mask, that it felt good at last to have an honest confrontation, one that would not unveil his attempts to solve Ezra's murder.

No, this was just one man against another. Spider could handle that.

"You might find me a rather difficult man to kill," Spider said in a calm, even voice. "Others have. But all I did was speak truth. I know you have designs on that girl. I also know there are whores aplenty in Port Royal. You can wait a few days."

Addison blew out a gust of breath, and Spider tried not to wince at the odors of tobacco, rum, and rotting teeth. "I can wait a few days. I can wait a few days to get some quim, and I can wait a few days to drive my dirk through your goddamned chin."

"You'd best not be slow about it when you try," Spider said. "I am damned quick."

Spider turned away, headed for the ladder, and never looked back.

23

*S*pider was working in naught but his britches under a blazing sun, touching up the paint on the busty wooden wench looted from *Loon*. He'd painted her earlier, of course, and given her time to dry in the hot sun, but the ropes had scraped a bit of her paint as she was lowered into place, and she had suffered a few scuffs as she was secured beneath the bowsprit. Spider wasn't willing to leave her in poor condition, so now he was touching up the bad spots.

Red Viper's former figurehead, the poor bitch decapitated by a cannonball sometime in the vessel's past, had been relegated to the lumber hold. Addison said he did not give a damn whether *Loon* had a figurehead or not, and Dowd seemed not to want the headless figurehead, so Spider tried not to care himself. It pained him, though, as a seaman and a carpenter and a wood-carver, to see *Loon* go about with ugly scars and naked wood where her figurehead should be.

Maybe, he thought, *if I survive this death trap of a voyage, I will carve her one.*

Above him, Thomas the cat lazed in the sun, stretched along the bowsprit and stirring only to lick his leg now and then.

Peg and a crew had painted *Viper*'s new name on the stern and touched up some rough spots elsewhere at Spider's insistence. Work was getting done, but the ship's mysteries remained unsolved.

No one had come forth with the missing gadget, but Addison had remained outwardly patient—although he had cast many greedy glances toward the forecastle where May was locked away and under guard.

Addison spent much of his time the last two days in quiet conversations, reminding his crew that they could profit together if the thief turned himself in. He did not bully his men, and he did not randomly execute anyone. It was a marked change from Barlow's command, but Spider could see the anger and impatience behind Addison's pretense of reasonableness.

The captain seldom missed a chance to glare at Spider.

Addison's assumption of command, and the steady, warm weather, plus the heady wind that pushed the ship south and west at eleven knots or better, would have lifted the mood considerably on any vessel not under the devil's curse. *Loon*, ordered by Addison to lag astern just within sight as a rearguard to keep an eye out for the naval frigate, would signal with a shot if that pesky ship made another appearance. Meanwhile, *Viper* beat hell for Jamaica, the voyage's end, and the big payday—if it came to pass.

Dangling from the prow and dripping red paint on himself thanks to *Viper*'s ups and downs on a choppy sea, Spider smoothed the paint on the figurehead's flaming crimson dress. He'd already dabbed paint on her bare nipples. He had worked more quickly than he liked, for he could feel time closing in on him, but he could not leave her with scarred paint. Details mattered in work, as in everything else.

Below him, *Viper*'s bow cut through the water at a steady clip. To port, dolphins jumped in pairs, blowing water skyward and plunging gracefully into the sea. Spider felt sorry, indeed, for lubbers who had never seen a dolphin leap into the sky; he greatly wished to describe such things to Em and little Johnny someday.

Ezra had loved dolphins, too, and that thought pulled Spider away from his unobtainable fantasies and back into the real world, where Ezra Coombs had been murdered and no one cared save for Spider.

If he had truly believed Barlow had killed Ezra, Spider could have relaxed, knowing he had avenged his friend. But he did not believe that. Instead, he suspected a murderer still trod the decks of the renamed vessel.

He was determined to solve the mystery, and having actual work assigned to him slowed him down. For once he envied the dullards who had nothing to do until there was a ship to seize or the king's men to fight off.

He knew his bad mood put him at risk. Noticed, it might make someone realize that Spider knew Ezra had been murdered. So he shucked it off as best he could and tried to put some cheer into his voice.

"Well, then, lads, I think this wench is finally as pretty as she is like to get," Spider called. "Hoist up the bucket, if you please."

"Aye."

He gave a tug on the rope, and someone above tugged on the line attached to the bucket of paint. Spider let go, and the bucket swung gracefully away to be hoisted up. Next, it would be his turn. Then, he would avoid Addison's sight in hopes of evading work long enough to see how Hob was recovering.

He had checked on Hob every morning and was assured by Doctor Boddings that the lad was doing remarkably well. Still, the surgeon would not let anyone pester Hob. He chased Spider off every day, telling him to go find some useful work to do and to leave him and his patient bloody well alone.

This morning had been different, however, and Boddings had told Spider he might be able to sit with Hob a bit in the afternoon. "He is a strong boy, I dare say, and will emerge from this none the worse," Boddings had said, "but he is sleeping and I shall not wake him. Go nail something or screw something"—the surgeon had chuckled—"and return in a few hours."

Eager to speak to the boy, Spider had rushed his labor. Once the paint bucket was out of his way, he detached the safety line that ran from the prow to his belt. "Well, then, I am ready." He pulled on the rope that led above and prepared to swing away and be hoisted upward.

Thomas, above on the bowsprit, hissed angrily and leapt out of sight.

"Are you, then?"

The voice was full of menace. Spider leaned out, looked upward, and saw Tellam's dark, tattooed face peering back at him.

"I spelled your helpers," he said. "Sent them off for a tot of grog. Thought we might have words, you and I."

Spider spat into the sea and glanced downward. *Viper* was still making eleven knots, perhaps more, he reckoned. A fall might smack the breath from him, the hull would certainly pummel him, and he might bloody well be left to drown. Spider imagined himself delirious below the surface, the ship's keel battering him, his lungs filling with water, sharks tearing at his flesh. . . .

He thought furiously, but he seemed to be at Tellam's mercy. *Loon*, on patrol in case the phantom frigate reappeared, was too far aft to do him any good.

Tellam stood, knife in hand, and Spider calculated how easily the tattooed son of a bitch could sever a line and send him plunging. Too damned easily. He clutched at the figurehead and felt some relief in knowing he'd done a damned fine job of securing her to *Viper's* bow.

"I suppose I'll have to agree," Spider said, trying to reattach his safety line. Climbing up would be pointless; Tellam could stab him or shove him with ease while Spider clung to the bowsprit and clambered his way up.

"I wonder if you might know more about that missing item than you let on," Tellam said. "I wonder if you might tell me where it is hidden?"

"I wonder the same about you, Peter," Spider replied, tying off a good knot in his line.

"Oh, I doubt that," Tellam growled, brandishing the knife. "Every time I see you, you are sneaking about, listening in to what other men are saying. You've been up to something this whole bloody trip."

"Just learning the ropes on a new vessel," Spider said. "Don't really know anyone here, yet."

"I do not believe you, Spider John." Tellam set his blade against the hoisting line. "I do not believe a word you say, you who befriends witch boys. Might be best we lose you. Maybe you are no better than your witchy friend. Hell, you brought him aboard with you, right? Maybe that's why we still sail under a curse, because you are still with us."

"Few men are better than Ezra Coombs," Spider growled. "And if you'd like to discuss that over crossed swords, I will gladly do so. I don't know that Addison would mind me killing you so much as Barlow might have."

"Well, then, aren't we a brave one?" Tellam laughed. "I would like that, Spider John. I truly, truly would like that."

Then the tattooed man vanished.

Spider waited, listening to the hull cut water below and controlling his breath. Then he called out.

"Here I am, then," Peg answered, grabbing the line. "Just went for a drink. We are all in place now. Tug when ready."

A few minutes later, none the worse for the encounter but watching out for both Tellam and Addison, Spider worked his way along the port rail toward the surgery. Ahead of him, Addison ducked beneath a boom and loomed in his path. Spider whirled, leapt over a hatch, and dashed along *Viper's* starboard rail, breathing a sigh of relief upon realizing Addison had not seen him.

He did not see Tellam, but he imagined eyes on his back, followed by sharp knives.

Spider arrived at the surgery just as Doctor Boddings was climbing out. "Well, then, John, good of you to come just now. I have orders to cook something for this lot of ruffians, and I have a patient below who is feeling well and wants for company. You can sit with him until I return, if you please."

"I should like that, Doctor, thanks," Spider said.

Boddings lifted himself out of the hatch, and Spider started below. "Oh, John," Boddings said. "A moment, please."

Spider halted his descent and looked at the surgeon. "Yes?"

"I understand you uncorked the keg, so to speak, and precipitated the retribution upon that bastard Barlow. I know we've had harsh words, you and I. I spoke ill of your friend . . . but, well, that was a brave thing you did, and Barlow damned well deserved his fate."

"He certainly did," Spider said.

"Had you not struck, I do not know that any man aboard would have done so. I mean to say thank you, Spider John. Thank you."

"You might thank me by praying, Doctor," Spider said. "For my soul and for my friend's."

"I will do that." Doctor Boddings nodded, then turned his bulk toward the galley. He halted after two steps and turned slowly to face Spider once again. "I cannot promise it will do you any good," he said. "And I certainly will not promise it will do your friend any good. Witch blood carries a powerful curse, Spider. I am sorry, but I believe it to be true. Though I should have left judgment to the Lord and lent you my Bible. I sometimes forget myself. It is the Lord's place to judge your friend, not mine, and I failed in my Christian duty to you. I should have lent my Bible for your sake, if not for that of your friend. I . . . well, I am as fallen as anyone else, redeemed in Christ but not always acting with grace."

Spider bristled a bit. "If Ezra Coombs had not earned a measure of grace, well . . . Hell, Doctor. I don't reckon I know much about the next life. But I shall take prayers, nonetheless, as a goodwill effort on your part, and I will try not to hold it against you that you would not lend me your Good Book."

Spider dropped down into the surgery. He was happy to see Smith no longer took up a berth.

Hob reclined in the bunk farthest aft, a tiny, horizontal closet where Barlow had once slept. "Spider!" The boy's eyes were wide with enthusiasm, and Spider imagined himself at that age, cooped up in a small berth and wishing to be out and doing things.

"Well, is the surgeon going to ever let you work again, Hob, or do you get to just sleep and eat the rest of this cruise?"

"I feel well enough, now, honestly, but Doctor Boddings insists I need to rest more. He worries me, though. I think he is drunk all the time."

"I do not ever recall not smelling a whiff of rum upon him, but you live and I would have sworn you wouldn't, so bless him. I shall pour him a drink myself if I get the opportunity. You look spry, lad, so I reckon he has done well by you."

Hob pointed to a medical chest under the table in the common space. "If you truly want some rum, he keeps it in there"—the boy winked—"and the key is hidden in that lantern."

Spider retrieved the key and opened the chest. Three clay bottles, with the wax seal broken on one. Spider lifted the one with the ripped seal, popped the cork, and took a thirsty swallow. "I shall be damned," he declared. "This is the finest rum I have ever had."

"He finished a bottle last night and opened this one this morning," Hob said. "He let me try some. Better than what Barlow gave the crew, no doubt."

"Aye," Spider said. "Hob, I want you to promise me something."

"If I can."

"When we reach port, I want you to leap from this bloody ship and never look back. Get out of this life, Hob. Don't dream of riches. Don't dream of beautiful ports and beautiful girls. Those lure you in, but you never get them in any amounts worth all the blood and pain and the risk to your immortal soul. Promise me."

"What shall I do, then?"

"There's work for a smart lad, repairing ships, loading cargo," Spider said. "Honest work. I plan to get the hell off the account myself. I'll teach you woodwork, if you wish, and we'll earn our way in Jamaica's harbor until we can find a decent vessel headed back north. I'm for Nantucket, if I can get there. You may join me, if you will."

"It sounds like running away," Hob said. "I ain't no coward."

"I know you ain't a coward, Hob. I know you ain't. We won't be running away, boy. We'll be running to. And the world being what it is, we'll still have to do some cut and thrust along the way, so you shall have many a chance to show your mettle. We shall have to watch one another's backs, I dare say. It ain't a world for cowards, no matter what we do."

"Well," Hob said after a deep breath. "You showed the cap'n, so I reckon you can watch my back." He grinned.

"It is a deal, blood brother," Spider answered, taking another quaff of the doctor's rum and offering Hob a drink, too. After drinking to their future success, Spider corked the bottle, hid it away, and returned the key to its hiding place. "The doctor is a sneaky bastard, I'll say, for being a fat man and all that. He's got far better rum than the piss he serves the rest of us."

"You don't know all," Hob said. "I tried to tell you before Cap'n went all off course. I seen the doctor sneaking into the cap'n's stores."

"Under the poop deck?" Spider pointed to the deck above. That was where most of the ship's charts were stored, and many of the weapons, along with some of the captain's personal belongings.

"Aye."

Spider knelt close to Hob and whispered, "When, boy?"

"The night before Barlow called us all out and searched us."

"The night his goddamn cylinder disappeared?"

"Aye."

The aft cabin was a likely hiding place for Barlow's item, Spider thought. It was where Barlow hid when he wanted to avoid the crew.

"Why did you not say something before this, Hob?"

"I tried," the boy said, "and then, well . . ." He pointed to his bandaged shoulder.

"Aye, sorry." Spider nodded. "Sorry. Does Boddings have any other hidey-holes in here?"

"Not that I seen," Hob said. "He sleeps there, and keeps his Bible there." He indicated a bunk on the port side.

Spider opened the tattered curtain. The bunk contained a pillow, a partly shredded red wool blanket, a couple of linen shirts, the doctor's coat and hat, and his New Testament. Seeing the book reminded him of Ezra's death, and he drew a deep breath. Spider tossed the blanket and pillow but found nothing hidden. If the doctor had stolen Barlow's device, it was not concealed here.

He looked around the chamber. The other bunk, to starboard, was Addison's, Hob told him. Spider gave it a quick look, too. There were two pillows, a better wool blanket than the doctor's, and a very nice knife in a leather scabbard. That was it.

"Damn," Spider said, looking about for other hiding places. The doctor's medical chest was large, with several drawers and cabinets.

Spider grabbed the key again and opened it. He rifled through, aware he was making something of a mess but determined to find a clue. He noted many a medical device he could not recognize, along with scalpels, forceps, and more, but nothing that resembled the mystery item. That damned brass cylinder had been the focus of a great deal of bloodshed, and Spider could not set aside the notion that the deaths surrounding it had started with Ezra Coombs.

Spider lifted a cheesecloth and exclaimed, "Jesus!" He'd uncovered a skull, its empty sockets staring back at him and its crooked teeth grinning.

"What the hell is this for, and what is the bloody smell?"

An unholy stench rose from the chest, worse than the odor in the crew quarters. Spider poked around and found a bottle of blue fluid, its cork popped, lifting the stench into the hold. Spider was fairly certain he had not been the one to disturb the bottle.

"It is horrible," Hob said.

Spider wanted to cork the jar but did not want Boddings to know someone had been poking about. He held his nose and pressed on.

A thorough search turned up plenty of potions and surgical tools and herbs tied together with leather cords, but no clues. Spider dared a deep breath and spat hard. "Damn! It is not here. Maybe he keeps it on him."

"It?"

"The bloody goddamned cylinder that got us all poked and prodded," Spider growled.

"Oh. Perhaps," Hob said.

"Hold on there," Spider replied, turning to Hob. "I have a thought."

He removed the unopened rum bottles and gave each a shake. They were sealed with wax, but it would have been no difficult trick to open one, insert the cylinder, and seal it up again. Boddings had sealing wax among the many items in his chest.

Shaking and swirling each bottle, however, produced no sound or sensation other than that of liquid within. "Damn again," Spider said. He began trying to restore some order to the chest. "Keep an eye, Hob, and see if he hides anything else in here. Tell him you feel weak yet, if you need to, and stay in here another day."

"I already feel like cargo lashed down tight," Hob said. "I want out of this hold, Spider."

"I know, boy. I know. But the doctor's sneaking about is the closest thing I have heard to a clue here. If Boddings took that ... that ... whatever it may be, a decoder, Addison called it, he may have killed Ezra. Maybe Ezra saw him lurking, or heard him speak to an accomplice, or something."

A sinister thought entered Spider's mind, and he stared Hob in the face.

"Does Boddings know you saw him in the cap'n's stores?"

"No, sir."

"Are you certain?"

"Aye, certain as can ever be."

"Well then, good. Make sure he does not learn of it."

"I am not a fool, Spider."

"Of course you are not a fool," Spider said. "Of course not."

24

After leaving Hob's side, Spider headed toward the galley. Doctor Boddings was passing out slices of crusty, stale bread and slabs of cold, salted pork, and filling mugs from a barrel of stale beer. It had been nothing but salted pork since the surgeon had stewed a few of Barlow's precious egg hens to celebrate the tyrant's death. Addison fussed less over meals and seemed content with the doctor's explanation that Hob needed his attention more than the hungry crew did. Spider couldn't imagine Boddings working any harder than he had to, aside from tending to patients. The man did seem engaged when performing his chosen trade.

Spider joined the line, grabbed a plank from the crate, and pulled a leather jack from a peg on a post. "Your patient seems well, Doctor."

"Aye, tough lad he is," Boddings said. "I feared fever might take him, but once that broke I suspected he would do well. Prayer and medicine, sir, in conjunction, will do wonders, mark my words." As he talked, the doctor poked a slab of cold pork with a fork and laid it upon Spider's plank, then tossed a hunk of bread next to it. Spider saw nothing crawling in the meat or bread, much to his surprise. Boddings then ladled the beer into Spider's jack. The aroma from the brew was bitter hops and wet wheat.

"I have been suffering pain here, on my left hand, where the finger used to be," Spider said before ambling away. "It ain't pained me in years, but it is now. Can I see you after the meal? Maybe you got something to help."

"That is odd, I dare say, but I have an ointment or two that may suffice," Doctor Boddings answered. "See me later."

"Aye."

Spider found an empty spot on a four-pounder to eat as *Red Viper's* bow rose and fell, rose and fell. Somewhere aft, Weatherall coaxed a somber tune from his fiddle.

Spider watched Boddings serve the men. The burly man had given up trying to wear a coat on deck many days ago and toiled now in just a linen shirt, suspenders, britches, and boots. Still, sweat dripped from him, especially from his meager gray hair, adding a little extra salt to the pork for some lads. The doctor clearly did not relish what he saw as a servile role, but he filled it nonetheless.

Could such a man hatch plots of theft and murder? Spider tried to recall the night Doctor Boddings had come aboard along with Ezra and himself. The surgeon merely sought working passage to Jamaica, he'd said. Since that day, the man had spoken little of his plans.

He was an educated man, probably from a moneyed family, and likely retired from His Majesty's Navy. Such a man potentially had a home and inheritance and could likely find medical work in London or Boston. So why was he here, sailing with brigands to Jamaica? Had he come aboard specifically to steal Barlow's brass cylinder? Had Ezra caught him poking around the captain's stores?

Spider sighed. The meat and bread, scarcely tasted, vanished in a few absentminded bites. He saved the beer for last and drained the jack at once. The thin fluid did not satisfy at all.

The hour passed slowly. Weatherall switched to a brighter tune, and Boddings began to gather up the greasy planks and wet mugs dropped into the crate by crewmen upon finishing their meals. Spider watched him work and noted he wrapped bread and pork into a cheesecloth, probably for Hob. Spider pondered whether to confront the doctor in the surgery, with Hob present, or risk doing so on deck. He told himself he had already decided to trust the boy, and so, by God, he would. Better to rely on that stout lad's promises than to be overheard on deck.

The doctor headed aft, and Spider followed discreetly. Now that he had something upon which to focus his attention, his energy was renewed. He could feel an alertness swell within him, and he kissed Em's pendant as though he were going into battle.

Perhaps, he realized, he was.

Spider's fingers brushed the hilt of his work knife, assuring he would know exactly where to snatch it if need arose. He had not noted a blade on the doctor's belt, and all the sharp surgical things were in a chest under a table. Still, Boddings had proven to be a sneak, and the captain's stores he'd broken into also held the ship's weapons, so Spider would be prepared for anything.

He would give Boddings a moment or two down in the surgery before hailing him, but Spider could not afford to wait long. The surgery was where Addison bunked as well; the man was kneeling with Peg on the poop deck, discussing their westerly course with a chart unrolled between them. Addison almost always stayed up top until late, especially if Weatherall was fiddling, but Spider wanted no surprises. He would confront the doctor quickly, and as quietly as he could, and hope not to draw Addison's attention.

Spider counted slowly to fifty, then knelt by the ladder. "Ahoy, surgeon. Can you see a patient?" He waved his left hand, with its scarred tissue where a finger had once been.

"A moment," Boddings said. Spider heard some rattling, followed by the medical chest's lid clamping down. "Very well, come down."

The sun was just low enough, and blocked by shadows thrown by mast and sail, to keep its light from reaching below, so Boddings had lit his lantern. It swung on a hook, casting dancing shadows and oozing its oily, smoky odor into the air.

Spider nodded at Hob. "Hello again, boy," he said.

To Boddings, he asked, "Might the lad take some air? He has been hidden away here for days, and I'd like to discuss my ailment in privacy, if you please."

The surgeon pondered, glanced at Hob, and saw the boy smiling and nodding. "Very well," Boddings said. "When the sun goes down, you return to your bunk. Understood?"

"Aye," Hob answered, rolling out of his bunk and practically racing up the ladder.

"Slow and careful, you jackrabbit!" As Boddings yelled, the rum scent wafted from his breath and competed with the lantern to render the cabin air unbreathable.

Boddings sat on the table. "A good boy, he is, but if he rips my sutures I shall have to be persuaded to replace them."

"Aye," Spider said.

"Now then, hold out your injured hand, under the lantern here. Does it pain you all the time, or when you move it, or when the weather changes?"

Spider took a deep breath. "The hand is fine, Doctor. I just wanted to talk."

Boddings looked immediately suspicious. "Talk?"

"Aye, about Jesus," Spider said.

"The Savior? Well, what is it you would know?"

"Does sneaking about and stealing from shipmates sit well with the Lord, I wonder?" Spider raised his eyebrows and tilted his head slightly beneath the lantern light. "Seems I was taught otherwise, but I see other examples set by them what claim to know these matters better than I do."

Boddings stammered a bit, looking very confused. "Now see here. Are you seeking some absolution for your pirate soul? I am not a priest, Spider John."

Spider pulled his knife slowly and let the lantern light gleam on it. "Scream, and I will cut your throat," he said quietly.

Boddings swallowed. "In a vessel full of thieves, what is it you accuse me of, John Rush? I dare say I shall fare better in the ultimate accounting than any other man aboard, certainly better than you."

"I saw you skulking about the cap'n's stores," Spider answered. "Saw you go in, saw you come out." He said no more, instead letting the knife and his hard eyes fill Boddings's mind. It was rather like playing cards, and Spider wondered what cards the surgeon would throw down.

"Well, then," Boddings said in a hushed tone. "May I presume from your presence here, weapon and threats at the ready, that you wish not to involve others in the matter? You've said nothing to Addison, I take it, or to anyone else?" The doctor's stringy, thin hair trickled rivers now.

"I have held my tongue to this point," Spider said. He waved the knife slowly. "And I shall very soon hold your tongue if you do not tell me the truth."

Boddings gulped, and Spider inhaled deeply. It felt good to be on the offensive.

"Very well," the doctor said. "I understand you completely. I have been in such situations before, in my long years of service. You seek a cut for yourself, aye? A share of the spoils?"

"Where are the spoils, Doctor? Show me."

Boddings nodded and stood, moving like a dismasted ship on a still sea. "It is in here," he said, pointing toward the medical chest under the table.

"Open it slowly, and if I see anything I don't like in your hands, I will end your life quick as you please," Spider whispered. The tension in him, building now for weeks, grew, and he half hoped the doctor would pull a flintlock out of that bloody chest.

"I understand, I say," the doctor said, "although, I must say, I find your attitude somewhat out of kilter." He pulled the chest's key from the lantern, opened the lock, and lifted the lid. He kept his left hand high, where Spider could see it, and reached in with his right. Spider leaned forward and touched his dirk to the doctor's neck, with just enough of a poke to remind the man of the stakes. A red dot appeared under the doctor's jaw.

Boddings slowly pulled out a clay bottle. Spider could see the broken seal, and the rum scent grew.

The surgeon handed the bottle to Spider.

"It is in here?"

Boddings nodded, confused. "Aye."

Spider locked eyes with the physician and bit the cork from the bottle. He lifted it and drank slowly, listening for the clatter of the brass cylinder inside. He heard only the swoosh of liquor.

Spider swallowed, enjoying the fine rum but unsure of what was happening. "Is it held firm with wax?"

"I beg your pardon? I broke the wax."

"Not the wax on the cork, damn ye! The cylinder! The brass cylinder that supposedly is worth more than all our carcasses! Is it in the bottle, secured with wax to keep it from shaking about?"

The doctor shook his head, and a smile slowly broke across his grizzled face. "I stole only rum, Spider John. Only rum."

Spider pointed the knife. "You were in those stores the night before Barlow stripped us all in search of the damned thing."

"Aye," Boddings said, "and twice before that."

Spider took another swig. It was, indeed, fantastic rum, and he loved the burn at the back of his throat.

"Captains, naval or otherwise, always keep the best stuff for themselves, Spider." Boddings sat on the table. "It is universal and hardly fair. I have pilfered drink from every captain I have ever sailed under. It is why, alas, I no longer sail for His Majesty. I'm twice the surgeon with drink in me than the next man is dead sober, but a board of captains assessed things differently. I was drummed out. It shames me to admit it, but there you have it." He reached for the bottle, and Spider handed it to him. Spider also tucked the knife back into his belt.

"The stores were locked, and men all about the decks. How the devil . . . ?"

"Spider John, I have pulled musket balls and bone from men's brains, and from their arses, too, and done that with half a pint of rum in me. I assure you no simple padlock will stand between me and a good drink." As if to prove his point, he took a healthy swallow.

"And the sneaking about? You are not the most graceful of men, nor the smallest."

"Mister Dowd, of the night watch, enjoys a tot of the good rum, too," Boddings said. "He sends the night men out of my way, I pilfer the bottles, and I deliver some to him. Child's play. Barlow has so many tucked away in three chests, he'd never have missed the bottles I took, not before I was well off this blasted ship, anyway. But I did not steal the captain's gewgaw, I assure you of that. I have no idea what the bloody thing is, nor ever heard of it until the bastard stripped us and had his trained dog poke our bums."

Spider sighed. The doctor's tale seemed plausible, and the man looked to be telling the truth. He had the exquisite rum to back up his story. The stuff they were drinking now was far better than the watery swill given to the crew.

Still, Spider had questions. "Why are you on this floating den of thieves and scoundrels, Doctor Boddings?"

Boddings swallowed more rum. "I'm a thief, am I not? At least, a thief of rum. Heh. The navy is done with me, Spider John. My family spent its fortune—misspent, I should say—and Jamaica is the prettiest place I have ever been, and home to the prettiest girl I've ever loved. Where else might I go? And His Majesty was in no mind to book me passage, I'm afraid. I make do with what the Lord gives me."

"That hardly seems enough reason to go pirate at your age, Doctor," Spider said. "There are merchant vessels."

Boddings stared at him, and his eyes went watery. He waited several awkward seconds to respond. "You are correct, of course," he answered. "There are legitimate enterprises and vessels to carry them out. But none were sailing for Jamaica soon, you see, and I am rather in haste."

Boddings took another swallow. "You see, Spider John, I am dying."

"Dying?"

"Aye," Boddings said, taking another huge swig of rum. He swallowed, grimaced, peered into the empty bottle, then stared at Spider. "I do not know precisely how long I have, but I am as fine a physician as has ever sailed under the king's flag, and I know my prospects. I am dying. And I damn well was not going to die alone in a Boston winter."

Spider sighed. "Go on."

"I could not sail on a naval ship, of course. None would have me. And I looked, you see, for a merchant vessel Jamaica-bound. But there were none, at least, none departing in a timely fashion."

The surgeon's eyes welled up with tears.

"I overheard Addison, you see, recruiting, searching for a carpenter and other hands." He sniffed and swallowed hard. "He was leaving soon, and there is a lady in Jamaica I wish to see before . . . before . . . while I still can."

A quiet filled the cabin then, and neither man talked for a long while.

Spider spat. "Keep your bottles, surgeon. I shall take a sip now and again, in payment for my silence."

Boddings looked at him, swallowed, and nodded.

"Well enough, Spider John, well enough."

They locked eyes for a few moments, while Boddings chased away whatever demons filled his mind.

"You really thought I had the damned thing that drove Barlow off course? What the hell is it, anyway?" Boddings asked at last, tossing the empty bottle into his chest. "And what is your interest? Do you think to cheat Addison with it, steal it for yourself?"

"I do not know what I thought," Spider said, feeling the booze in his head and unwilling to say more. "Good night, Doctor Boddings. I will send Hob back this way."

Spider started climbing back up to the deck.

"If you ask me," Boddings said, "Barlow himself was the thief. He knew men were talking, whispering of the Frenchman. I believe his tale of theft to be a complete fabrication and his damned search a mere pretense for him to give vent to his perverse nature. He wanted the men fighting each other, spying on each other, while he snuck away and sold the bloody damned thing himself. He wanted to cut Addison and Dowd and all the rest out of it. He was a devil for plots, Spider John, and no more trustworthy than a man selling a horse."

"Perhaps," Spider said. "Perhaps. But if that be the case, then where is the bloody thing?"

He climbed up and stared into the lowering sun. He was no closer to solving the mystery of Ezra's death than he had been, and time was growing short.

25

"**M**urphy," Addison called. "Get up top and signal *Loon*. I want all hands on the main deck, smart as may be."

"Aye, sir."

"Peg, Odin, let us furl sails and drift a bit here, give Dowd and his lads a chance to come alongside."

"Aye." Peg ran off, his oak leg drumming on the planks. Odin went up the mainmast. Orders were barked, men responded, and soon Spider could feel the vessel slowing beneath him.

Spider sat on a gun and waited, hardly noticing the early-morning breeze. It had been a bad night for sleep, filled with dreams of Ezra. Spider shuddered at the memory—Ezra and his grandmother beckoning him to the fire, reminding him he was a witch-spawn like them, while the sailors of *Red Viper* laughed and fired pistols into his brain.

Spider shrugged, shook, took a bite of hardtack, and washed it down with watered wine. *Forget the nightmares*, he told himself. *Figure out who killed your best friend.*

Rumor said they were no more than a few days from Jamaica, and still no one had produced the mystery item. Each day, the situation grew tenser as the days of relatively empty seas were behind them.

Soon, they would weather the Turks and Caicos, and then make a run south through the Windward Passage and on to Jamaica. The French had islands in these waters, as did the English and Spanish, and God alone knew who controlled which lands at this particular moment. Men long at sea often were the last to hear of a new flag hoisted above a conquered island town.

This was the Spanish Main, and they could cross paths with flags from any of the European powers. They might meet convoys of Spanish galleons loaded with precious metals, or ships of the line patrolling for pirates, or more bloody pirates or privateers on the hunt. Blackbeard had haunted these waters, and Henry Morgan, and Bartholomew Roberts, and Calico Jack with his vicious girl pirates, Mary Read and Anne Bonny.

Lookouts would have to keep open eyes for reefs as well, the farther into the Main they reached. These were legendarily dangerous waters.

It took a couple of hours for *Loon* to come alongside. Most of her crew came aboard *Viper*, but a handful stayed behind and listened from the rail of the other ship.

"Gents, you are a stubborn lot," Addison began, cane held in clasped hands behind his back, the shadow of a wide-brimmed hat hiding his eyes. "I have set it straight for you, I have, and it is as plain a case as I can make it. Surrender to me the brass cylinder, and I sell it and we all get rich. Keep it, and you've kept an item that will get you killed before you find a buyer. It is ungodly simple, gents. A schoolboy could parse it easy."

"Barlow took it with him to his grave," Doctor Boddings called. "He only accused us of theft to give him an excuse for his beatings and shootings."

"No," Addison said. "He described the item in plain terms for you. He'd not have done so if he still had it himself, no matter how much he loved firing his damned pistols and watching men bleed. No. One of you has it. Who?"

"Perhaps the thief knows a buyer, too," Peg said. "You may not be the only one here who knows someone interested in buying something."

"Perhaps," Addison answered. "But I have a rendezvous, and it will be a quick score. I doubt any other among you could arrange something as quickly, and I will certainly shoot any man of you who tries to break from this ship before I have the damned thing in my hands. I dare say, lads, it is in all our interests to work together, and quickly."

Spider watched the men as they listened, trying to discern whether the captain's words were making anyone nervous. He noted a lot of men with the jitters, but no one stood out as especially worried.

"These are crowded waters, tough to navigate, full of reefs and potential enemies, and we had best get in, sell our package, and get out again to rendezvous with our little fleet. I am for wintering in Bermuda, lads, and then retiring!" Addison raised his arms, as if to embrace them all. "But if I cannot do that, by thunder, I will wait for the son of a bitch who is holding the goods to make his move. And the rest of you will stick with me and keep *Viper* away from port until that happens, because the bastard is robbing you as much as he's robbing me. Aye?"

"Aye!" the men bellowed, but Spider could see their enthusiasm was false. No one wanted to remain on this ship of the damned any longer than necessary.

"So we will wait you out, you dirty son of a bitch," Addison said. "I can find the Frenchman again if I must. You will not profit from this. You will not, except by showing me your cooperation."

No one came forward.

"Fool." Addison cracked the cane against the deck with a sound like a gunshot. "Bloody, goddamned fool. Back to work, then, damn ye."

The captain headed aft toward the officers' quarters, gave Spider a shove, then disappeared belowdecks. Dowd waved his *Loon* crewmen together. "Let us go," he said. Turning to Peg, he added, "We shall resume patrol."

"Aye," Peg said, his chest swelling a bit. He seemed to have become Addison's first mate aboard *Viper* and appeared to be glad Dowd had noticed.

Spider scratched his head and tried to make sense of the situation. Addison's spot was more precarious than he let on, Spider realized. He was vastly outnumbered, and every man aboard was on edge. Addison might seethe, curse, and bellow, but if he dared slay a man, or even beat one, he risked touching off the same sort of powder keg that had gotten Barlow killed.

If Spider had been in Addison's place, he'd have drawn up new articles, closer to those on other pirate vessels that gave the crew the right to vote on virtually all matters until the ship went into battle. Then, in combat, and only then, the captain's commands were sacred, for there was no time for a discussion in parliament when cannonballs were flying. But on other occasions, the crews had a voice.

Addison could have given his men such a voice, but he had instead pressed on with Barlow's strict articles, and he was stuck with them. He was not the type to show weakness, so he would not change his mind.

Addison's best hope now was for the thief to confess, in private, and try to cut himself a larger share; Addison could then get his hands on the gewgaw and deal with the thief as he pleased. That seemed ever more unlikely, though, because Addison could not conceal his anger, try though as he might. Anyone coming forward now faced certain death once the bauble was in the captain's hands—of that, Spider was convinced. Addison would be able to dispense with the man and would sell the idea to the crew by claiming the fellow had tried to cut everyone else out of their share of profit. Surely, the crewmen realized that. Surely, the thief did.

Spider thought more on Peg's suggestion that the thief already had a buyer in mind. It would account for the stubborn refusal to play along with Addison if the thief thought he could sell the bloody thing himself and keep all the profit. Addison's threat to remain at sea would thwart such a plan, it seemed. Spider tried to imagine what a clever man might do to get around that obstacle. Another mutiny? No. That would require a conspiracy, and Addison had not built up animosity among the crew the way Barlow had. Addison was being cautious not to stir up anger, and he would be alert for anyone whispering. The thief also would have to persuade men that he could sell the thing and would share the profit. No. That plan would take time and would be unlikely to succeed.

So what, then? Murder Addison in his sleep? Let him be found dead and see if the Vipers were of a mind to reach Jamaica and place themselves as far from this wretched curse as possible? Then lay low awhile and sell the precious item, perhaps even suss out the mysterious Frenchman? That sort of cold-blooded plan might work. It would take a certain boldness, perhaps the kind Peter Tellam displayed.

The big drawback to that scenario, of course, was navigation.

Addison alone had that skill, as far as Spider knew, although it was said Dowd had been studying the art, and Peg had recently begun doing so as well. These were not waters for an amateur to try to learn quickly. Whatever else happened, Addison was needed, and he was smart enough to subtly remind his crew of that at every turn.

Up top, Elijah raised flags to signal *Loon* their course. Spider watched as *Loon* responded. Ships could communicate across an expanse of sea; he wished he could communicate with Ezra across the widest of all expanses.

He shook himself and spat overboard. Mourning was not getting the job done. He had to think. He watched *Loon*'s signal flags and pondered the murder and the stolen bauble. There had to be a connection.

So how would the thief get the thing off the ship in Port Royal without the captain knowing? Spider sighed. He had exhausted one scenario after another.

Staring across the sea at *Loon* and watching her return signal, a new possibility occurred to Spider, and it hit him like a sudden gale. As soon as the notion formed in his mind he cursed himself for a lubber. He whirled the idea around, turned it upside down, and examined it from every angle, and the more he thought it over, the more convinced he became.

He reviewed his experiences aboard this damned ship.

Jigsaw pieces clicked together and fit.

Damn, he thought.

If he was correct, *Red Viper* would not reach Port Royal at all.

26

The noon bell had scarcely stopped echoing when the call came from above: "Sail off the port beam! Sail off the port beam!"

Spider did not join the others rushing to the rail or climbing the lines for a view of the ship. He was fairly certain it was the bloody phantom frigate, and he was more interested in seeing the reactions of *Red Viper*'s crew.

"It is that English bitch, I dare say," said Tellam, clutching a mainsail stay. "I knew we'd not seen the last of her."

"Hell and damnation!" Weatherall waved his arms. "Bugger you, George's lads, every damn one of ye!" Similar calls and shouts lifted all across the deck and in the trees as well. The frigate was too far off for her crew to hear any of the shouting, but that hardly seemed to matter. *Red Viper*'s crew had come to view the frigate with great disdain, and had hardly seemed to notice that it showed up time after time.

Fools, Spider thought. *We're mice, and that's the cat.*

Peg, in the crow's nest with a spyglass, called out, "It is her, I say, our English navy friend! She is beating north by northwest!"

Spider parsed that quickly. *Viper* was headed south by southwest, with the wind out of the east. The two vessels were on merging courses.

Addison, who had not been seen since scurrying below in aggravation, emerged from the officers' bunks, bearing a scope of his own. "Our present speed, helm?"

"Nine knots, Cap'n, at last reading ten minutes ago," came the answer.

Addison ran to the port rail and shoved Weatherall out of the way. He raised his glass, aimed it at the frigate, and cursed very quietly. Spider could not make out the words. Then Addison spoke aloud. "Well, ain't this a complication? *Loon* is on rearguard far off our starboard stern, barely within sight, so naturally our Royal Navy friend makes his hello off our port beam. It would appear, sirs, that my attempts to alter our vessel's bloody bad luck have been, as they say, to no fucking avail."

He smiled as he spoke and shrugged theatrically. "I dare say, we must rely upon the general incompetence of His Majesty's imbecile crew once again and fend off the assault upon our honor. She has not bent all her sheets, bless her, and so we might put some distance between us if we act smartly. Prepare to come about, north by northwest! And let us press all sail, if you please. We shall outrun the bitch."

"Aye, aye. North by northwest," the helmsman answered.

A chorus of "Aye, Cap'n!" arose, and Peg and Odin started shouting in the trees to put Addison's words into action. Elijah scurried nimbly up the ratlines, with an ease a cat might envy. The crew pressed on more canvas quickly, the booms swung, and *Viper* soon was under topgallants and coursing north by northwest. The frigate trailed behind, with full sails and charging hard. She might be within musket range before long.

Weatherall emerged from the crew hold, a red sheet in his hand. Spider had not noticed him vanishing and cursed. He wanted to see and hear everything that transpired, because he believed he was on the cusp of a vital clue, but keeping an eye on everyone was impossible. Busy men were scurrying and shouting all over the ship. Now was not the time for his powers of observation to fail him. If he had surmised correctly, this brush with the royal frigate would differ greatly—and dangerously—from the previous encounters. And if he paid attention, he might well notice the clue that would reveal Ezra's murderer.

He took a deep breath and blew it out hard. More than once Ezra had praised Spider's attention to small details. *By God*, Spider told himself, *don't let Ezra down now. Something will be different this time. It will be the key. It will point like a reaper's finger straight at the killer.*

"Catch us if you can, ye dog buggerers! Hey ho!" Weatherall hollered like a drunk, waving his impromptu scarlet banner for all he was worth. "We shall show how real seamen work, you bloody sons of whores!"

Spider looked to see how the frigate fared and was not surprised at all to see her under all sail, and her canvas swelling with wind. There was no sign of laziness this time, by God, nor did Spider expect to see any. The frigate, built for speed and maneuverability, would not be undone by the slow work of her crew this day. In previous encounters, she'd been slow to turn, slow to make sail, as though crewed by still-drunken lubbers newly pressed from a tavern sweep. This day, however, they behaved like a crew of His Majesty's Navy ought to behave, and that spelled trouble for a bloated, converted whaler. The English vessel would ride wind and wave smartly, and cut through the sea far more quickly than *Viper*. Barlow had loved his large ship and her cavernous central hold and all the hidden nooks and crannies he'd had built into her, but his crew soon was going to regret his choice.

"She's going to catch us," Spider said under his breath.

Addison realized the truth of it, too. "Blazes! They must've got her a better crew, or lashed the lads into doing some real work at last. Hob!"

The captain was spinning excitedly, eyeing the crew. "Where are ye, lad?"

Hob ran up, shouting, "Here, sir!"

Addison tugged a leather cord from around his neck and tossed it to the boy. Spider could see something small attached to it. "That's the key to the cap'n's stores, Hob. Open 'em up and start passing out weapons! Get guns up in the trees, too! You there, and you, ye sons of bitches, help the lad out and disperse arms! We may have to convince these damned naval bastards that we aim to live another day!"

"Aye, sir!" Crewmen scrambled to obey.

"Lookout! Signal *Loon*, if you please, and tell Dowd to make haste and come about and get into the bloody fight! We shall lead yon frigate on a merry chase, and if they stay focused on us, *Loon* may well sweep in behind and do some real damage! Yonder king's men shall not find us eager to swing on a rope, aye!"

"Aye, Cap'n." Murphy, who had replaced Peg in the lookout once real action commenced so the one-legged man could lead crews in the rigging, started the hectic business of whipping signal flags onto the line. "And hoist that goddamn bloody skull," Addison roared. "Raise our black banner! Raise our bloody black flag! We are *Red Viper*, by God, not some pissant merchant! Get our damned colors aloft, I say!"

"Aye, sir!"

Spider did not have a spyglass, but he could tell the frigate had picked up significant speed. She was cutting a fine white wake, and drum rolls carried across the waves. Her captain had called beat to quarters, and marines were lining up on the deck, bayonets glinting in the sun in neat, disciplined rows.

It was exactly what Spider expected to see, and he suspected he would see something different aboard *Viper* this time as well. He looked across *Viper*'s deck, seeking a sign that would confirm his speculation, but he did not see a damned thing that lent weight to his theory.

There was Addison, pacing and barking orders. There was Peg, laughing nervously up above and joking about death. There was Weatherall, whipping his banner in defiance and cursing the representatives of King George's might upon the ocean. There was Murphy up above, shouting updates on the frigate's course and sending signals to *Loon*.

Signals.

Spider shielded his eyes and looked harder at the crow's nest. He was not an expert signalman, but Murphy was not using any unfamiliar flags, nor was he making any unexpected signals with his arms. The man's attention seemed entirely focused on *Loon*. Certainly Addison, whose gaze pivoted from the charging frigate to Murphy's signals, then to the distant *Loon*, had not noticed anything amiss in Murphy's work.

Spider spat; he had thought for a moment he had parsed it all out. He suspected the frigate's dogged pursuit and the disappearance of the captain's stolen bauble were connected, for he had never been much of a believer in coincidences. When the captain still had his precious item, the pursuit had been amateurish. Now that someone else apparently had the bauble, the chase was conducted professionally.

The frigate had been after the mystery item the whole time and had waited only for a signal to come and get it. That signal had been given, but Spider had missed it. He cursed himself because he was convinced Ezra's death was related to the spy's mission. Ezra had seen something, or heard something, and it had cost him his life.

Spider's mind raced like a dolphin. What had he missed? There was Hob, distributing guns and powder with the help of men bearing buckets of arms and armloads of swords. There were men forming relay lines, moving packets of powder from the forecastle to the four-pounders and swivel guns mounted on *Viper*'s deck. There were muskets and powder and ammo, being hauled up on ropes so that men in the trees could pick off gunners and officers. There was beautiful May, visible now that the forecastle was open, wide-eyed and straining at the ropes that bound her, as no one seemed to be paying her any attention now. There was Dobbin, with a bright gash across his toothless cheeks earned in the slaying of Barlow, now cursing at Weatherall.

Dobbin snatched at the man's makeshift banner, which had flapped on his face, and a gust lifted it out over the sea. It danced on the wind, like a crimson wraith or a bloody, fleeting soul, before dropping into the sea.

If there had been a signal to that cursed frigate, Spider had missed it. Or had he? A thought started to take hold—then the crack of a musket and a battle cry brought him to the present. Battle was about to be joined, and any chance of avenging Ezra Coombs soon would be lost. Ezra's murderer might be killed in the fight, or hung later, but he would not be unmasked, and he would not die by Spider John's hand. The bloody son of a bitch would die for the wrong reasons.

He lowered his head and shut his eyes tight. It was almost too much, this thought that Ezra's murder might not be avenged. Spider could feel tears building and covered his eyes with a hand to dam them.

He clenched his jaw, yanked the hand away from his face, and forced himself to stare at the frigate rushing toward them. That was his competition. He had to find his killer before that damned naval vessel cut *Viper*'s crew to bloody tatters.

Spider pushed his way through the men crowding around Hob and the others. After several seconds of shoving and pushing, he snagged two pistols, some shot, powder and wadding, and his rusty sword on its pitiful rope cord.

"'Luck in battle, Spider John," Hob said.

"I hope you take a sword through the eye," said Peter Tellam.

"I hope you live long enough that I might kill you m'self," Spider told Tellam. Then he pushed his way out of the crowd and set upon loading his guns. All around him, men did the same, and the tension mounted.

"She gains," someone said. Spider looked up. Sure enough, the frigate was making good headway on the slower *Viper*. She rode the wind like an avenging angel, and everyone saw it.

There was no real hope of outmaneuvering the king's ship. The frigate could sail far closer to the wind than their converted whaler. *Viper* was vastly, ridiculously outgunned as well.

It would be a bloodbath, unless Addison surrendered.

Spider noted the man's wide eyes, the way his tongue smacked at his dry lips, and the way his hands fidgeted and his body paced the deck.

Surrender was not in the offing.

Addison grumbled. "Goddamn all English shipwrights," he said.

Spider finished his preparations and shot a glance at Hob. "You get the hell out of sight, Hob. This is going to be bloody work."

"I ain't no coward!" The lad tucked a pistol into his own belt for emphasis, then spun away.

"Damn it," Spider said.

"We shall need more powder and balls, lads!" Addison had mounted the poop deck. "Stern chaser first, boys! And the ribbons, boys, the blue ribbons! It will be a fracas, I dare say!"

Discipline was not a word that might have described *Viper*'s crew most days, but when it came to battle everyone knew his role. Spider's job in a fight was to prepare for close combat, either to repel boarders or charge across the enemy's rail, unless *Viper* had been hulled or otherwise needed immediate repairs. He took his place and watched the frigate's steady, tireless advance. He could just see faces now, peering back at him from the king's vessel.

Spider kissed Em's pendant, and prayed, as he moved among the men. Some muttered quietly, to God or Satan. Others stared blankly. Still others stared wide-eyed, swung swords restlessly, and fidgeted with their guns. They were nervous, and they had every reason to be.

The frigate likely mounted twenty-eight guns at least, and those guns would be full of grape and chain to tear bloody shreds out of *Viper*'s crew and rigging. She would not be satisfied with sinking *Viper*; indeed, she would not dare, for there was something aboard the pirate vessel that the frigate's captain desperately sought.

"To arms, lads, and let us cut a fucking gory path to glory!" That was Tellam, breathing hard already, eyes blazing, nostrils flaring. "Death to tyrants!" He bore a sword in his right hand and a pistol in his left.

In seeming answer to Tellam's bellows, ragged musket fire thundered from the frigate. Tellam's tattoos gleamed darkly with sweat, and his eyes shone with fury. Spider feared that if the enemy did not close quickly enough, battle-mad Tellam might start killing his own mates.

"Are you ready, Spider?" Hob had suddenly appeared next to him, brandishing a sword and nearly slashing Spider's chest. Only the carpenter's quick step back saved him from harm.

"For the love of God, be careful, you fool! You are supposed to cut them with that thing, not me!"

The boy already had an identifying blue ribbon tied to his arm and held one out to Spider. Spider held his arm out, and Hob deftly tied the ribbon on.

"Keep low, if you won't keep hid," Spider said. "Don't give them much of a target, and stay on the move until it is done!"

"Right, Spider, I will."

Spider sighed. The lad was far too eager for this fight.

Addison called out: "Fire stern chaser!" The rear-mounted swivel gun belched out seconds later. Spider doubted it had hit the frigate. It most likely was a ranging shot.

"Reload, smartly, lads! Smartly!"

Spider glanced about. All seemed in order for a ship heading into battle. Nothing seemed amiss.

"Elijah! Goddamn you, there's a tuck needed!" That was Addison, pointing into the rigging where a topsail had partially ripped from its mizzenmast spar, possibly the result of a lucky musket shot from the frigate. It was flapping and threatening to carry away more sail—and the last thing *Viper* could afford now was to lose even a square inch of canvas.

Elijah had that post, but Elijah was not aloft. Spider's gaze pierced the rigging, darting along every yardarm and ratline, but saw no sign of Elijah.

"I will fix it," Peg growled, swinging across from the mainmast to the mizzenmast.

Spider furrowed his brows. Where was Elijah? Had he gone below to hide out until the battle was done, when he could present the frigate's captain with whatever the hell it was that was at the heart of all this? Was Elijah the spy? Was he the killer?

The stern chaser thundered again, and this time an answering salvo roared from the frigate, and grape and chain shot whistled through the air, chewing up wood and men. At least four men fell dead. Spider saw the naval ship drawing closer, coming about to bring more guns to bear so she could rip up *Viper*'s crew and sail, confident that she could resume her former tack and make up any lost ground.

Red Viper was doomed.

An explosion rang in Spider's ears, and a bright flash erupted from the cargo hold. It was as if a thundercloud had dropped right out of the sky and onto his head. The searing flash blinded Spider a moment, and his ears felt heavy and full of mud. He fell, skinning his nose against the deck. The acrid tang of burnt powder filled his nostrils, and a billowing ghost of black smoke rose from the hatch.

That blast had not been the result of cannon fire from the frigate, Spider knew. Something down there had exploded. It had to have been a powder keg, a bloody powder keg set off somewhere below. Sabotage. On an undisciplined ship like this, the culprit could have set his damned traps anytime he bloody well pleased, and all of Barlow's little built-in cabinets meant there were dozens of places to hide the powder keg. The spy, the man who had stolen from Barlow whatever the hell it was the Royal Navy sought, had crippled the ship.

Spider rose, but another blast rumbled through the lower decks, shaking *Viper* and nearly causing him to fall again.

"Carpenter!" Addison roared. "Get ye ass below and fix what ye can, goddamn it! We're listing! Pump crews, get ye below!"

Spider yelled a reply. He was already headed to the hold, not to fix anything, but because Ezra's killer likely was hiding below.

He would be blind down there. Any lights below would have been extinguished at the first sign of battle, for you could not have open flames unattended in a ship-to-ship affair, and all hands were needed above. Roiling smoke from the fire below added weight to the darkness, and Spider was choking on the hot air. He reminded himself that Ezra's killer was down there, somewhere, and clenched his knife between his teeth before descending. The twin pistols in his belt comforted him, as did the sword across his back.

A volley of grape shredded its way across *Viper*'s deck, shearing splinters from the mast and skin from crewmen in a sudden rain that fell on Spider during his descent.

Spider heard Addison shout, "Bloody hell!" Someone responded: "I said rudder's gone, Cap'n!"

Spider could feel *Viper* growing sluggish. *Taking on water*, he thought. *We will not outrun the frigate. We're all out of miracles, and undeserving of them, by any account.*

Once he reached the bottom of the ladder, Spider crouched below the rising smoke and took advantage of the thin sunlight that fought through the hatch above him. *Viper* had heeled over mightily, and the deck tilted at a frightening angle. Trunks in the crew hold had tipped and burst, blankets hung like draperies from hammocks, and Weatherall's fiddle had somehow been shattered in the violence.

Four men followed him down. He stepped aside. A hatchway led farther below, toward the source of the gray-and-black snake of smoke and toward the holes that now were letting the sea pour into *Viper*. There were pumps down there, too, and these men would go fight the water.

Spider knew their fight would be in vain, because he wasn't going to waste time shoring up a busted hull while Ezra's killer lurked in the darkness, waiting for the frigate to complete her capture.

Once the pump crew had gone deeper into the ship, Spider stepped toward the hatch to follow. A cough halted him. Someone was behind him, hiding.

Ezra's killer, concealed in smoke and darkness.

Spider drew a gun and started to turn. "You filthy, murdering..."

His sentence halted there, snapped off like a life at the end of a hangman's rope. He never saw the weapon that crashed against his skull. He spun and fell, hitting his forehead against the bulkhead and nearly tumbling into the hold below. His gun did drop below.

Despite the pain, despite the fear, his mind remained clear enough to know it was Ezra's killer who had attacked him. The bastard had waited in the chaos and pounced like a scorpion fish springing from a coral reef.

Spider reached back with his right arm and grabbed the first bit of flesh his fingers found. He clawed into skin, his grasp mimicking a grappling hook, and yanked forward. He twisted, brought his adversary around hard, and then drove himself backward to pin his attacker against the bulkhead. The yawning hatch below their feet threatened to swallow them both. Spider heard his foe cry out in pain, and he redoubled his efforts to slam the bastard against the hard wood again. He still had a vise grip on the son of a bitch's arm, and his fingers had partially shredded a bandage. One thin ray of light from the hatch poked through the swirling smoke and illuminated the exposed flesh, and Spider could make out a dark patch against the man's skin. It was only part of a pattern, but it was a familiar pattern.

He had seen it every day, for years, on the arm of his best friend.

Every man who had served aboard the ill-fated *Trusty*, which had exploded and left few survivors, bore that tattoo. Ezra Coombs had borne it—and so had his killer.

"He recognized you," Spider said, coughing. He slammed himself backward once again, knocking wind from his opponent, as *Viper's* tilt grew more outrageous. Spider growled. "You were here to steal the cap'n's . . . thing, for the navy, and Ezra knew you from *Trusty*, knew you were Royal Navy."

"Aye," the man said, breathlessly, and Spider tried in vain to identify the voice as the murderer's fingers raked at Spider's eyes.

"You bloody son of a bitch."

"I did not want to kill him," the man said. Spider still could not recognize the voice, weakened as it was by heavy gasps and a fog of pain. Then the man's fingers hooked Spider's mouth and spun him around quickly. Spider bit down as hard as he could and tasted blood, but he could not make out the man's face before his own nose was grinding into the bulkhead.

Next, Spider found himself plummeting through the hatch. He caught himself, his arms spread wide and holding his head and shoulders above the hatch, but the blindness of pain and a fresh billowing of smoke closed off all sight. He choked, coughed, and winced—and heard Ezra's killer get away. He heard boots on the ladder rungs and noted how the man's passage momentarily killed the sunlight that tried to pierce the smoke.

Spider, grimacing in pain, pulled himself out of the hatch. *Viper's* tilt made that more difficult. "I am going to get that son of a bitch, whoever the hell he is, God help me or damn me," he said.

Shouts and gun blasts and the whir of shots through the air brought him back to reality. He headed toward the grotesquely angled ladder. Spider was climbing out of one hell and into another.

27

Spider checked that his remaining gun was still tucked into his belt, then emerged into the chaos above. He took two steps and tripped over Peg. The man's good leg was a tattered red mess, and his chest was open to the sky. His eyes were open, but they saw nothing. The back of his head had splashed a pool of red against the deck when he'd fallen from the trees.

Spider gulped, then moved on. Shreds of sail, cut to ribbon by cannon fire, flapped uselessly, and *Red Viper*'s deck was tilted bow-upward and listing to starboard with the heavy water gathering below.

"Blast that bastard!" Addison was red with anger, waving Barlow's cane wildly while gripping a pistol in his other hand. "Dowd! You stupid, cowardly, bloody . . ." He stopped, as if he was unable to conjure up an epithet foul enough to suit him.

Spider spotted Hob at the larboard rail with weapons in hand. He sprang to the boy's side.

"What did Dowd do, Hob?"

"He ran," Hob said. "Ain't gonna fight."

"A wise choice on his part," Spider growled, watching the frigate pull up alongside, mere yards away. Her gun ports were wide open, like the maws of lions, ready for a tremendous broadside. Black coils still rose like pipe smoke from the guns' last salvo. He could hear the calm orders of the gun crew leaders, the cannonballs clunking into place.

Spider scanned *Viper*'s deck and the rigging, looking for someone with a torn bandage on his arm, but had no luck.

"Dowd can barely navigate," Hob said.

"His odds of finding land are better than his odds of staying afloat if he stays here," Spider answered. He almost wished he were on *Loon* right now—but Ezra's killer was here.

On *Viper*'s deck, nearly decimated gun crews worked furiously to ram home powder and balls; there were not enough men to handle all of *Viper*'s guns. Those men still alive had to work over the corpses of their crewmates.

"Pour on the fire, Vipers!" Addison cast his hat into the air. "We live or we die today, not in an English prison! Not on a rope!"

The frigate closed in at a shockingly fast clip. Spider now could see the very efficient work of the frigate's gun crews and the officers behind them calculating the rise and fall of the ship.

The Englishmen could hardly miss at this range, Spider thought, yet their crews would work in an orderly and efficient manner just the same. Death angels would feast.

"Come," Spider said, grabbing Hob's shirt and pulling him away from the rail. "We can't stay for this."

"I am not a coward!"

"I know!" Spider yanked Hob across the bloody deck to the starboard side as quickly as he could, with the deck's tilt working in their favor, then shoved him down and dove beside him. He'd picked a spot behind a ship's boat for cover. He heard the shouted order to fire, and the frigate's guns roared in a ragged symphony of thunder. Grape and chain shot sliced through rope and sail and bodies; men fell and died as splintered wood and blood rained across *Viper*'s deck. Splinters showered Spider and Hob, and a chicken flapping and squawking in fright exploded on the hill of the inverted boat that shielded them. "Jesus," Hob exclaimed as feathers and blood stuck to his face.

The mizzen boom shattered, and a portion of the sail hung over the rail and dipped into the sea. A black gunpowder cloud drifted slowly across it all.

The frigate's salvo spent, Spider risked a quick look around and spat a chicken feather from his mouth. He saw only chaos and death. He did not see a murderer with a torn bandage and a tattoo.

A hale of musket fire came next, and then grappling hooks flew from the frigate, finding purchase on the rail. Another order rang out: "Heave!"

"Charge, Vipers!" Addison threw aside his cane, drew a second pistol, then ran uphill across the poop deck, a gun in each hand. "No nooses for us!"

The captain leapt to the rail and fired both pistols into the frigate's boarding party. He prepared to jump aboard the frigate, but a pair of slender black arms grabbed his belt from behind and pulled him back down to the deck. He landed on his back with a thump that winded him and stared up into the vengeful face of May.

She had somehow freed herself from her bonds and had grabbed a knife. She knelt swiftly and ran the blade through Addison's throat quickly and efficiently. A gush of blood flew upward and fell in red rain into Addison's surprised, dying eyes.

May spat in the man's face, rose swiftly, and turned to meet another pirate. She ducked under his sword stroke and plunged the knife into his crotch with a ferocity that made Spider wince. He could almost feel the pain himself.

Another Viper prepared to leap onto the frigate, only to be impaled upon a bayonet as a marine swung aboard *Red Viper*. The marine fired the weapon, and the man's back erupted in a gusher of gore. The man's corpse toppled overboard in a sticky, bloody heap.

None of the other Vipers tried to board the frigate. They hid by the rail, ready to fight when the navy came aboard, but they were not rushing to their ends. Musket fire flew over the gunwale, over their heads.

"Spider John." The voice was from behind him. He turned. Peter Tellam crouched behind a chest, glaring, aiming his gun at Spider's head. "You are supposed to be below, pumping water and fixing the hole."

"It ain't getting fixed."

The next salvo of musket and pistol fire was followed by screaming English sailors. They poured over the rail, swords and guns in hand, as *Viper*'s defenders met them with steel and pistol shots to their bellies.

Meanwhile, Spider and Tellam glared at one another. Spider hoped to see a ripped bandage on the man's arm, but there was naught but scars and tattoos.

"Fuck the navy," Tellam said, aiming his pistol toward the invaders and firing without ever taking his gaze off Spider. "We're going to die today, Spider, or swing tomorrow. I'd rather kill you myself than let the king's men do it." He dropped the gun, drew his fine cutlass, and licked his lips.

Tellam had plagued him for weeks. Spider was going to make him pay.

"Well, then," Spider said. He calmly drew his pistol and shot Tellam in the left knee, then tossed his expended gun away.

"Bastard! I used up my shot!"

"Well, that was stupid, wasn't it?" Spider rose and drew his sword.

Tellam glared.

"I know you didn't kill my friend. But you enjoyed Ezra's death a bit too goddamned much, I'd say." Spider raised his rusty old sword and ignored the battles elsewhere. Tellam had all of his attention, and Tellam was going to regret it.

Tellam, clutching at his bloody knee, leered. "I knew you were a coward." He straightened up and wielded his cutlass.

"Not a coward," Spider answered. "Just not wasting time."

He rushed Tellam, who parried Spider's backhand sweep with surprising efficiency. He did not parry Spider's left foot. Heel crashed into bleeding knee. Tellam staggered, and Spider followed up by driving the knuckle guard of his own sword into Tellam's face.

The tattooed man backed away two steps, rose into a defensive posture far too slowly, and Spider cut his throat.

Tellam stumbled backward, his head tilted back farther than seemed possible, his eyes staring toward heaven, and his neck gushing blood. Then he fell onto his back, convulsed, and died, eyes wide open.

A spar, *Viper*'s black, bloody skull flag trailing from it, fell from above and covered Tellam's corpse.

Spider heard Hob fire a shot behind him. He turned and grabbed the boy. "Listen, you say nothing. Nothing! Your life depends upon it, boy."

Swords clattered on the deck, and most of those Vipers who had not already fallen to their deaths fell to their knees. A pair carrying one of *Viper*'s miserable boats toward the rail opposite the frigate was cut down by musket fire.

Spider knelt and stared hard into Hob's eyes. "We are done for, Hob, so listen. Let me do the talking, and you just heed what I say and be smart. We might just escape the noose. I can't promise, but we might. Trust me."

"Aye."

Spider wished he actually felt the confidence he'd tried to portray.

He dropped his sword and put his hands on his head. Hob followed suit.

They knelt, surrounded by blood and bodies, shattered wood and ripped sail, dangling rope and wafting smoke. An odd silence prevailed as navy men watched and waited, weapons at the ready, wondering if anyone hid with a gun below. Spider noted that May had wisely thrown aside her knife and knelt in surrender.

Viper's tilt grew, and a stray four-pound ball rolled astern. It crushed the skull of a man already dead.

"Take your men below, Mister Rogerson," said a stern young lieutenant, pointing his sword at a midshipman. "See if our man is below. Others may be lurking, too. It is a big vessel, plenty of places to hide, so be smart about it."

"Aye, sir."

Spider's eyes darted among the surrendered and the dead. He saw no sign of a ripped arm bandage or an exposed tattoo. Nor did he see any sign of Elijah, but blood and gore and burns rendered many of the dead unrecognizable. He wished he could recall whether the arm he'd glimpsed during that battle in the hold had been black or white, but it had been too dark.

A midshipman brought May forward. "Probably an escaped slave, sir."

"No," Spider said. "A free woman, before we took her, anyway. She was wife to the cap'n of a vessel Barlow took. And I hope you noticed who she was killing before she dropped her knife. It wasn't your lads."

The lieutenant stared at Spider, disgusted. He strode forth, all blazing green eyes behind a hawk's beak of a nose. "That will be sorted out," he said, his voice full of sneering unconcern. He turned to the midshipman. "Take her aboard *Austen Castle*, inform the captain and treat her well. Find her a place away from the rest of these dogs, but do not be overly trustful," he said. "I've known woman pirates to be as deadly as any other, and twice as deceptive."

"Aye, sir." The midshipman took his charge by the arm and went away. May cast a glance and a nod back toward Spider, who gulped when it took him a moment to recall Em's face.

Spider shook his head, tried to concentrate. "Do you want to find your man? Or the prize he came for?"

The lieutenant stabbed him with a cold stare. "What did you say?"

"I know you had a spy aboard us," Spider said. He was determined to say nothing more. He hoped only to sow enough doubt in the officer's mind to delay a hanging, to give him time for a miracle. It was a lousy cast of the dice, but it was all he could do for himself, and for Hob.

The lieutenant then said softly, "Smithson, take these pirates aboard *Austen Castle*, place them under guard."

"Aye," the man said.

28

*D*own in the belly of *Austen Castle*, secured to one another by lengths of chain and manacles on their ankles, six survivors of *Red Viper*'s demise sat quietly in a makeshift pen of crates and planks. Two armed marines stood in the hold's shadows nearby. This would be their home for the length of their journey to an Admiralty trial in England. Captain Raintree had questioned each of them individually and said *Austen Castle* would lay in new supplies in Kingston, then set sail for Plymouth.

Spider had expected they would see a trial in Port Royal, followed soon after by a spectacle upon Gallows Point. But the captain had been clear about England, and Spider supposed it was because the mystery bauble was considered too vital a matter to be left to the governor of Jamaica. The Admiralty wanted to know what the pirates knew and what Barlow planned to do with the damned thing he had pilfered.

Raintree, a bewhiskered gentleman in his fifties who obviously had celebrated the capture of *Red Viper* with generous amounts of wine, had talked almost as much as he'd questioned when it came Spider's turn for an interview. Apparently, he'd been in a similar state while interrogating the others. By the time they'd all discussed their talks with the captain, Spider understood this much: the mystery item, a small cylinder with several brass rings on it, was a decoder, and thus was something the king of England and the Admiralty wanted very much to keep out of the hands of France. A Spaniard had stolen the decoder from an English agent and had hired Barlow to take him to Spain. Barlow, instead, had killed the Spaniard and taken the decoder. A naval officer had pretended to a piratical past and joined Barlow's crew in hopes of retrieving it.

And Ezra Coombs had died because of it.

Spider spat, now battered and chained and weary to his soul. Ezra had not died because someone feared his witch blood, or for mere greed or for any other reason Spider could understand. Ezra, his best friend, had died because of a king's spy games.

Whether Ezra's killer had died in the carnage aboard *Red Viper*, or lived to turn over the damned decoder to the navy, remained a mystery to Spider, a mystery that he doubted would ever be solved.

And he doubted Ezra would ever be avenged.

Spider expected to remain chained in this hold for several weeks, at least. Months, perhaps, if *Austen Castle* laid over in Africa before heading to England. *That is a long time to contemplate hanging*, he thought. *It would be more merciful to line us up and shoot us.* His left hand wrapped around Em's pendant, still dangling from his neck.

Six men lived, out of more than seventy who had been aboard that night Spider and Ezra set foot on the cursed deck of *Plymouth Dream* off the Massachusetts coast. Spider, Hob, Doctor Boddings, tooth-less Dobbin, one-eyed Odin, and a mute fellow named Jones who had come over from *Loon* when Barlow's crew had taken her prize. None of them, to Spider's thinking, was a likely suspect in Ezra's death.

Others had come over as prisoners, too, but they were wounded badly and had not lived long. Doctor Boddings had asked permission to treat them, but he had been denied.

Spider had been denied, too. He had wanted to unmask the killer, stare into his eyes, and plunge sharp steel between his ribs.

Weariness seeped into Spider's bones, and he half believed that he would simply die here, in chains, in the belly of a king's frigate.

A meow interrupted that maudlin thought, and Spider glanced in that direction to see Thomas, the yellow-and-white mouser from *Red Viper*, perched upon Hob's shoulder. The cat looked none the worse for all the gunfire and smoke and bloodshed. Spider wondered how many of its nine purported lives the cat had forfeited.

A suspended lantern swung with the ship's rolls, most of its light blocked from the prisoners by the guards, who talked quietly while keeping watch. The prisoners had said nothing since their capture the day before, save for the surgeon praying quietly and Odin chuckling as always. Now, they muttered among themselves a bit, in a probably feeble attempt to stave away thoughts of their eventual end on a noose.

"Wish Weatherall was here to fiddle," Boddings said after a heavy sigh.

"Or waving his banner and telling these bastards to bugger," Hob said.

"Did anyone see Elijah?" Spider looked around at his shipmates. "Anyone? I never saw him once battle was joined."

"No," Boddings said. "I did not." The others echoed him.

"Hmm." Odin chuckled. "Maybe he's the bastard they snuck aboard us. Sneaky, tricky bastard."

"He seemed a decent man," Hob said.

"Men can wear decency like a mask," Boddings added.

Spider wondered whether the surgeon might be spared the ignominy of prison and the gallows. He had not taken part in any of the violence, but he had abetted the crimes by serving as physician and saving pirate lives. Spider could not quite forgive the man's behavior after Ezra had been killed, denying use of his Bible for rites, but he determined to do what he could for the old gent anyway. The man's ghastly pallor and obvious fear seemed punishment enough.

As for Odin? God alone knew what was going on in the labyrinth of that man's mind. Spider imagined him laughing even after the rope had gone tight, peering at his executioners with his one good eye.

Dobbin and Jones looked as though they might not survive the trip home. Neither man had a lick of fight left in him.

None of the six survivors had witnessed *Red Viper*'s final moments. They had already been locked below by then, but they had heard the winches and the calls of men as they pulled everything of value from the vessel. They had heard the captain order *Castle* to shove off, and they had heard the frigate's mighty broadsides reduce what was left of *Red Viper* to kindling and fire. Captain Raintree had used the doomed vessel to train his gunners. That was naval discipline for you.

Castle's men had cheered as the pirate ship finally dropped below the surface.

Spider wished like hell he had a pipe to smoke.

Even for a man as accustomed to violent death as he, Spider could not fathom the forces behind Ezra's slaying.

Death in the commission of piracy, death on the end of the Admiralty's rope, even death in a damned drunken brawl over a card game, these all were things familiar in Spider's world. Deliberate death delivered by the agent of one world power, just to keep secrets from the hands of another world power, all in the name of wars past and future . . . these things Spider could not understand.

His friend, a good man despite the hard life he'd fallen into, had died a criminal, while the man who'd murdered him in a spy game, if he hadn't died in the carnage aboard *Viper*, would be hailed as a hero. No one in power would have given a farthing to see Ezra's murderer punished.

"Poor Peg," Boddings murmured. "I saw him plunge. Such a good spirit he had."

"Silence, you," one of the guards admonished.

"Bugger!" Hob laughed and tore off part of his already tattered shirt, waving it like Weatherall had waved his own flags at the English tars. "Bugger!"

"Hush, lad," Spider said tersely. "You are a pirate. They'll not hesitate to kill you."

Fortunately, the silence that followed Spider's admonishment seemed to satisfy the guards, and they did not threaten the prisoners. Spider let the frigate rock him into some semblance of real sleep and clutched Em's charm against his heart. Still, images flitted through his mind: Peg's mangled body after he plummeted like a meteor, Weatherall defiantly waving his banner, May slitting Addison's throat, Doctor Boddings admonishing men for tending their own wounds when there was a perfectly fine surgeon at hand, Hob ripping his shirt and taunting the guards with it.

Spider startled, suddenly awake. He spat. He blinked. He shuffled those images, looked at them one by one.

By God, he thought, *I know who killed Ezra Coombs.*

His next thought was a prayer: *Please, Lord, let the killer be alive still.*

His third thought was determination. *I am going to get out of here and kill the fucking bastard.*

29

An unknown number of hours of sleep—honest, deep sleep—left Spider John's mind clearer than it had been in weeks, clear like the shallow waters in a Caribbean lagoon.

He knew what he had to do, and his friend's memory seemed suddenly more real to him, spurring him on in death as Ezra always had in life. Ezra would not have submitted meekly to a hanging. Ezra would have pointed out things were as bleak as they could possibly be, so one last great snatch at freedom was fully merited. Escape, he would have counseled, or die in the attempt. Better a quick musket ball through the brain than waiting and waiting and waiting for the inevitable gallows.

Usually, it had been Ezra's role to hatch the outrageous goals and Spider's job to whittle everything down to some kind of plan that might actually work. So Spider now simply imagined that Ezra was there with him, saying they could make a break for it in Jamaica. Now all Spider had to do was figure out how to do the deed.

Spider watched dust motes dance in the morning light pouring through the hatch. That dim beam of light had filtered down a long way into the bowels of *Austen Castle*, but the intense darkness made it seem a bright beacon, nonetheless. Two new guards had replaced those of the night watch. They talked quietly, with occasional glances at their sleeping prisoners. Spider heard what he wanted to hear; *Austen Castle* expected to put into Kingston Harbour by morning.

Spider edged slowly to his left, where Doctor Boddings snored. The carpenter blew on the surgeon's face, hoping to wake him. He dared not speak or startle the man.

After long moments, in which Odin mumbled in his slumber,

the doctor opened his eyes. Spider put a finger to his own lips to urge silence, then looked to see if the guards had noticed anything.

They hadn't.

"Doctor," Spider whispered, "can you swim?"

Boddings peered back wide-eyed. He looked dubious but nodded slowly.

"Good," Spider said as softly as he could. "Now, if you had a tool, do you think these irons on our ankles would trouble you any more than the locks on Cap'n Barlow's liquor stores?"

The surgeon's eyebrows rose quickly. He looked at the manacles on his own ankles, then glanced back at Spider. "Simple," he said, so quietly that Spider relied more on reading the man's lips and expression than on his voice.

"Odin has hairpins," Spider said.

Doctor Boddings grinned.

30

They spent the day preparing to carry out Spider's plan. The *Red Viper* survivors prayed, sang quiet hymns, and drummed on the bulkhead and clapped hands, mostly to cover the click-clack noise of the doctor's work on their manacles. Spider tapped the surgeon anytime the soldiers glanced their way. The guards urged them to sing quietly and clearly wished the captives would just sleep away the whole journey, but they did not otherwise harass the condemned men.

Whenever the guards were occupied in talk with each other or the men above, Doctor Boddings went to work with Odin's brass hairpins. Spider had to marvel at his skill. Even though he had not had rum for many hours now, and his hands quaked as a result, the doctor opened the locks on the manacles almost as easily as if he'd been given the key. No wonder no captain's liquor was safe from Doctor Eustace Boddings.

It would have been better to work by night, Spider reckoned, but then there would be no light for the surgeon to see by, and their singing likely would not have been tolerated. They worked now, so as to be ready to spring next morning.

As the surgeon freed them, they left their manacles unlocked but seemingly in place. They made several clever adjustments to hide the fact that they were no longer bound to one another or to the bulkhead; Hob tucked an ankle beneath Spider's knee, and Odin knelt and then sat on his own ankles in an attitude of prayer that looked painful, although he grinned oddly the entire time.

Spider was busy plotting. There was no telling what went on in Odin's mind, but Hob, Jones, and Dobbin had a tough time concealing their excitement. Spider gave them harsh admonishing glances more than once, and when the ship's boy brought them their water, bread, and moldy cheese, Spider was certain the guilty expression on Dobbin's face would ruin the entire scheme. But it didn't.

Spider kept an ear open as the men working above called out familiar landmarks and hollered at passing vessels. He tried to discern a particular voice, a killer's voice, out of the din, but could not. *Let him be alive*, he thought. *Let him be alive.*

By evening, he heard the names of Morant Point and Yallahs Bay shouted above, and, just after dark, he heard mention of the long east-west spit of the Palisadoes. Spider could envision the night lights of Port Royal, sitting like a pommel gem on the tip of the spit.

The Palisadoes separated Kingston Harbour from the rest of the sea. Spider knew the harbor itself would be crowded with ships, some preparing to leave and others having just arrived, and some anchored for repairs or just so her captains and crews could haunt the taverns and brothels and gambling houses of Port Royal and Kingston, the city across the bay from the Palisadoes. There was little chance Captain Raintree would attempt to enter the harbor by night. When dawn came and the captain ordered *Austen Castle* into the sheltered waters, the Vipers would make their move.

That was the most difficult part, the waiting. The doctor had freed them all, and Spider wanted nothing more than to release his manacles completely and rub his chafed leg. He knew the others were just as eager to be free, and if he could have risked a scouting run to determine whether they were close enough to the Palisadoes or the harbor mouth to make their break here, he'd have done so in a heartbeat.

But he could see nothing, and he could not discern much from the distant ship's bells and occasional gunshots he heard.

They had to wait.

The plan was a desperate one, indeed. Spider could scarce imagine anything so desperate, and part of him was glad they could not talk openly. Kingston Harbour held horrors, and his shipmates would have to get past those if they were to survive.

The graves of the dead were one such horror.

It had been about thirty years since an earthquake and the resulting tidal wave had laid waste to Port Royal, once known as a pirate haven and decried as the wickedest city in the Christian world, a new manifestation of Sodom and Gomorrah. The quake—hailed by many as a justly deserved divine retribution—had leveled two-thirds of city, and the tidal wave had reduced the packed sand beneath the city to sludge that could not support any weight. Buildings and people slid into the harbor, to be battered by the waves and buried beneath the stirred mud.

At least three thousand people had died.

Spider doubted every one of those people deserved God's wrath, but he was no expert in such things.

Hundreds already dead had their graves torn asunder and their remains dashed out into the sea. Henry Morgan, famed privateer and once governor of Jamaica, was among the dead whose eternal sleep had been interrupted.

Spider recalled Hob's tale of Blackbeard returning from the deep one day to reclaim his severed head and silently prayed that none of the ghosts dwelling in Kingston Harbour would arise.

Spider tried to convince himself there was no such thing as ghosts, at least outside of nightmares. His shipmates would have to swim through that damned harbor regardless, or await the certain death of the noose.

There were more immediate concerns than Henry Morgan's ghost, however.

There were sharks.

Spider had been present, years ago, aboard an oar boat when a man foolishly trailing his fingers in the harbor lost most of his hand to a tiger shark. The bay was home to hundreds of them, and you could often watch their dorsal fins cut the water in the wake of a ship's boat, the sharks waiting for someone to slip overboard or for a boat to capsize.

Spider had visited Jamaica three times previously and had seen sharks in that harbor every time. Some topped fifteen feet in length, and their razor teeth could sever an arm or leg in an instant.

He was glad he could not discuss the peril with his small command, for he feared it would unnerve them. When the time came, he would simply shout to them to swim as though hell's dogs were snapping at their heels—for it very likely would be true.

For a moment, he envisioned himself holding Ezra's killer below the surface while sharks gnawed the man's face.

If the sharks did not finish the Vipers off, men with muskets might. The fugitives would be plowing their way through open water, and the marines likely would get off a couple of volleys at least before any one of the captives could reach any sort of cover.

Even if they survived all those terrors, there was Port Royal itself. Once, men could wander freely, drink copiously, and brag of their exploits loudly, without the slightest danger of a jail cell or a noose.

Those days of piratical glory had slowly faded since the quake, and after a fire years later that undid much of the rebuilding, and the town no longer provided reliably safe haven for pirates.

These days, pirates were hung and their corpses put on public display. Hell, even Calico Jack Rackham—the famed dandy of a pirate who dressed in almost womanish fashion and sailed with women, too—had found his end here, just a couple of years earlier.

But the governor had not been able to erase every sign of Port Royal's piratical past, and Spider had whispered to his co-captives the name of one place of refuge—the Phoenix, home of fine ale and a former shipmate who would provide a safe harbor. If they could just reach the Phoenix, they had a chance to live out the rest of their lives.

It was, of course, a ridiculously dangerous plan. Spider reminded himself he wouldn't be any deader if the plan failed than he would be if they didn't try to escape, and if there was the slightest chance of avenging Ezra, well, he had to roll those bones.

The sun's rosy touch brushed the sky and sent weak tendrils of light down through the hatches and into the hold where Spider and his friends—for he had now come to think of them as such—were held. A new pair of guards came on to relieve those who had stood through the night. Spider heard orders shouted above, felt the wind gather in *Austen Castle*'s sails, and noted the ship was coming around.

The time to act was now. Once *Austen Castle* was anchored, her captain might order a detail to lead the prisoners above, ship them into a boat, and haul them off to prison to await questioning. There would be no hope of escape from that; the captives would be surrounded by attentive guards whenever they were not safely locked behind iron bars, and they would languish in cells until they were hauled back to the ship for the journey to England. Or, Captain Raintree might just leave his prisoners in the hold, where guards would have nothing to do but watch them.

For now, though, *Austen Castle*'s men were anxious to see their long journey ended, and thus were distracted. They were thinking about shore leave, good drink, and women.

Before they could enjoy any of that, though, they had to work their way into the harbor. They must navigate reefs, keep an eye out for other vessels, and choose their anchoring spot. They would be preparing at the capstan, freeing the anchors. A gig would be made ready for the captain to go ashore. Guns would be loaded, too, to fire a salute as *Austen Castle* drew past the harbor fort.

Everyone was busy, and little attention was being paid to the prisoners. Swift action now, while the men were distracted, might just prevail.

Or it might lead to a quick death—still a better option than hanging.

Spider waited until he heard the frigate's cannons fire a thundering salute and her crew shouting helloes and other vessels answering. He waited until he could not possibly imagine *Austen Castle* had not entered the harbor, and until he knew the men above must be focused on the ceremonies of arrival.

He gave the men of his small command a knowing look.

One, he mouthed.

He watched the guards. Their attention was focused above.

Hob and the others quietly slipped off their bonds and their boots.

Two.

Odin suppressed a cackle, and it seemed to take an effort worthy of the one-eyed Norse god who inspired his name.

Three.

Spider, Hob, Dobbin, Jones, and Odin rushed the two guards. Spider clapped a hand over one soldier's mouth; Dobbin did likewise on the other. The guards went down under the weight of their attackers. Hob took a musket from one guard and drove the butt of it into his head, then did the same for the other.

"Again," Spider said. "Make certain."

Hob bashed each man in the skull twice more.

"Let us go," Spider said tersely. "Be quick! And swim fast, lads. Muskets and sharks."

"Sharks?" That was Dobbin, his toothless mouth making the word sound like something spoken in French.

Hob went up the ladder first, followed closely by Spider. The plan was brazen and foolish—get to the deck, run for the starboard rail, and dive into the harbor, then swim faster than musket balls and tiger sharks.

That was the plan for Hob and the others, anyway. Spider had another role to play.

It was a long way up. They had been placed in a lower hold, where everything stank of bilge water and where the chatter of rats was a constant noise. They had to climb their way past a lumber storage and a gun deck. The latter was manned by men who had fired salutes moments before; Spider counted on their attention being aimed at the town and urged his small command to simply rush upward. Speed was their ally. Wasting time in worrying would get them killed.

His calculation proved to be imprecise, and a man on the gun deck yelled, "Escape!" and snatched at Spider's shirt. Spider kicked him in the groin, grabbed his hair, and sent him tumbling below to where the other guards bled in the hold. He had already climbed higher by the time he heard the horrid thunk of the man's impact reverberate through the hatchway.

Spider reached the main deck just on Hob's heels.

Bright morning sun stung Spider's eyes, and he had difficulty seeing. *Austen Castle*'s men crowded the rail, waving hats at ships, boats, and gulls. Hob sprinted for the rail and dove through the gap between a pair of seamen. Startled, they hardly reacted.

The other Vipers followed suit. Spider, though, stood his ground and spun around, shielding his eyes from the sun. He heard the splashes of his companions in the harbor but saw out of the corner of his eye Doctor Boddings being held back by a couple of sailors. Spider did not spare time to pray for his friends, though. He was searching for a killer and praying he found him before a musket ball or bayonet ended his search.

Then he saw Ezra's killer, plain as day, freshly shaved and dressed in a lieutenant's uniform, bellowing orders to stop the escape.

Ezra had never said "I miss her," referring to some mystery woman. Peg had misheard, Spider realized. Ezra had said, "Aye, mister," upon being addressed by an officer he recognized.

John Weatherall, the navy officer who had posed as a pirate to recover a spy decoder. The man who had wrapped a bandage on his arm instead of seeking Doctor Boddings's aid, because he was not wounded; he was covering up a tattoo that said "Trusty 1716." The man who had waved a white sheet at the pursuing frigate during every encounter save the last, when he'd switched to a red one to signal to Captain Raintree that the goddamned spy bauble was safe in hand.

The man who had clubbed Ezra Coombs over the head with Peg's stolen spare leg, because Ezra could identify him, and then tossed a flask of booze by the corpse to make it look like an accident. The killer might have stolen the flask from anyone.

A marine poked a bayonet at Spider's belly. Spider knocked the blade aside, punched the marine in the nose, and bolted toward Weatherall. The killer stood on the quarterdeck, next to Captain Raintree, a place of honor for the hero welcomed home. Spider ran at his foe, shoving men aside. He gambled that anyone carrying a gun would hold fire on a crowded deck. Most of the men on the deck were unarmed, or at least were armed with nothing more significant than a knife tucked into a belt, and none of them was motivated like Spider John.

He bounded up the ladder with an energy that sprang from pure fury, fueling his sore and stiff limbs. A snarl erupted from his throat and grew in intensity as he closed the distance.

Weatherall stepped in front of Raintree and drew his sword as Spider approached, and a wicked slash caught Spider across the chin. A better-timed stroke would have slashed his throat. Spider ignored the pain and barreled into Weatherall, planting the crown of his head squarely on the man's breastbone. Weatherall went down hard, the sword clattering to the deck, and Spider dropped on him, his knees driving hard into Weatherall's gut and forcing air out in a miniature gale.

Nearby, men shouted and muskets fired and acrid smoke rose in the sun. Whether they were shooting at him or at his shipmates swimming in the harbor, Spider could not say.

Spider grabbed for Weatherall's loose sword, even as men clutched at his shoulders. He drew the blade across Weatherall's uniform sleeve and ripped at the fabric. There was the tattoo.

"You killed Ezra Coombs, and you will die for it!" Spider swung the blade around in a wicked arc, forcing the surrounding men back.

"It was my duty," Weatherall said.

"And this is mine." Spider drew the blade neatly across Weatherall's throat and glared steadily at the man as a red ribbon blossomed below the dying man's chin. Spider was still glaring at Weatherall when a strong grip tore into his shoulder, and glaring still when a knife touched his own throat, and glaring still when rough hands lifted him to his feet.

Men held Spider by the arms, but no one said a thing for several heartbeats, until Raintree broke the silence.

"You will hang," Raintree said, hate and shock filling his eyes.

Spider took his gaze off Weatherall once he was certain the man's last breath had joined the gun smoke in the air around him. He glanced past the line of musketeers firing over the gunwale and looked out into the harbor. He saw his small command, some of them, anyway, swimming for freedom. He heard a voice that could only be Odin's shout something about Blackbeard, and saw a small but strong figure that had to be Hob vanish behind a rowboat. And was that Elijah, pulling Dobbin into a rowboat? How the hell had Elijah managed to vanish from the midst of that battle and appear now? Spider wished he could hear that tale.

He swallowed hard. Spider was glad his shipmates had a chance to be free. He wished he could have gone with them, but it would have cost him any chance of avenging the best man he ever knew.

Spider returned Raintree's hard gaze. "There are hundreds of crimes you can hang me for," he said. "Killing John Weatherall ain't one of them."

Spider looked across the deck and imagined he saw Ezra there, towering over the others and wearing a silly grin. He knew what Ezra would advise. Damn the muskets! Damn the sharks! Anything but the gallows! Anything but that!

Spider wrenched himself free just before the manacles were locked onto his wrists. Cat-quick, he was over the rail, plummeting to death or freedom, and shouting thanks to his best friend.

Acknowledgments

I t is sometimes said that writing is a lonely, solitary endeavor. That is bullshit.

The truth is I could not have written this story, nor gotten it published, without a solid crew to back me up.

My longtime friend and partner in crime Tom Williams, whose work I am sure you will be reading one day, provided strong copyedits and much sage advice, along with friendship and encouragement. Look for the byline Mas Williams.

Fantasy author Tyrone Johnston set the example, by getting his ass in a chair every day and producing works at an impressive pace.

Fantasy authors Howard Andrew Jones and James Enge are sword brothers of mine from a different era, and both helped me along the way.

My agent, Evan Marshall, was enthusiastic from the start and offered keen editorial insight. He also found me a publisher.

Dan Mayer, the editorial director at Seventh Street Books, decided a pirate murder mystery would be a fine thing to unleash upon the world. I thank him profusely for that and for his patience and guidance in editing.

I also want to thank you, dear reader. Book people are the best people.

More than anyone, though, I have to thank my wife and kid, Gere and Rowan. They gave me the time and space to write this, and the love and support needed to get me through the agony of seeking an agent and selling the book. Gere, in particular, did some stellar copyediting and provided full-time muse service, helping me sort out plot problems and listening to my endless thinking out loud. I could not have done this, or anything, without her. When she gets a book out there, you all are going to love it.

About the Author

Steve Goble is a career journalist, working for USA Today Network–Ohio. Before he started writing about murder on the high seas, he wrote a weekly craft beer column called Brewologist. He lives in rural Ohio with his lovely and patient wife, a supremely sarcastic teenager, and two occasionally well-behaved dogs. Learn more at SteveGoble.com.

Author photo by Jason J. Molyet